GIRL

OF

RAGE

CHARLES SHEEHAN MILES

Books by Charles Sheehan-Miles

Thompson Sisters
A Song for Julia
Falling Stars
Just Remember to Breathe
The Last Hour

Rachel's Peril
Girl of Lies
Girl of Rage
Girl of Vengeance

America's Future
Republic
Insurgent

Nocturne (with Andrea Randall)

Prayer at Rumayla
A Novel of the Gulf War

Saving the World on Thirty Dollars a Day: An Activist's Guide
to Starting, Organizing and Running a Non-Profit Organization

GIRL OF RAGE

If you enjoyed this book, please share it with a friend, write a review online, or send feedback to the author!

www.sheehanmiles.com

ISBN-13: 9781632020017

Printed in the United States of America
Cincinnatus Press
PO Box 814
South Hadley, MA 01075

www.cincinnatuspress.com

v091314

Dedication

for Khalil
I am proud of you

Acknowledgements

This book took a lot of help along the way to complete. I'll probably forget some people but I especially want to thank Lori Sabin for your fantastic editing, and Sally Bouley and Jackie Yeadon for your extensive assistance reading through the book.

Thanks to my beta readers: Tanya Hall, Kristen Teaff, Emma Corcoran, Kathy Baker, Wendy Wilken, Dimitra Fleissner, Laura Wilson, Bryan James, Michelle Kannan, Sarah Griffen, Amy Burt, Jennifer Mirabelli, Stacey Grice, Kirsten Papi, Beth Suit, Rita Jenkins Post, Kelly Moorhouse and Kirsty Lander. You guys looked at a lot of first draft material and have my everlasting gratitude.

To the baristas at The Thirsty Mind and Amherst Coffee, where I wrote the bulk of the book: you guys and gals are awesome. Khalil and Amirah: thanks for putting up with your dad being distracted, overworked and sometimes addled. It's been one of the toughest years of your lives, and I'm proud of you both.

To my partner and love of my life, Andrea Randall: thank you for listening to my brainstorms and crazy ideas as I worked through this book. Living with another author means we understand each other, and it also means sometimes we're both in worlds of our own creation. But we always return home to each other. I love you.

Cast of Characters

The Thompson Family
Richard Thompson
Adelina Thompson
Julia Wilson (Thompson)
— Crank Wilson
Carrie Thompson-Sherman
— Ray Sherman
— Rachel Sherman
Alexandra Paris (Thompson)
— Dylan Paris
Sarah Thompson
Jessica Thompson
Andrea Thompson

The Wakhan File
Roshan al Saud
Leslie Collins
Mitch Filner
Vasily Karatygin
George-Phillip Patrick Nicholas
Chuck Rainsley

Diplomatic Security
John "Bear" Wyden
Leah Simpson

The Washington Post
Anthony Walker

PROLOGUE

Do You Trust Me?

Andrea Thompson , May 1, 12:04 am

"Dylan?"

As she saw the lean figure limping toward her in the darkness, Andrea Thompson stepped out of her hiding place. Dylan Paris walked unevenly toward her through the dimly lit entrance to the Bethesda Metro Station. He wore a light jacket, even though it was really too warm for it, and a canvas backpack was casually thrown over his shoulder. His face was grim, mouth turned into a deep frown, and his eyes were focused somewhere else, far away from her. At first she thought he was going to walk right by her.

"Dylan?"

He stopped, his hands tightening into fists. His pause gave her a second to look closer at him, but he wasn't reassuring. His face, already unshaven, had dark flecks of dirt or something along his jawline. One of his hands shook, and his shoes were soaked. *Why?*

She'd last seen him as she went over the rail of the balcony. He'd been standing in the darkness, knives in hand, ready to protect her.

Get into the condo below us then meet me ... in thirty minutes. At the war memorial on Norfolk. If we miss each other there, then the Metro station at midnight. Got it?

Looking at him now, she wondered what the delay had cost him. Gunmen had been coming down that hallway. She shivered as the realization sank in that this man, who she barely knew, must have killed their attackers with his bare hands. The flecks on his face weren't dirt.

They were *blood*.

"We need to get out of here," he said. His voice was low, and barely contained a hint of savagery.

She nodded. "Where to?"

"I'm gonna make a couple calls, see if I can get us a place to hole up."

"What about the *policia*?" She corrected herself. "The *police*."

Dylan just stared at her, his expression unreadable. Then he said, "Come on." He turned and walked out into the darkness. Andrea followed, down an alley, then onto a crowded street. Bars, people crowded onto the sidewalk. Cars were parallel parked along the street.

Dylan took her upper arm in his hands and said, "We can't go to the police because it was police who came after you in the first place. I don't know who they are. But for now, we're getting you under cover."

She nodded, then said, "I don't know."

Dylan stopped and looked at her. "Your sister's my wife, Andrea. Do you trust me?"

She met his eyes. Dylan—he'd put himself between her and killers. "Yes. I trust you."

"All right, then. No more questions, for now."

He turned and strode away. Three cars down, she saw a Chrysler convertible, the top down, parked illegally next to the fire hydrant, its emergency lights flashing. Dylan paused and glanced around. Then he reached in his pocket and took out a cell phone. He looked at it with cold eyes, his jaw firmly set. He quickly tapped a message into the phone, and with one last glance at the people walking by on the street, he tossed it into the back seat of the convertible.

Then he turned and began quickly walking away, pushing his way through the crowd of young professionals out for drinks. At the next corner, he extended his right arm in the air and flagged down a cab.

The car came to an abrupt stop. Andrea peered inside. The cab itself was light blue, with dark blue and orange lettering on the side. Barwood taxi. Hybrid vehicle. The driver looked East Asian.

Dylan opened the door and said, "Get in."

She didn't hesitate, sliding across to the seat behind the driver. The car was small and clean, and the radio was loud, tuned to a news station. He got in beside her and leaned forward, resting one hand on the back of the seat in front of him.

"Where to?" the cab driver asked.

Dylan shifted in his seat, then he said, "You know any good hotels? Like on the other side of town?"

The driver shook his head. "No good hotels there."

"No, listen … good like … I don't want to get asked too many questions. Pay cash." Dylan reached in his pocket and slid out a hundred dollar bill, then slid it into the driver's hands.

The driver looked at Andrea in the rearview mirror. Creepy eyes.

Then his eyes shifted back to Dylan. "I know place in Maryland. Cash only. No ID."

"Perfect," Dylan said.

As the driver put the car into gear, a raindrop splashed on the windshield. The traffic was slow, but they were moving. Three police cars, lights flashing, rolled by going in the opposite direction. Back toward the condo.

Andrea leaned back in her seat. The last three days had been a nightmare. She'd been kidnapped, escaped, then watched her family fall apart with the realization that she and Carrie had a different father than the rest of their sisters. She'd been faced with assault and attempted murder.

She was exhausted and terrified.

"What's the plan?" she whispered, pitching her voice beneath the prattle on the radio so the driver couldn't hear.

"We hide. Get some rest in a place where we can't be tracked. Then we figure out a plan." His voice was low enough she didn't worry about the driver hearing them over the car radio.

"Why did you throw away your phone?"

He shrugged. "GPS. Someone wants you dead badly enough to either be a federal agent or impersonate one. I don't want to be found. I sent a text to Alex to warn her she wouldn't hear from us."

She sighed. "I thought so."

The raindrops fell steadily now, a rapid drumbeat against the roof of the car. For a few minutes she just listened as the taxi driver navigated traffic and the rain fell against the roof. For just a second, the drumming of the rain took her back to Calella, driving along the beach in the summer rain with her best friends. She wanted to go home.

All of this chaos stemmed from ... what? Something about her mother? Her real father, whoever that was? She didn't even believe Richard Thompson's assertion that Senator Rainsley was her father. He'd never said anything true to her before. Why should she believe him now?

She needed answers. She needed to know why she'd been virtually abandoned by her parents. She needed to know why strangers had been trying to kill her.

She needed to know who her father was.

"I need answers, Dylan," she whispered.

He didn't answer right away. Instead he stared out into the rain, his face turned away from her. "I know," he finally said. His tone was desolate.

"I need to know who my father is. And who is trying to hurt me and my sisters."

He nodded.

"Will you help me?"

A handful of raindrops pattered against the roof before he turned and put a hand on her shoulder. "Of course," he said. "I'll help."

PART
ONE

CHAPTER ONE
Them's the rules

Adelina. May 1, 10:15 pm Pacific

The little man grimaced, rubbing his eyes. Adelina Thompson had called three times during the drive north, and he'd promised to stay awake until she arrived. But he hadn't been gracious or polite about it. He was short, with thick glasses that magnified his rheumy eyes, and his pale blue pajamas were threadbare, the vertical blue stripes faded into obscurity. She imagined that winter was tough for him—his knuckles were swollen and arthritic.

He had a business here in the shadow of the northern California redwoods, but it was a business that merely limped along. The prospect of the twenty extra dollars she'd offered for late arrival had been powerful.

The campsite was deep in the woods, and the air was moist and warm. Crickets and frogs and God only knew what else made a continuous buzzing, and the darkness hid the trees and cabins and dangers beyond. It was oppressive. Claustrophobic.

"Here's the key. No noise, everybody's already asleep. You're in the second cabin on the left."

"Thank you," Adelina said. "We won't be making any noise. My daughter's asleep in the car."

"I'll just need to make a copy of your driver's license, please."

She lay her hand on the counter and said, "Oh no ... I'm afraid I forgot it."

The old man narrowed his eyes. "Can't rent a cabin without a driver's license."

She frowned. "We're only here for the night. Can you make an exception? You wouldn't make me and my daughter sleep in the car, would you?"

He grimaced. "Them's the rules," he said, sounding unsure of himself. It was after midnight, after all, and temperatures had been dropping.

"Please?" she asked, leaning slightly forward. "I wouldn't ask if it wasn't urgent. You see…"

"I don't need any trouble," the man said.

"We're no trouble. It's just … my husband…" As she said the words, she dropped her eyes to the floor.

He grimaced. "Left him, did you?"

"He hurt me," she whispered.

The man exhaled. "All right, then. Fine. I guess the copier's not working. You make sure you're out of here early, mind you. We don't get inspected often, but if the county finds out I'm letting people stay without ID, there'll be hell to pay."

She breathed a sigh of relief. "Thank you."

He frowned. "That'll be forty dollars. Plus the twenty you promised on the phone."

¡Gilipollas! It didn't matter. Right now, the important thing was to get Jessica into a bed and get under cover for the night. She couldn't drive without sleep and Jessica couldn't continue at all. Despite the adrenaline and shock of the news of Andrea's kidnapping and finding their home burning away, Jessica had still slipped into a deep sleep within minutes of getting on the highway. She'd tossed and turned, moaning and resistant when Adelina woke her to eat at a fast-food chain along US 101.

That was the withdrawals.

She won't suffer through the same kind of physical withdrawals you see from alcohol or heroin, Sister Kiara had told her. *But it will be almost as bad in its own way. She's only been doing meth a few weeks, but it might be two years before she laughs again, or feels any joy. That's just what happens to the brain. She's done a tremendous amount of damage to herself. In the meantime, all you can do is love her.*

That, and keep her alive. Jessica had been through a harrowing ordeal on an emotional level, but Adelina knew that the only way she could keep her daughter safe now was to run as far and as fast as she possibly could.

She thought about the voice on the phone ... the voice she hadn't heard in more than a decade.

Always, Adelina. Always.

Hearing his voice again gave her a thick pain like a fist buried in her chest, slowly squeezing the breath out of her. He'd been the love of her life. He'd gone away, at her insistence.

Hearing his voice gave her something she hadn't had in years. Hope.

So she ran. It's not that she thought Richard would hurt Jessica. He was a monster, but in some ways a predictable one. He wouldn't hesitate to hurt Andrea, most likely, reasoning that she wasn't actually his daughter. But Jessica was his, and he knew it.

But Richard wasn't the only threat. She never knew the details, but something terrible had happened in Afghanistan when Richard was there thirty years ago. Something so terrible it had lain dormant, a secret which had floated some careers and killed others. She thought she knew who some of the players were. Prince Roshan, a charming snake of a man who kept his wives in veils in Saudi Arabia while sporting around Washington with twenty-year-old call girls on his arm, a man who had smiled at her and been charming and had the same cold, lifeless look in his eyes as her husband.

She thought the other threat was likely to be Leslie Collins, who Richard had insisted for years was nothing more than an accountant. He thought she was stupid, and at times through the years it had served her well to let him think that. It had protected her and her daughters. But Collins was no accountant, and when he finally reached a level where further promotion required Senate approval, the now Director of Operations for the Central Intelligence Agency finally had to go public about his career.

Collins wouldn't hesitate to torture small children to accomplish his goals. She just hoped the rest of her daughters had heeded her instructions to run.

If only she knew what had happened in Washington. She'd called the condo that afternoon and gotten Dylan, her son-in-law. Her instructions were simple. Run, and get Andrea out. She heard a loud crack over the phone, then more, and then Dylan hung up. She knew what the sound was. Gunshots. She'd called again, but it was too late. She kept trying, stopping at rare pay phones along the road—there were few enough of those left—but no one answered at the condo.

It wasn't safe to use cell phones. She'd thrown them into the San Francisco Bay as they left town. Then drove, for hours, north, stopping only for one meal and restroom breaks. In a way, Jessica's deep depression and withdrawal made the trip easier.

But Adelina kept questioning herself. Second guessing. Jessica needed to be in heavy therapy. She needed to be in an environment where she could get treatment. She needed to be examined by a doctor. Instead, she was on the run, and the only thing Adelina could do for her daughter was pray.

Finally they had reached her destination for the first night—a campground in Crescent City, California, surrounded by redwoods and quiet. As she got out of the car, Adelina took a deep breath, the scent of pine and spring flowing into her nose. It was a smell of hope.

She stumbled in the darkness to the cabin and unlocked it, the latch opening with a loud, audible click. The door swung wide. A queen bed and a bunk bed. A small table. No sheets or pillows. They would make do. She had a blanket in the back of the mini-van, and bundles of clothing from their bags would have to serve as pillows.

First, she needed to get her daughter inside.

Adelina opened the sliding side door to the van. Jessica was sprawled across the middle seat. Her lifeless brown hair was splayed across her face, eyes closed, and mouth open. Since Adelina had taken her to the retreat to dry out less than ten days ago, Jessica had begun to gain weight. But it still wasn't enough. Her face, red and marked with acne, was gaunt, the hollows in her cheeks heartbreakingly prominent, her ribs clearly visible under her tank top.

"Jessica, wake up. Come inside the cabin and you can sleep in a bed."

Jessica groaned and turned her head into the seat.

"Come on, Jessica. I need you to get up for just a minute."

Jessica didn't stir. Adelina closed her eyes. Her daughter was eighteen years old.

Her daughter was a wreck.

She leaned into the van and tilted Jessica out of the seat, pulling the girl to her shoulder. Jessica groaned and flailed, and Adelina staggered a little under the weight, her knees bending. With a lot of effort, she got her arms around Jessica and dragged her out of the van, Jessica's sneaker-clad feet hitting the ground with a thud.

Jessica groaned and said, "All right, all right. Head hurts." Then she stood, and staggered toward the door of the cabin.

As she stepped inside, Adelina sighed and whispered a prayer. For now—for the next few hours—they were safe.

She leaned against the doorframe for just a second, staring in at her daughter, indirectly lit from the headlights of the car. Jessica had staggered in and fallen into one of the bunk beds. Anyone else who saw this scene would see a strung out kid who might be a drug addict or might be anorexic, a kid who couldn't keep her eyes open, brush her hair or take basic care of herself.

Adelina knew what they saw. She'd seen the looks, in the weeks leading up to their final departure from San Francisco. When Adelina had first returned home, switching places with Richard, she'd given Jessica plenty of leash. But it became clear, quickly, that her daughter was out of control. Conflict and rage. Sadness and grief. It was clear Jessica needed help and wasn't getting it.

In February, she had to drag Jessica out of the house when her daughter refused to even get dressed. They'd gone into the grocery store with Jessica padding behind her, wearing pajamas and flip flops, muttering and cursing at her mother all the way through the store.

She'd seen the looks of curiosity and pity from the young mothers. Disgust from single men. Understanding and empathy from the older mothers and grandmothers.

Nothing was as simple as it seemed. Adelina didn't see an eighteen-year-old drug addict lying on the bare mattress in the cabin. What she saw was a three-year-old daughter twirling in her ballet shoes. She saw the daughter who seemed to take on the pain of her daring, sometimes reckless twin. She saw a young teen, fifteen years old at the time, serious expression on her face, as she played Paganini's 24th Caprice for a packed recital at the Green Music Center. One of the most difficult pieces for violin, and Jessica had mastered it. Of all of her daughters, Jessica was probably the only one who had both the musical talent and discipline to match her mother, and until a few months ago, it had seemed likely she was destined for the San Francisco Conservatory.

When Adelina looked at her daughter, she saw the four-year-old who had once followed Sarah around the house, both of them leaving a trail of chaos everywhere they went.

Adelina walked out to the minivan. She looked around in the darkness. She couldn't see anyone, so she reached far back under the driver's seat and removed the thick envelope full of cash. She wouldn't risk leaving that in the van. She removed the blanket and their bags from the back seat, then carefully locked up the van and went inside.

She closed and locked the door, covered her daughter with the blanket, then curled up beside her in the darkness

Adelina suppressed a tear. She didn't have time to fall apart right now. She'd already done that too many times in her life. For now, she needed to hold it together.

All the same, she missed her little girl.

CHAPTER TWO
Insider

"**A**re we *finished*? I need to get my daughter to sleep somewhere appropriate."

When Carrie Sherman said the words, her daughter stirred in the sling. The baby had cried most of the last hour, finally drifting off into a fitful sleep. They were inside a sterile office in a building she'd never paid attention to before, a few blocks from the main State Department building. A stream of investigators, uniformed officers, and God only knew who else continued to demand answers. The noise had made for a challenging time, as the team of federal investigators asked questions and then asked them again, over and over.

Where was Dylan? Why hadn't he or Andrea come out with them?

Why were drugs found in Andrea's room?

What did they know about their father's career?

Bear Wyden knew the questions wouldn't get any answers, because he knew that the three sisters knew nothing. But her demanding, arrogant tone infuriated him. People were *dying* out there.

"We're done," he said. "For now, we've got you in a safe house in Alexandria. I'm going to need to get clothes sizes for all of you."

"What?" Carrie asked. "We're not going to a safe house."

"Just for a couple days. Your condo is a crime scene, Mrs. Sherman."

"Fine. I'll need all new baby supplies then too. Diapers. Clothes. Formula. Bottles. Breast pump. Either we get that stuff from my condo or someone buys it. And where are my sisters?"

Bear closed his eyes and heard the phone call with Leah in his mind again.

Bear, is there supposed to be a relief team here?

No, he'd said. There wasn't time to say anything more, because the supposed relief team, led by Ralph Myers—an insider, a fifteen year DSS agent Bear had known for at least a decade—killed Mick Stanton and critically injured Leah.

He'd been frantic. Two hours he'd attended to duty instead of running to the hospital. Two hours. And now he had to listen to this spoiled woman demand diapers and bottles.

"Just in case you missed it, Mrs. Sherman, two of my agents died protecting your family. Leah Simpson is in the hospital. Don't take that demanding tone with me."

Carrie wasn't cowed. "Just in case *you* missed it, Mr. Wyden, my sister and brother-in-law are missing because your team failed to protect them. So don't take that judgmental tone with me."

Bear felt his chest and throat tighten. He closed his eyes and struggled to take a deep breath. His mother had suggested breathing exercises to keep his temper under control through the divorce. Sometimes they actually worked. He turned and walked out of the room and into the hall. He could *not* stay in the same room with that woman another moment.

He paced in the hallway for just a moment then reached for his phone. It rang before he had a chance to start dialing.

Secretary Perry.

Secretary James Perry. Former soldier. Vietnam veteran. US Senator for three decades, then presidential candidate. He'd been Secretary of State for six months, and for reasons that didn't mean one lick of shit to Bear, he'd taken a liking to Bear Wyden.

Bear answered the phone. "Wyden, here."

"It's James Perry, Bear."

"Yes, sir."

"I'm going to ask you about progress in just a moment. But first, how's Leah Simpson?"

Jesus. Bear muttered under his breath, then said, "Critical condition, sir. That's all I know. Hospital wouldn't tell me shit when I called."

Damn it. He couldn't recall the words, but using profanity with the Secretary of State was never a good idea.

"And you're downstairs?"

"Yes, sir."

"Put someone else in charge for the next two hours. You go to the hospital."

Bear choked a little. "Sir, I can—"

"That's not a request. She's your ex-wife. Go find out if she's okay."

"Yeah," Bear replied.

Perry disconnected without any further courtesies. Bear leaned against the wall for a moment.

Bear, is there supposed to be a relief team here?

She was calm. Not panicked. Not even anxious. Concerned. Businesslike. Within two minutes of that call she was lying on the floor, a bullet through her hip and another in her chest. And he was here, babysitting the investigation. Screw that.

He walked down the hall and pushed open the door to the offices assigned to the investigation team. His eyes scanned the room and fell on Scott Kelly.

Kelly was a forty-four-year-old former federal prosecutor from Boston. Precise, competent, exacting. Four years prior, his wife had left him, and he decided he wanted to travel the world. He resigned from his position and joined DSS as a high-level investigator, where his first three-year tour had been in Bangkok. He had slightly prominent jowls and dark circles under his red rimmed eyes, and looked perpetually exhausted. His performance reviews, however, were stellar.

"Kelly," Bear called across the room.

"Yeah?"

"I'm going to the hospital to check on Leah, then out to the crime scene. You're in charge."

Kelly raised his eyebrows. "Yeah? When do I get to sleep?"

"You can sleep when the investigation is over."

"Yeah, yeah, whatever. Go check on Leah."

Bear didn't stick around to figure out what else Kelly might have to say. Everyone on the team knew he and Leah had been married for fifteen years. He didn't need them looking at him, wondering, speculating, whatever. He had a job to do.

He was soaking wet by the time he got to the parking deck, and the drive to the hospital felt like it took days. Even though it was well past midnight, traffic near downtown DC was snarled from the downpour. Bear didn't like to drive at all, not in DC, but under the circumstances he had little choice. It pissed him off that he was stuck in traffic. It pissed him off that someone out there was running circles around his investigation. It especially pissed him off that he still had feelings for his ex-wife. His ex-wife, who left him and remarried a college professor of all things. It pissed him off that from the moment he'd gotten her phone call, he hadn't been able to think about *anything else.*

So he drove through the storm in a fog, the rain drumming against the roof of the car, then he walked through the hospital paying little attention to his surroundings, until he finally reached the trauma center at George-Washington University Hospital—the epicenter of the convulsion which had taken one of his daughters and destroyed his marriage.

He'd been here before. Four years before, to be exact. It was the end, really, of his and Leah's marriage, although neither of them knew it at the time. At the time they thought they were there because their eldest daughter was diagnosed with encephalitis. They thought they were there because loving couples support each other through crises.

But when Leanne died of the brain infection, their marriage died too. Part of Bear's soul died, really. He tried to be there for Leah. He did. But all he could see was their daughter. Dying. He had nightmares—nightmares where he woke up choking, nightmares where Leah was shot on duty, and he'd begun to fight for her to switch to a desk job.

Their mild arguments turned into loud ones, and that was fine, until they went silent. When *she* went silent. One year after Leanne's death, an angry silence reigned over their home. Until she left him. Then Bear was transferred overseas—without her.

The thing was, Bear never said goodbye. Not to Leanne. Not to Leah. Not to his marriage, or his life. So now, being back in Washington—even if only briefly—supervising his ex-wife? Not something Bear wanted. It was old wounds being torn open, problems being stirred up. If it hadn't been for Andrea Thompson's kidnapping, Bear would have spent a quiet week in Washington before being reassigned.

Wouldn't that have been nice?

Shit.

Gary Simpson was pacing in the waiting area. Leah's *husband*.

She hadn't been married long. Only a year ago, Bear had been up to his ears in terrorists and jihadis in Islamabad. But he still called Jimmy and Rebecca, via Skype every Sunday afternoon. The kids were getting older, and it had been a couple of years since the divorce was final, so the fact that Leah was dating shouldn't have been any surprise to him.

Married though? That was a surprise. To Bear, her getting re-married was *final* in a way the divorce hadn't been. So when she broke the news one day via Skype, he congratulated her, and then got off the line as quickly as possible.

He'd never admitted to himself that he'd secretly believed they'd one day get back together.

He'd never admitted to himself that their divorce had broken his heart.

Now he was faced with Gary Simpson, who approached him with a wounded, red-faced expression. Simpson was everything Bear wasn't—an intellectual, a college professor, an academic. Simpson would have set off every alarm Bear had for a limp wrist-ed pretty boy. Except for the fact that he was built like a truck and had earned his first degree, a Bachelors in Economics, with a full scholarship as a fullback at Notre Dame. He'd gone on to earn a Masters and a PhD at Harvard.

In short, Gary Simpson was a man to be reckoned with. And right now his face reflected nothing but rage.

Bear started to back up when Gary got close.

"Gary, chill," he said.

"Motherfucker," Simpson said, preparing to take a swing.

"Gary! This isn't going to help Leah!" Bear got his arms up in a protective stance as he shouted the words.

"You got her shot. Doctors said she might die."

"I didn't *get* her shot, Gary."

Simpson moved to attack again, and Bear stepped back. "Gary. I just came to find out how she is."

"What do you care?"

Bear sighed and dropped his arms to his side. "Fine. Hit me. Whatever. I don't care, Gary. I just want to know how she is." As a final step, Bear closed his eyes and waited, because he knew if Simpson hit him, he was going to *feel* it.

The punch didn't come. After a few seconds, he opened his eyes. Gary Simpson had turned away. "They don't know if she's going to make it, Bear."

Bear muttered under his breath, "Motherfuckers."

"Who *did* this?"

"Don't know yet. It was partly an inside job. And I didn't tell you that. We're working on it, all right? Whoever did this—we'll find them. They won't get away it. I promise."

Simpson leaned close. Bear braced himself, but Gary didn't have any fight left in him. Instead, he whispered in Bear's ear. "Don't just find them, Bear. *Kill* them. Do you hear me?"

"Yeah, buddy, I hear you."

Twenty minutes later, Bear was back on the road. He was grateful, for the ten thousandth time, for Leah's parents. As they had in more than one crisis in the past, they'd stepped in, Leah's mom watching the kids while her dad held a vigil at the hospital. He ached to go to them right now. What kind of father stayed at work at a time like this?

The type of father Bear was. He couldn't go to his kids right now, because he needed to find out who had hurt their mother.

So, he drove from the hospital to the Thompson family's condominium in Bethesda.

The crime scene.

Despite the very late hour, traffic was snarled on Wisconsin Avenue. A cluster of police vehicles—both federal and Montgomery County, Maryland—spread out in front of and around the 20-story building, blue lights flashing. One lane of Wisconsin was blocked. Bear pulled his car to a stop, parking half on the sidewalk, and a local police officer in a heavy rain poncho approached rapidly. Bear flashed his badge and said, "I'm Bear Wyden. Diplomatic Security."

The cop backed off immediately. They knew who he was, of course.

Bear sprinted through the rain to the entrance of the building. Two more local cops were there, and they scrutinized his ID while he stood there dripping on the tile floor. One of them made a quick phone call, presumably to ensure Bear was cleared to enter the crime scene.

"Forensics team is upstairs," the officer finally said.

"Thanks," Bear replied. Then he walked toward the elevator.

The ride up to the 20th floor seemed to take hours, and the soft music playing in the elevator didn't help. Finally, the doors opened. A uniformed officer—this one from Diplomatic Security—blocked the elevator.

"Bear," the officer said. Now that he'd verified Bear's identity, he stepped back.

The FBI forensics team had spread out across the entire top floor of the building. From the door of the elevator, the hall went off in two directions, with two doors at each end, a total of four penthouse apartments. As he stepped off the elevator, Bear saw that large sections of the floor were taped off.

Ejected cartridges littered the floor near the elevator, each of them neatly marked. It was clear, from here, what had happened. The shooters—as best they could tell there were three of them—sailed past the ground floor security by flashing their IDs. They rode up the elevator just as Leah was calling Bear to ask why a relief team was coming on duty.

On arrival, they opened fire the moment the elevator opened up. Mick Stanton had been halfway down the hall to the left. Twenty-eight years old. Unmarried. He finished law school at Georgetown and decided a future of poring over the books and writing briefs didn't suit him, so he'd joined the Diplomatic Security Service two years before. A promising young agent, shot in the head.

The shooters shifted their fire to Leah. They'd missed her with their first round of bullets, probably because she'd instinctively ducked. She took out one shooter, midway down the hall, and wounded another before she got hit.

The position of the dead shooter was marked clearly on the floor. That one was Ralph Myers.

Ralph Myers. Bear had known him ten years. He and Leah, back when they were married, had hosted Ralph for dinner at their house. Bear knew a lot about him. He was single. Late thirties. Myers was smart as hell, ambitious. He volunteered for dangerous and sticky assignments, and had spent a lot of years in the Middle East, including Iraq, Pakistan and Afghanistan.

Huh. Suddenly it occurred to Bear to wonder. Was Ralph agency? Did this have something to do with the CIA?

Bear walked on further. On the left side of the hall, in the alcove across from the Thompsons' doorway, was a large bloodstain. Leah's blood. She'd taken two bullets and probably looked dead to the attackers when they busted through the door into the Thompsons.

What happened after that was ... less clear.

The first attacker didn't make it through the front door, and the reason was clear enough. His gun-hand had been removed at the wrist with a large meat-cleaver. When they ran the fingerprints they got an immediate hit from the military database. Dylan Paris's fingerprints were on the knife, which was partially embedded in the wall.

The second attacker made it into the condo, but not much further. Another knife—this was a sharp, fourteen-inch kitchen knife—was embedded in the man's back. He lay on the ground, arms splayed out, in the middle of the living area. He had a shoulder holster under his coat, but no weapon.

Presumably, after Dylan killed both attackers, he took their weapons. But there were a lot of unexplained questions here. Who were the attackers? Who were they after? Presumably Andrea Thompson, but what was she up to? After the assorted dead bodies, the second big surprise in this investigation was the discovery of four kilos of cocaine in Andrea's room, along with a lot of cash. The cash and the cocaine were out on the floor, and the cash had been tampered with.

Who did it belong to? Andrea?

Bear didn't buy it. But it looked bad. Especially after she apparently abandoned Dylan and busted through the apartment below in an effort to get away from the gunmen.

If it hadn't been for the insider, it looked very much like Andrea's kidnapping—and the subsequent attacks—had to do with some kind of drug war more than anything else.

Which made absolutely no sense at all, unless she was working for someone else.

If so, that was one cool actress. He'd seen her right after she was rescued from the kidnapping. And not in a million years would he believe she'd been faking the shock and terror of that experience.

But something was clearly wrong here, and the Thompson sisters were right in the middle of it.

CHAPTER THREE

"Damn it, Crank."

Julia. May 1. 11:30 pm Pacific

Julia Wilson ran her fingers through her hair. She was frustrated. It was eleven-thirty, and she and Crank had been at the Hall of Justice, the headquarters of the San Francisco police, for hours. She was more than a little bit tired of being stuck there, answering questions hour after hour.

For the last forty-five minutes, she'd been left alone. That didn't fit well with Julia's normal mode of operating. As the manager of one of the most successful bands in the world and the CEO of her own company, Julia didn't spend time cooling her heels waiting on other people. So less than five minutes after her questioners left the last time, she'd gotten up and walked to the door to demand that the questioning be brought to an end.

That was when she discovered that the door was locked.

Julia didn't panic. She didn't raise hell, or bang on the door, or yell. Instead, cold as ice, she turned and walked from the door and sat back down at the small table. She sat with her back straight, one knee crossed over the other, and she stared at the mirror prominently placed on the wall.

She waited. Minutes went by, then more. She resisted the urge to take out her phone. She'd already received a text message from Carrie with the most essential information. Carrie, Rachel, Sarah and Alexandra were under protective custody somewhere in northern Virginia, under the protection of Diplomatic Security. Dylan and Andrea were missing, but Alexandra had received one last text from Dylan shortly after midnight.

I'm with Andrea. We're safe for now. I'll be in touch. Dylan.

Not enough information to do anything with, but at least they knew he was alive. Which was more than they knew about her mother or sister Jessica. Carrie had filled her in on that, too. Jessica had called, after being missing for days. She was with their mother, and according to their mother, everyone needed to run and hide.

That was oh-so-helpful. Typical of their mother, really. Make a short, cryptic phone call about something urgent and expect everyone to drop everything. It didn't make any sense. But then again, little about Adelina Thompson made sense. Julia had long since made her peace with her mother, and generally wasn't bothered anymore. But moments like this—when the entire family was in danger—she couldn't help but be a little cynical.

But then she remembered the photos. The file.

It was pretty clear-cut. Carrie—Julia's next youngest sister—wasn't related to their father. Therefore, Adelina must have had an affair. That didn't really surprise her—she had known for years that neither of her parents had been entirely faithful.

But the result was a surprise. In her father's files, she'd found the report with the genetic testing. And filed away with it, she found a police report, documenting her mother's brutal beating and rape.

The beating took place one day after the date of the test results.

The conclusion was inescapable. Her father—Richard Thompson—her *father*—had beaten her mother nearly to death. Raped her. *Impregnated her.*

Julia had run it through her mind a thousand times in the last six or so hours and it still made no sense at all. The whole concept was unbelievable. How was any of this possible?

Julia didn't have a chance to completely absorb the news however, because two men had shown up at the house. Normally that wouldn't have fazed her in the least—but Andrea had *just* been kidnapped, everything was confused, and as they tried to figure out what to do, the men broke in. Julia and Crank—along with the reporter from the Washington Post who had been along for the confusing ride—tried to escape out the back door, only to be shot at. They made it out, but it was close.

Then, the unthinkable happened. The men had set off a bomb of some kind in the house. Julia stood there in shock, watching her parents' home burning, until the police and fire department showed up.

And so here she was. Waiting. Because the police had apparently disappeared, leaving her locked in this room. She had to go the bathroom, she didn't know where her husband or sisters were, and every second that went by without answers she got more and more angry. The more she thought about it, the more angry she became. Finally she gave in and began pacing.

And that, of course, was when the police came back in. Julia froze and said in a cool voice, "Unless you're planning on pressing charges for some crime, you need to let me go to the bathroom, then talk to my family, right now. I've done nothing wrong and I don't know why I'm locked in this room."

The detective who had originally talked to her—Detective Sergeant Pam Larson—raised her eyebrows. An attractive woman with dark hair and a slightly red face, she had red cheeks and nose—broken capillaries—the obvious look of someone who drank too much.

Sergeant Larson said, "I think you're going to want to talk to the gentleman."

She didn't say anything else, as a man in an off-the-rack grey suit walked into the room.

He set a briefcase on the table in front of him and said, "Mrs. Wilson, have a seat."

A woman followed him, also in a grey suit. She had prematurely white hair, but unlined skin.

"And you are?"

The man nodded and gave a half smile. "I'm Wolfram Schmidt. Special Agent, Internal Revenue Service, Criminal Investigation Division. This is my partner, Emma Smith."

His voice was smooth as butter, his accent odd, part Texas, part eastern European.

Julia stood there, frozen in place. *Internal Revenue Service?* "I'm sorry ... what? Who did you say you were?"

"IRS, Mrs. Wilson. Criminal Investigation Division. Please ... have a seat."

Julia moved on autopilot, sliding into the seat across from ... what was his name? Wolfram Schmidt. Who inflicts that kind of name on their child? "What can I do for you, Mr. Schmidt?"

He smiled and slid a business card across the table toward her. "Mrs. Wilson. First, I want to make it clear, you are not under criminal investigation at this time."

"I'm sorry?" she said, suddenly alarmed. *At this time?* "Why would I think I would be under investigation?"

What the hell was going on? She thought about the last week. Her mother going missing. Her father preparing to go into confirmation hearings as Secretary of Defense. Andrea kidnapped, then attacked by gunmen. Her heart was beating forcefully in her chest.

What would the IRS want to do with her?

Schmidt seemed unperturbed. He opened his briefcase, took out a manila folder, and flipped through it. His attention appeared to be on the folder, but the game he was playing was familiar. He knew what was in that file. This was all about intimidation.

Julia wasn't easily intimidated.

"Mrs. Wilson. In 2011, there were a series of transactions involving your Barclays International accounts that don't have proper documentation in your tax return. Specifically, there was a sale of stock in Beta Pharmaceuticals. Are you familiar with the transactions in question?"

Julia blinked. She didn't have the first clue what he was talking about.

She did, however, know that she was in over her head. She picked up his card, then said, "I don't think I'm going to answer any questions at this time. My attorney will be in touch."

Schmidt raised his eyebrows. "Are you sure you want to go that route, Mrs. Wilson? We can probably settle this all here and now, plain and simple. I don't see any need to make this an adversarial process."

She shook her head. "First of all, as I'm sure you're aware if you've been researching my company, I deal in hundreds of transactions a year. I have no idea about the specific ones you are talking about. Second of all, I think it would be best if you spoke with my attorney. In fact," she said, standing up, "unless you or the San Francisco Police Department plan on pressing charges or coming up with some other reason to hold me further, I'll be leaving right now."

She backed away from the table.

Schmidt looked up at her. His eyes were blue and clear. Menacing eyes.

"Mrs. Wilson. I wouldn't recommend that."

"Thanks for the advice," she said. "But I'm leaving."

For a second, she thought the police were going to stop her, which wouldn't make any sense, because she hadn't done anything wrong—but who knew what made sense? She was intimately familiar with her business dealings, and there was absolutely nothing of interest to the IRS. If anything, Wilson Enterprises, the holding company for the band and all its assets, overpaid its federal taxes. She was scrupulous about such details, and even if she wasn't, her tax attorneys were.

Something was seriously wrong.

Sergeant Larson, the local cop who had originally questioned her, followed her at the door. "Mrs. Wilson, I'm going to have to ask you not to leave town."

Julia froze in place. Then she turned toward the detective. "Sergeant, are you filing criminal charges against me? Yes, or no?"

The sergeant swallowed, then said, "Not at this time."

"In that case, I'll ignore your request. I don't live in San Francisco; my home is in Boston. If you need to reach me, you can do so via my attorney. Where is my husband?"

"He's being questioned, ma'am," the sergeant said.

"No. Neither of us has committed a crime. We were in my parents' house, which was attacked, and instead of helping us, you've been treating us like criminals. We are *finished*."

As she spoke the words in a sharp tone, she saw a familiar face. Anthony Walker—the reporter from the *Washington Post* who had been with them in the house.

"I'm calling my attorney right now. My husband's attorney. He's going to advise you to release my husband *this instant*. Am I clear?"

"Wait here, ma'am," the Sergeant said. Then she hurried off.

Walker sauntered up. "I was wondering when you would get fed up."

She raised her eyebrows. "What do you mean?"

"I told them to call *The Post's* attorneys hours ago. They've been bluffing. Fishing for information because they don't have a clue what's going on."

"I don't have a clue either," Julia replied. At that moment, she let out a sigh of relief, releasing tension she hadn't even known she was holding in. A door down the hall opened, and her husband came walking out toward her.

Crank Wilson was considerably taller than Julia. Bleached and spiked hair. He wore half a dozen earrings, spread unevenly between his ears.

He gave her a lopsided grin, the same grin she'd fallen in love with when she was a college student and he was struggling as a musician, trading gigs for beer.

They'd had their share of conflict, especially their first three years together. Misunderstandings. Raging arguments. They'd thrown dishes, and on one memorable occasion, Crank had smashed an acoustic guitar against their dinner table, shattering it. Each time they'd apologized, with tears and emotion and love. And over time, they'd mellowed. Her barriers came down as she slowly learned to trust for the first time in her life. He grew up, and over time they discovered that on top of being passionately in love—they also liked each other, a lot. They laughed, and played silly games. They traveled the world together.

As soon as she saw his smile, Julia melted, walking to him and wrapping her arms hard around him.

"You okay, baby?" he asked.

"Let's go," she replied. "We need to go, now."

"Right," he said.

Five minutes later they walked out the front door of the Hall of Justice, both Crank and Anthony trotting to keep up with Julia's pace. At the corner, she raised an arm high, and held it there. It took no more than thirty seconds before a cab pulled up.

"Never fails," Crank said. "Takes me half an hour to get a cab, usually."

"I wonder why?" Anthony said with a smirk.

"No one asked you," Crank replied in a friendly tone.

They all climbed into the cab, and Julia leaned forward. "Hayward Airport, please."

"Yes, ma'am," the cab driver said. "You've got a flight arranged there?"

Hayward was a general aviation airport, of course, and the easiest place to get a private jet in and out of San Francisco. She was happy to be leaving San Francisco. It was her family's home, in theory, but it had never been hers.

Julia, normally scrupulously polite even to people she intensely disliked, didn't reply. It's not that she didn't hear the cab driver. She did, but the words didn't really sink in until Crank said, "Yeah, we've got a flight. We're a little late, so it would be great if you could get us there quick."

As he finished saying the words, he leaned back and whispered in her ear, "You okay, babe?"

She shook her head and crossed her arms over her chest.

I want to make it clear, you are not under criminal investigation at this time.

Which meant nothing. It meant they didn't have anything yet, or they were on a fishing expedition, or they thought she'd done something and might confess. The whole thing reminded her all too vividly of the incredibly painful ordeal her sister Carrie had gone through less than a year before. Investigation at NIH. Husband court-martialed by the Army.

For a second, a flash of shame passed through her. She remembered shying away from Ray when she first heard the news. On trial for war crimes. For killing a little boy. For a few minutes, she'd let herself believe the crappy news she saw in the papers and on CNN.

Oh, Carrie. She wished she'd been better to her sister. She wished *the world* had been better to her sister.

Finally she answered, "I don't want to talk about it here, Crank. Let's get to the plane. I need to know where everyone is."

"All right, babe," he said in a low, deeply concerned voice. "I'll make the calls. You just ... relax."

She could hear the worry in his tone. And she knew it was her own fault in a way. Julia didn't fall apart. Julia didn't freak out. She didn't panic or get hung up on anything and maybe sometimes she just *needed* to. Because right now, all she could think of was her sisters, wondering whether they were okay. Without thought, she found herself dialing her phone.

"Babe, it's almost three in the morning back east," Crank said.

"What about Jessica? Where is she?"

He shook his head. "Carrie texted earlier. Jessica called this afternoon. She's out there somewhere."

"Damn it, Crank."

He put his hands on both sides of her face and leaned close. "Julia. Calm. Okay? It's going to be okay. I promise."

"You don't know that. You can't know that."

"I know you can't fix it all from this cab. We'll fix this, Julia. Okay? But we can't do it, *right now, right here.*"

She swallowed and nodded. Of course he was right. But that didn't make it any easier.

CHAPTER FOUR
Safe House

I **'m with Andrea. We're safe for now. I'll be in touch. Dylan.**
That was all she had. She didn't know where he was. She didn't know if he was hurt. She didn't know if he was *drinking.* She didn't know if something horrible had happened. All she knew was he was with her sixteen-year-old sister, and that they were safe. *For now.*

Alex had messaged Dylan back at least a hundred times through the night. But no luck. She'd gotten desperate enough that while they were still being questioned at the State Department, she'd shown his text message to her questioners. That had started a flurry of activity, which resulted in absolutely nothing that she could tell.

Sometimes Alex Paris thought she was going to explode from the stress. It seemed like nothing she did made things easier. She'd forgiven Dylan. She'd forgiven herself. She'd done everything she could to protect herself and make herself stronger. She'd stood by him when he struggled with the physical therapy. She'd stood by him when he was drowning in post-traumatic stress. And after a long fight, it had seemed things were getting better. That life was getting better. It had seemed that she was going to get her happily ever after, after all.

But real life didn't work that way, did it?

It didn't. Because shit happened. Best friends showed up with the news that people you loved were criminals. Best friends got killed, leaving behind young widows and unborn children. *Ray* had been killed, leaving a gaping wound in her sister *and* in her husband, and it wasn't fair, because there was nothing Alex could do to heal either one of them. She'd spent the last nine months holding their hands and watching them cry, and watching her husband fall to pieces.

Because that's what Dylan had done. No question. When Ray died, he took part of Dylan with him. In some ways, he'd taken the best part of Dylan. The honorable part, the part who would never lie to his wife. When Ray left, he left behind a shell of Dylan, a Dylan who looked the same and sometimes acted the same, but was actually hollow.

Sometimes Alex felt like it was *her* husband who died, not Carrie's.

That's exactly how she'd felt when they'd gone out. Was it only eight hours ago? It felt like a lifetime. His last words to her had been, *I'm just exhausted, Alex. I miss Ray and I'm tired and sick and just ... please. Go without me tonight, okay? I'll be fine.*

So she did. She went out with Carrie and Sarah and the baby. While she was having dinner, armed gunmen had gone after Andrea and Dylan. *Why?* The questioning had been pointed. Did she know about the drugs? Did she know about the money? Both had been found in the condo. Did Dylan have something to do with it? Did she know where he had gone? Where Andrea had gone?

Nothing they said made sense. None of it.

It was nearly two in the morning before the DSS agents had brought them in an armored SUV to a nondescript ranch house in northern Virginia. They could have been anywhere in America. Drab brick. Scuffed hardwood floors. Sliding glass doors to a dark backyard. Well-stocked guest rooms, clean and impersonal. One of the rooms had a crib and was fully stocked with diapers, bottles, powdered formula, zinc oxide, and a hundred other possible needs for Rachel. Someone had been thorough.

The only thing the house didn't have was safety. It was in the middle of nowhere. It was a *safe house*. It merely underscored the fact that someone had tried their best to kill Andrea and Dylan tonight, and that neither of them had surfaced since, except for that one, cryptic text message. Alex already knew every inch of the bare bedroom she'd been impersonally assigned. Roughly 120 square feet. A closet with a sliding panel door. Crappy carpet. Crappy windows, frosted to make her invisible to snipers, she supposed. A queen-sized bed that was far more comfortable than her and Dylan's second-hand bed in New York, but not nearly as welcoming.

It was cold. And she missed her husband.

But missing Dylan was nothing new, was it? She'd had plenty of practice at that.

So Alex lay in bed, watching her phone, waiting to hear from the man she loved. Waiting to hear from the man she knew was fighting to keep his head above water but wouldn't reach out to her for help. Waiting to hear from the man who she'd have done anything for. She didn't cry. Alex Paris was all out of tears. Now she just lay there, waiting. Waiting, and wishing.

In the nearby rooms, she knew her sister Carrie slept, baby Rachel in her crib. At the opposite end of the hall, Sarah. None of the three of them were in good shape, but Sarah, in particular, seemed shaky. She hadn't talked at all in the last couple of hours before they reached the safe house, only answering questions in monotone with as few words as possible.

They'd been in the safe house for two hours almost, but Alex hadn't slept. Instead, she lay there in the bed, staring at the ceiling, wishing she could go back in time and change everything. Her wishing was futile. Frustrating.

She felt like she'd spent most of her relationship with Dylan separated. When they met and fell in love, they'd lived thousands of miles from each other, and that distance had almost killed them. She went to college; Dylan went into the Army. Only through a series of improbable coincidences and near miracles did they have a chance to become a couple again.

Then Ray had to go and die.

She knew it was irrational. It wasn't Ray's fault. It's not like he committed suicide. He was *murdered*. But irrational or not, she was angry with him. She was angry with fate, or God, or whatever it was about the universe that allowed her husband's best friend to die under those circumstances, leaving behind little more than a messy pile of survivor guilt.

Alex sighed. She was wasting her time, rethinking about the same things over and over again. She was exhausted and stressed and worried and there was absolutely nothing she could do about it. She rolled over, staring at the wall. Pale moonlight shone through. She could see the vague shadows of the trees in the frosted glass, swaying and rolling in the wind, the raindrops rattling against the gutters. It must be blowing like crazy, because occasionally the window rapped slightly in its frame.

Dylan and Andrea were out in that.

Somewhere.

CHAPTER FIVE
Something bothering you?

Meredith Collins. May 2. 4:30 am.

Meredith Collins lay in her cold bed alone, staring at the ceiling, listening to the drumming of the rain outside and the echo of her own breath against walls which were too far away in an empty room.

It was half an hour before Leslie usually rose for the day, and he'd already been out of bed for half an hour. It hardly mattered— she knew he hadn't slept. For a week or more, he'd been short with her, he'd been late nearly every night, and he'd spent long hours locked away in his office on the phone.

She sighed. *Poor Leslie.* He'd spent decades working his way up, enduring dangerous tours in places like Afghanistan and Indonesia. He'd devoted his life to his country, to the safety of others, and now he'd finally reached the pinnacle of his career. And instead of being able to relax, instead of being able to slow down and give orders, he'd become more stressed, more overworked, more—*cold.*

It wasn't fair. Logically she knew that high office meant a lot of pressure. More pressure than ever before, because now not only did he have to do a good job, but he had to navigate the political waters of the White House with a fickle, inexperienced President and a Congress which had a vendetta against the federal government itself. It wasn't enough to be good in that environment. You had to be perfect.

But knowing that intellectually wasn't enough to ease her heart. It wasn't enough to stop her from worrying as she watched her husband age before her very eyes.

She slid out of the bed. It was early, but she could at least get some coffee going and prepare to greet the day with some semblance of calm.

The truth was, she rarely knew what to do with her days anymore. Susan, their eldest, had graduated from Princeton and gone on to the FBI—she was now at the academy at Quantico and reportedly doing well. Woodrow and Franklin, the twins, were undergraduates at Columbia.

Since the twins had gone to college, her days were frightfully empty. Quiet. Leslie was gone from 5:30 in the morning until late in the evening sometimes, and their house had been too big even for a family of five, much more so for the two of them. Even when he was home, he wasn't really here anymore. She sometimes filled her days with friends in her bridge club, and served on the board of the McLean Women's Club, but when she was honest with herself, she had to admit that she was unbearably lonely.

She padded down the hall in her bare feet, passing his office on her way to the kitchen. Unusually, the door was cracked. Leslie had soundproofed his office when the children were very young, and out of habit, he always closed the door.

She paused just for a second, her feet faltering, when she overheard Leslie say words that shook her to the core.

"I don't really care, Danny. I want them found, and I want them dead. No more fuckups. Andrea Thompson and Dylan Paris need to turn up in the Potomac. Am I clear?"

She stopped, her feet buried in the thick plush carpet.

Andrea Thompson. Wasn't that—Richard Thompson's daughter? She'd been kidnapped earlier in the week; it had been all over the news. What would Leslie have to do with that? It didn't make any sense. Even though she never got involved in his work, even though she'd never asked questions or wondered or doubted, she found herself paralyzed in the hallway, listening.

"Yeah, I know," he was saying. "But don't worry about that. The Justice Department's going to be holding a press conference this morning. Richard Thompson is going down. We don't have to worry about him anymore."

A trickle of sweat ran down between her breasts, and she felt her chin involuntarily shaking. Richard and Adelina had been friends for twenty years. This—it didn't make sense. Why would Leslie be up in the middle of the night plotting against his friend? Taking about *killing* his friend's daughter?

She stumbled as she moved backward away from the door, and her nightgown caught on a closet doorknob. The thin fabric tore along the seam as she yanked the nightgown. She ignored the damage, instead moving as quickly as she could down the hall to the kitchen. Hands shaking, she poured water into the coffee pot and started it brewing.

She took a breath, trying to calm herself, and looked out the kitchen window into the wet darkness outside. Even though it was very early in the morning, she knew the traffic would already be backed up along Old Dominion Drive, a third of a mile down their driveway. She rarely heard any traffic—the trees fronting the property were too thick to allow much sound through, and the long driveway took a sharp turn halfway there, effectively blocking any lights from the road. Their house was old—a converted farmhouse built in 1842, which was often included in the annual Tour of Homes sponsored by the Women's Club. The house had been a sore point with her and Leslie—he'd wanted to add a substantial addition, but the Women's Club and the Historical Society had fought the addition. So, unfortunately, had Meredith. That was five years ago, but she was afraid he still hadn't forgiven her.

She realized her hands were still shaking as she stood at the window. What had the phone call been about? The coffee pot was almost finished, the machine making the loud bubbling sounds it always made when it was finished brewing. She turned around and let out a startled squeak.

Leslie was in the doorway.

"You scared me!" she admonished.

He walked to the coffee pot casually, then took the carafe out and shook his head. "The machine generally works better if you put coffee grounds in it, dear." He poured out the hot water that had collected in the pot. She'd completely forgotten to put grounds in. She stood there, wringing her hands as he started a new pot, grinding the beans for an unusually long time before scooping the grounds into the filter.

His eyes were lifeless as he restarted the pot. "Something bothering you, Meredith?"

"I... I—"

"Perhaps you overheard something?"

She nodded, still wringing her hands.

"Meredith, what was it your father used to say?"

She knew instantly what he was talking about. Her father—George Mason Cutter—had been a Navy admiral. During World War II he'd flown a F2A Buffalo aircraft off the deck of the USS Hornet before he was shot down and spent nearly 24 hours in the water before being rescued. By the Korean War he was squadron commander and a fleet admiral by the late 1960s, but his career ended under a cloud. An accident and subsequent fire on the aircraft carrier USS Forrestal killed 134 sailors and destroyed millions of dollars worth of equipment. Admiral Cutter wasn't officially held responsible—but he'd been forced to retire, a bitter, aggrieved man. Right up until his death in 2004 at the age of 82, he'd frequently said that no one understood what patriots were forced to do to protect their country.

Civilians never understand, he would say. *Of course it was horrible we lost those sailors. But it was a war. You can't win a war if you don't take risks.*

She sighed. "He used to say civilians didn't understand."

Leslie nodded. In a slow, condescending tone he said, "That's right, Meredith."

"Les … what don't I understand?"

He turned away from her, a troubled expression in his face. Slowly, he pulled two coffee mugs down from their hooks and walked to the refrigerator, getting out a carton of half-and-half. She stood anxiously; still wringing her hands as he poured the coffee, then poured a splash of half-and-half into each. Neither of them used sugar anymore. He slid her cup toward her.

"How much do you know about what I actually do for a living, Meredith?"

She shook her head and shrugged. The question made no sense. She knew *nothing* of what he did.

"Meredith. My job is to protect the security of the United States. You know that."

She grimaced. "What does that have to do with Richard and Adelina, or their daughter?"

"Well, it seems that there has been more going on there than we realized. In fact, Richard has been involved in some very shady dealings. Treasonous dealings."

"I don't understand."

"I can't explain it all, Meredith. He's involved in some kind of serious drug money laundering, and his daughter, the oldest one, has been assisting him with moving the cash around. Her husband's a rock musician, you know."

Meredith felt her heart slowing down. Of course. There was an explanation, and it was even one that made some sort of sense. Except she couldn't imagine Richard Thompson being involved in anything so sordid. "It all seems so … greedy."

"That's what happens when people have power, Meredith. They get greedy. I've uncovered some very disturbing history about Richard recently, unfortunately. I had to meet with the Justice Department to turn over a lot of it."

She shuddered. Poor Adelina. She must be heartbroken.

"Why didn't you tell me?"

Leslie raised an eyebrow. "You know the answer to that. It's all classified. You should never have heard what you did hear."

"Explain that, please. Classified or not. I heard you saying … saying…" She couldn't finish the words. She literally, physically could *not* finish the sentence. That she'd heard her husband ordering the killing of a teenage girl.

Leslie shook his head. "What did you hear, Meredith?"

She swallowed. And whispered, "Andrea Thompson. That … that…"

"That she was to be killed."

Meredith shuddered.

"Meredith, Andrea Thompson is not what she seems."

"She seems like a sixteen-year-old girl who was kidnapped."

"The news didn't report that the kidnappers were known, vicious killers. Both of them heavily involved in the drug trade and terrorism. The news didn't report that she killed *both* of them with her bare hands. She may be sixteen, but it's likely she's psychotic.

Didn't you ever wonder why the Thompson family never brought her around? As best as we can figure, this was some kind of deal gone bad. These are *not* nice people we're dealing with."

"But what about a trial? Bringing her into custody? Why would you—?"

Leslie shook his head. "Sometimes, we can't do things all nice and clean and neat. That's what it means to be in a position of power. You have to make decisions that are the best for all. You know that. Your father knew it too. But the thing is ... I can't sit around and wring my fingers and worry. I have to take action. Richard knows I'm on to him now, and I fully expect he's going to do everything he can to take me down. And—Meredith—he's the acting Secretary of Defense. He has resources at his disposal I can't even dream of."

"Are you in some kind of danger?" She didn't like the way her voice rose at the end of the sentence. It spoke of fear and anxiety and dependency.

He sipped his coffee, and from the set of his lips and eyebrow, she knew he was taking the question seriously. Finally, he nodded and said, "Yes. I'd say I'm in danger. Both professionally and personally. And it's essential I deal with that danger."

"I don't see—"

He held up a hand, cutting her off. "Meredith, Richard Thompson is a dangerous, ruthless man. He's at the top of his career, and he won't put up with any threats. He's right next to the President of the United States. If I don't deal with this, it's not just me in danger, dear. It's the country. It's the President. Now you tell me. What would your father say if he was still alive?"

She swallowed. Of course he was right. She knew Richard. She'd seen, at a few dinner parties over the years, how dominant he was. How occasionally he would say something to Adelina with *just the right tone* and she would go silent. Terrified of her husband. A husband Meredith knew was cold as ice. They'd been acquaintances over the years—friends even. But they'd never gotten *too* close. The Thompsons weren't people you got *that* close to, because it was clear that they only opened up so far.

She sucked in a breath and took a sip of her coffee. Then she said, "Leslie, I'm sorry. I didn't mean to overhear anything, and what I did overhear was none of my business. I trust you. I know you'll do what's right."

Leslie looked at her and said, "You're going to see a lot in the papers in the next few days and weeks about them. Things that will seem crazy—even unbelievable. Do you understand?"

She nodded. "I do."

"Trust me, Meredith."

"Of course."

He took her hand and gave her a smile. But it wasn't warm. Then he turned away, walking back to his office down the hall. Undoubtedly, he would close the soundproof door.

She turned back toward the window. The barest edge of the sunrise was visible above the trees, just a slight lightening of the sky. In another hour it would be completely light. Leslie would be gone to work by then, and she had a meeting this morning to plan the annual Tour of Homes.

Time to put Richard Thompson and his family out of her mind.

CHAPTER SIX
They took everything?

Crank. May 2. 9:25 am.

Crank's eyes jerked open when he felt the wheels of the plane touch down with a loud screech, the tiny jet bouncing and bumping down the runway at Stafford Regional Airport forty miles south of Washington, DC. Instantly awake and craving a cigarette, he slid up the plastic window cover and looked outside.

The sky was ominous, banks of grey and black clouds forming a roof above them. It had been nearly one o'clock in the morning in California before they finally got off the ground, and the second half of the flight had been interrupted by stomach-wrenching turbulence. Five and a half hours later, plus three time zones, and it was already mid-morning here.

Across the aisle from him, Julia stirred, sitting up. Crank looked outside as the plane taxied to the end of the runway and turned to the left. From here he could see Interstate 95, which they would take to get into the DC area.

It was a parking lot. Lines of cars were backed up, unmoving, as far as the eye could see. A moment later the plane turned again to taxi back toward the general aviation terminal, and the view shifted to blissful, peaceful woods, hangers and warehouses. No traffic. Sometimes ignorance *was* bliss. Soon enough, Crank would be stuck in that traffic.

"What time is it?" Julia groaned. This despite the fact that she *already* had her phone out and was checking her email.

Crank didn't answer. He recognized the expression already on her face—a line, slightly off center, creasing her forehead. She was irritated about something.

"What the hell?" she muttered. She started dialing her phone.

"Problems?" Anthony said.

Crank looked back over his shoulder. The *Washington Post* reporter was sitting in the seat behind Crank, covering his mouth as he yawned. His eyes were red and puffy.

"I don't know," Crank replied. "Seems like everything's problems lately."

He stopped talking as Julia finally reached whoever she'd been calling.

"Mary, it's Julia. Talk to me."

Quiet, as Julia listened. Her expression grew more severe, then in a high pitched, strained tone she said, "What do you mean they're taking everything?"

Crank met Anthony's eyes. That didn't sound good at all. It wasn't the sort of thing he'd ever discuss with a reporter, but they had been shot at and nearly blown up together the previous night. If he couldn't trust Anthony Walker at this point, they had even bigger problems than he'd imagined.

The plane came to a stop, lined up with other jets of similar size. Julia immediately unbuckled her seat and stood, walking a few paces behind them. A moment later the co-pilot stepped out of the cockpit. "We'll have you ready to exit in just a moment, Mr. Wilson."

Crank had no idea what the plan was for transportation or luggage. But usually Julia had a car arranged. While she was busy on the phone he asked the copilot, "Um ... our luggage? Has our transportation arrived?"

"Yes, sir, I understand there's a car here to take you to Arlington. We'll have your luggage offloaded in just a few minutes."

"Thanks," Crank said. He *did* know they were planning to check into a hotel in Arlington. Which one, he had no idea—he'd never really paid attention to that kind of detail.

"No!" Julia said, too loud, into the phone. "Of course everyone will get paid. Just—tell them to take the rest of the week off. Paid, of course. Yes ... I know it's Monday morning. Yes, I know what that will cost. But everybody gets paid. I'm in Washington, DC right now—or I will be in a couple of hours, depending on traffic. I'll find out what's going on."

Everyone will get paid?

Crank ran those words through his head. What was she talking about? Of course, everyone would get paid.

Julia hung up and looked at Crank, alarm in her eyes.

No. Not just alarm. Her eyes were ... almost hollow. She was terrified.

"Jesus, babe, what is it?"

"The IRS. They served a warrant at the Boston office. Everything's been seized."

"What?" Crank said. "What do you mean, everything?"

"I mean *everything*. They took the records, the files, the computers. Mary said they took everything out of the office, told everyone to go home, then hung a *sign* on the front door saying we were closed for business."

As her words slipped into the curse, her tone went higher and higher pitched. "The IRS said we were closed for business, Crank!"

"I'm sure it's just a misunderstanding," he said.

"Doubt it," Anthony muttered.

"What the hell is that supposed to mean?" Julia asked.

Anthony rolled his eyes. "A misunderstanding? The same day your house gets blown up and just a few days after your sister gets herself kidnapped? I'm pretty sure you're a smart lady, Julia. You need to start thinking this stuff through. Because if the IRS is after you, you've got real trouble."

Her eyes flared, and she said, "Thanks for the news, Anthony. Why are you along for this trip?"

He smirked. "Seems to me you could do worse right now than have a journalist on your side."

She took a breath then closed her eyes. Crank could almost hear her counting. He could imagine the words running through her head. *One ... two ... three ... four ... fuck it.* Julia wasn't the most patient person on earth. Her eyes snapped open. "My apologies. Let's get to the car. I've got a lot of work to do." She turned and walked toward the front of the plane.

Anthony didn't respond. Julia had the capability to turn on a dime, and Crank had years of experience dealing with her. Anthony Walker was a newcomer.

Ten minutes later, Julia and Crank were sitting on the sleek leather back seat of a Lincoln Town Car, with Anthony in the front passenger seat. The car pulled out of the airport silently. Crank could feel the tension as Julia dialed again.

"Marty? It's Julia Wilson."

Crank nodded, slipping his phone out of his pocket. Martin Barrymore was their attorney.

"We've got problems," Julia said. Then she launched into a narrative about the bombing of her family home, followed by their detention in San Francisco, the questioning by Wolfram Schmidt, that freak from the IRS, and then the news that the IRS had apparently seized their offices in Boston.

Crank was a musician. He was the lead singer and guitarist for one of the most successful bands in the world. He was, technically, a multimillionaire many times over. But when it came to legal or financial matters, he was out of his depth. Quite intentionally, he'd never really taken any interest in the business outside of supporting Julia's efforts. He listened. He knew all about the problems they had with the music being pirated, with declining sales revenue, with counterfeit merchandise. But in the end, it was his job to make music, and Julia's to make money.

So now, in the middle of a crisis?

He felt useless. Worse than useless. Because he couldn't help but wonder if he'd said something to Schmidt that might have gotten them into trouble.

You signed the tax returns, Schmidt had said. *So clearly you're responsible for them, right? Tell me about those stock sales.*

I don't know what you're talking about, Crank had replied. Over and over again.

Anthony twisted around in the front seat and said, "So, you just make the music, right?"

"Yeah," Crank replied. He felt defensive about it. Should he have taken a more active role? Julia loved the business side of things. She always had. But now he wondered if he should have stayed more involved. More engaged. Was he giving her the support she needed? Had his neglect of the business somehow put them in danger?

"You mind if I call in to some of my guys at the national desk? Something stinks here."

Crank met Anthony's eyes. Julia had trusted him this far. And it's not like he had to ask. The guy could go ask whatever questions he wanted.

"Yeah, knock yourself out. Whatever." *Whatevah*. He was tired, and he knew when he was tired his accent was wicked strong. And he didn't really care what Anthony thought anyway.

All the same, he listened as Anthony dialed and started talking.

"Hey, Ron? Anthony Walker. Yeah, listen, got a question for you. I'm sitting in a car right now with Crank and Julia Wilson ... yeah, really ... anyway, they've run into some issues with the IRS and something stinks ... *what?*"

Crank stiffened. Anthony had jerked in his seat, his back stiffening as he said the word *what?* What was that about?

Anthony had taken out his notebook and was scribbling in it as he nodded. "Uh-huh ... yeah ... okay. Isn't that pretty quick?"

The response was loud enough Crank heard it. The guy on the other end of the line said, "Hell, yes."

In the meantime, to his left, Julia was speaking into her phone. "Martin, I get they've got an investigation going. We'll deal with that. But there's due process. They can't just come in and send my employees home and take *everything* from the offices."

Her face blanched a little at the response. "What?" she said. She waited a second, then said, "All right, so they can. But they *shouldn't*. That's where you come in."

She listened, her face looking thoughtful. "Okay ... yeah. Yeah. Right. In the meantime, how do I pay my employees? Our payroll is fifty-thousand dollars every two weeks."

She frowned. "No. That's not acceptable. I can't tell them that."

Jesus Christ, Crank thought. None of this made any sense. And seriously? They paid that much every two weeks? He knew they had a large office full of employees in Boston—twenty-five people, actually—but that was still a lot of money. He tried to figure out the math and got lost. Then he got frustrated. Why the hell didn't he know this stuff?

He turned back to Anthony, who had disconnected his cell phone.

"What the hell was all that about?" Crank asked.

Anthony looked at him, surprise in his eyes, and said: "This is way bigger than I thought."

"What do you mean?"

Anthony grimaced and rubbed the bridge of his nose between his thumb and forefinger. Then he said, "The Attorney General just announced a special prosecutor is being convened to investigate Richard Thompson."

"*What?*" Crank and Julia said simultaneously. She set her phone down at her side, without any ceremony or word to the attorney on the other end of the line.

"Sorry, Julia. There's supposed to be a press conference at ten. But you know how it is—someone already leaked the story. Apparently there's evidence linking your father to major drug money laundering."

"Bullshit," Julia said.

"Yeah, well, the Attorney General doesn't think it's bullshit. Apparently the IRS doesn't either, because at the press conference they're going to accuse you of managing the whole operation."

CHAPTER SEVEN
Occam's Razor

Carrie. May 2. 9:35 am.

"**M**y computer," Carrie muttered, adding to the list she was compiling on her phone. Her list of things she needed from the condo, if they hadn't been seized as evidence.

"My guitar," Sarah said.

"Sure," Carrie replied. She added it to the list then took a sip of her coffee. Sarah sat across from her, reclined in the thickly padded dining chair, her legs stretched across to another chair. The table was thick glass that colored her legs with a pale blue and slightly obscured and blurred the thick, ropy scars on the outside of her left leg.

Across the economically furnished room from them, Alexandra paced back and forth in front of the sliding glass doors. Every few minutes she checked her phone. A few feet away, Rachel was asleep in the crib someone had managed to procure in the middle of the night.

All three of them jumped when they heard a knock at the front door. From the kitchen, Ben Crosby, one of their several guards, called out, "I got it."

Ben was in his mid-twenties, muscular, short-haired, and bore several weapons. A former soldier, he was jocular, with a ready smile and blue eyes that flashed intelligence and occasional danger. In some ways he reminded her of Ray. Optimistic. Honorable.

Probably doomed. Her husband, her poor, demented husband ... he'd walked into that trial ready to do battle, optimistic, somehow believing all the way through that doing the right thing would save him. He never expected someone to play outside the rules. He never expected a killer to try to save himself by committing murder.

He never even knew she was having a baby.

She dismissed Ben Crosby from her mind. Bitterness about Ray sometimes filled her thoughts, clouding her mouth with dust. But still, a lot had changed in nine months. Sometimes she went an entire day without falling apart, without her mind turning over again and again what had happened.

But she knew she would never be completely free of it. Free of the grief that continued to overwhelm her if she wasn't careful.

A moment later Crosby returned. Accompanying him was Bear Wyden.

Alexandra froze mid-pace, turning to face Bear, and Sarah looked up from the table, sudden interest in her eyes.

"Anything?" Alexandra asked.

No one had to ask her what she meant. Bear sighed and said, "No sign of Dylan. But we found his cell phone."

"Where?" she asked.

"Young couple from Gaithersburg—they were in Bethesda for drinks last night and left the top down on their convertible. Apparently Dylan threw his phone in the back seat of the convertible. We tracked it by GPS to their home."

Alexandra's face twitched. "No sign of him there? You searched their place?"

"Mrs. Paris—"

"I just want to know if you searched their place? What is the problem—?"

"Stop," Bear said. His tone was firm. "We're doing our best to find him, but this isn't helping."

She shook her head. "Just like you did to protect us, right?"

Carrie interceded, "Alexandra, this isn't helping."

"*You* stop. Just because you lost Ray doesn't mean I'm going to let the same thing happen to me!"

Carrie winced and stood up without thinking. She took a breath, ready to respond to Alexandra's verbal slap with a cutting response, but stopped herself. She took a deep breath and reminded herself how horrible those hours had been after the accident. Ray injured. In surgery. Dying.

She remembered the words he'd said to her over and over again, during their worst times. His words that had calmed, promised, and failed in the end, through no fault of his own. She walked around the table, toward her sister, even as Alexandra's eyes brimmed with tears and she said, "Carrie, I'm so sorry, I didn't mean it—"

"It's okay," Carrie whispered, lying. Sometimes you had to lie to serve a greater truth. She put her arms around her sister and said the words Ray had once said to her. "We'll get through this together. I promise."

At that, Alexandra's slight tears broke down into sobs. "Oh, shit, Carrie, I'm sorry!"

Carrie heard Sarah, behind her, talking to Bear. "Give her a second. She's been a mess all morning. In a few minutes she'll get it together."

Alexandra sniffed and started to try to pull herself together. Carrie took her hand, and said, "Come sit."

Alexandra followed, and Carrie said to Bear, "Can I get you anything? Coffee?"

Bear shook his head violently. "I had a million cups of coffee overnight. Last thing I need right now."

Sarah said, "You haven't slept?"

He gave her a dismissive glance then said, "I came out to brief you ladies on what we know so far, and to ask you a few more questions. Then I'm getting a couple hours of sleep."

"Wait," Carrie said. "I need to apologize for this morning, I was kind of a bitch."

He held up a hand, as if to forestall the apology, and as if she'd been waiting for the queue, Rachel made a tiny coughing sound then began to cry.

Carrie started to stir, but Sarah jumped to her feet. "I've got her, Carrie."

"Just bring her to me," Carrie whispered.

Sarah lifted the baby and gently carried her to her older sister. "I hope the sight of a woman's breasts don't offend you, Mr. Wyden."

He coughed, suddenly uneasy, and said, "Do what you gotta do." All the same, he looked away as Carrie rearranged herself. Awkwardly, his eyes fixed on a spot somewhere far to her left, he said, "No need to apologize. We're all under a lot of stress."

"How is Leah?" she asked. The baby was latched on now. She draped the baby blanket around Rachel and looked in her eyes. They were pale blue, searching, serious. Carrie rarely felt happy or at peace these days. But when she fed her daughter, for the first time in her life she felt the presence of God in the bond between her and that tiny, defenseless baby. Sometimes she looked into Rachel's eyes, and she could feel Ray's arms wrapped around her from behind. His legs clasping her thighs, his eyes as he looked over her shoulder into the eyes of their daughter.

Ray Sherman wasn't alive anymore, but when Carrie gave herself to her baby daughter, she could still feel his breath in her soul. She knew that no matter what happened, she would always feel it.

Now that Carrie had more or less covered herself, Bear looked back toward her and answered the question. His face was surprisingly emotional. "Leah's going to pull through. She took two bullets, and it was touch and go all night. But she's stabilized. Gary—he's her new husband—is staying at the hospital, and I'm going to spend the morning with the kids and hopefully get a couple hours of sleep in."

What? None of that made sense. Unless—wait... "Leah isn't..."

"My ex-wife? Yeah, she is."

"I had no idea," Carrie said, her voice low. She studied him. He was exhausted, his eyes red rimmed, dark bags permanently formed under them. But she could imagine the turmoil he was going through. Leah and Bear might be divorced, but he would have to be inhuman to not be turned upside down by this. "I'm doubly sorry for this morning. I was a raging bitch."

He waved a hand to dismiss it. "All right. So first things first, I want to go over a couple of things with you, and ask you some questions. First—any clue where Dylan and Andrea might be other than the text he sent? Any friends in town? Hideouts? Acquaintances?"

Alexandra shook her head. "I don't think Dylan knows anyone around here."

"No old Army buddies?"

Alexandra shook her head. "None that I know of. Most of..." Alex's voice trailed off.

Carrie leaned forward and spoke in a bitter tone. "Most of Dylan's *Army buddies* are dead, and the ones who aren't are in prison."

Bear grimaced. "Right. The shooting in Iraq."

"Afghanistan," Carrie corrected.

He nodded. "I'm gonna ask you a straight question here. Carrie, it's your condo. Any idea how the drugs or cash got in there?"

Carrie twisted her mouth a little, and Rachel stirred, grabbing at her with a tightly wound fist. "Someone planted it there. I guarantee you Andrea's not mixed up in drugs."

"What about Dylan? I understand they had him on some pretty powerful painkillers after his injury."

Alexandra said, "Dylan doesn't even drink. Much less do drugs." For a quarter second longer than they should have, Carrie's eyes locked on Sarah's. Then she looked away.

Alexandra was fooling herself if she didn't know Dylan was drinking again. Carrie had seen it in the furtive movements of his eyes, in the tension in his body when he was near Alexandra, in the slight shake of his hand. From Sarah's expression, she knew it too. All the same, while Dylan may be drinking again, he certainly wasn't dealing massive quantities of drugs. She didn't know where the drugs in the condo had come from, but it wasn't Dylan Paris.

"All right," Bear said. "So they didn't come from Dylan, and Andrea had literally just arrived in the country. And we *know* she had nothing, because she was kidnapped off the plane and her things were examined and catalogued before they were returned to her. Had anyone else been in and out of the condo?"

Carrie shrugged. "Not in the last week. Family. My father. The nanny. And a bunch of people from Diplomatic Security."

"Does the name Ralph Myers mean anything to you?"

It wasn't familiar, and Sarah also shook her head no. But Alexandra spoke up. "Isn't he one of the guys on your team? He asked me some questions about Columbia. Yesterday? I think so. It's all jumbled together."

"Where was he? Where were you?"

Alexandra closed her eyes and thought. "Carrie was out, gone to see Dad. Andrea and Sarah were at the doctor. Must have been yesterday."

"Where was Dylan?"

"Out on the deck reading a book. We'd ... we'd had an argument. Anyway, Ralph said he was on duty and was just curious about how Dylan and I met. He's a nice guy."

Bear frowned. "He was a nice guy. He's dead now."

Carrie flinched, and for just a second she felt a flash of irritation at Bear. She knew it was irrational. But she couldn't stop herself.

"The attackers killed him?"

Bear shook his head. "No, as best we can tell, Dylan Paris did. Myers was one of the attackers."

Alexandra gasped, and Carrie's irritation at Bear shifted to anger. "Mr. Wyden, do you think you can consider—"

"No. I need to know," Alexandra said. "What happened?"

Bear sighed. "We're still trying to reconstruct the events, and some of it I can't talk about. But as best we can figure, when the attack came, Andrea went over the side of the balcony, and Dylan stayed to ambush the attackers."

"Andrea did *what?*" Carrie asked.

"She tied a blanket to the balcony rail and used it to swing down to the floor below, then smashed in their sliding glass doors and let herself out on the 19th floor."

"Badass," Sarah murmured.

"And what happened after that?"

"The shooters killed Mick Stanton, and wounded Leah. Once she was down they busted open the door to the condo. As best we can tell, Dylan was hiding behind the door—he took down one right there, and the other one in the living room."

Carrie said, "He took them down?"

"The evidence seems to indicate he stabbed them with kitchen knives."

Alexandra gasped and covered her mouth.

"At that point," Bear said, "it's not clear what happened next. He had blood in his shoes—it looks like he went into Andrea's room and took some of the cash. We're still reconstructing the scene. But he left the building via the elevator at that point. The car he threw his phone into was near the Metro station, so we think he *may* have gone that way, or he might have taken a cab. We're having some trouble getting the surveillance video from the Metro station analyzed."

"Maybe you should leave him alone," Sarah said.

"Sarah," Alexandra commented. "We need to find him."

"Seriously," Sarah replied. "Think about it. He's taking Andrea underground, because someone is trying to kill her. Will you get that through your head? The last thing he needs is to have the cops breathing down his neck. And frankly," she said, looking now directly at Bear, "you need to spend more time figuring out who is trying to hurt Andrea and less time trying to stop her from getting away from them."

Bear frowned. "I'm going to be straight with you, but you've got to be straight with me. Why didn't any of you tell me the IRS was investigating the family? Don't you think that might have been relevant information?"

Carrie stared at Bear, stunned. "What are you talking about?"

"Don't bullshit me. The IRS seized your sister Julia's offices this morning. They've had an investigation running for some time."

She turned to Alexandra. "Do you know anything about this?" At Alexandra's head shake, she said, "This is the first I've heard of it. I haven't talked with Julia since the middle of the night last night. She's on her way here, last I heard."

Bear shook his head. "No one's questioned you? Asked any questions? Sent even a letter in the mail?"

"From the IRS? Nothing."

"I don't get it." Bear looked genuinely puzzled.

"Neither do I. Just in case you missed it, we've been basically housebound since the day Andrea arrived in the States."

Bear leaned forward and looked closely at Carrie. "Look, Carrie, I know you and I haven't exactly hit it off in the last few days. But I need you to level with me. I don't know exactly what's going on with all of this stuff, but you can bet if what I'm hearing about the IRS is true, you'll have agents coming to see you. FBI, treasury agents, who knows what. You're certain you know nothing of this?"

Carrie looked him in the eye. "I'm certain."

"All right," he said. "I'm going to do everything I can to make sure you're safe. You and your sisters and your daughter. What I need you to do is keep talking to me. You hear me? You *have* to let me know what's going on."

Carrie took a deep breath and sat back. She looked up at the ceiling. Did she really have any good reason to trust Bear Wyden? So far nothing in her experience led her to trust any federal agent. She remembered all too well sitting in a room across from Janice Smalls and Jared Coombs only a year ago as they prepared to destroy Ray's life.

Something about Bear, though ... made her want to believe. He wasn't a soldier—he never had been from what she knew. He looked nothing like Ray. He was a barrel of a man, with few social niceties. But the fact was, she *needed* to trust him.

Before she knew what she was doing, she said, "I think this is all somehow related to whoever my father is."

"Secretary Thompson?"

"No," she replied. "No. Apparently, he ... is not my father."

Bear nodded. "I suspected so. Nor is he Andrea's."

"That's right."

"What makes you think that has anything to do with all of this?"

Carrie shrugged. "Obvious, isn't it? No one's ever tried to kill any of us before. But now, when we're getting blood tests related to a genetic disease? Are you familiar with the term Occam's Razor?"

Bear shook his head. "Afraid not."

"Basically it's a principle used in science—in short, if you have a bunch of competing hypotheses, the one with the fewest assumptions is most often correct. You start out with the simplest explanation and work your way up."

He nodded. "Yeah, they teach the same principle to detectives. Because it's the truth—ninety percent of the time, the obvious perp is the one who did it."

"But not always," Alexandra said.

"No, not always."

Sarah asked the next question. "So what's the simplest explanation here?"

Bear shrugged. "Your father isn't Richard Thompson. Someone else is. And that someone else doesn't want to be found out."

"You would have to be one cold-hearted bastard to kill for that."

"If there's power and money involved, you can assume that. Who are our candidates to be your father?"

"My dad—shit..." Carrie stopped. "I've always called him that. My—whatever he is—says Senator Chuck Rainsley is my birth father. I have an appointment to see him later this morning. Or rather, Andrea and I had one."

"I'll take you," Bear said, sighing. "I'll get with the kids this afternoon."

Carrie sighed. "Thank you."

"There's one more thing you need to consider, Carrie."

"Yes?"

"Whoever is trying to hurt Andrea—if it's because of who her parents are—then we need to be concerned about your safety too. And Rachel's."

CHAPTER EIGHT
Open Up.
Police.

Andrea. May 2. 10:15 am.

The rhythmic thumping from the headboard of the room next door did nothing to ease Andrea Thompson's frustration, nor the fact that it had been going in spurts all night. The pattern was clear. Twenty minutes would go by. The door would open, and she'd hear voices. Then the building seemed to shake as the steel door slammed shut, and a few minutes later it would start, usually slow, then faster and faster. Never more than a few minutes. Then the door slammed again. The television Andrea kept on wasn't loud. She didn't bother—it would have to be all the way up to block out the noise from next door.

It was a few minutes after ten and this had been going on all night. An internal debate had been running through her head after she lost count sometime in the early morning, awakened every forty minutes or so. Was the woman next door a prisoner? Was she trafficked? Or a prisoner of her own addictions? Who knew?

What Andrea did know was that she herself was effectively a prisoner, a fugitive. It presented an interesting ethical problem for both her and Dylan. If the woman next door was a prisoner, they should call the police. But of course, the police had clearly demonstrated they couldn't protect her. And Andrea did not want to die.

Right now, however, she was nervous and frustrated and frightened. Dylan had left almost an hour before to get cigarettes and find out what he could of the news. An hour later he still hadn't returned, and she was worried that whoever was after them had somehow found him. Was he laying somewhere injured? Was he dead?

Andrea replayed her doubts and worries over and over again, a never ending loop of anxiety and stress, a film on repeat that kept showing her the same images. Hairy Chest, his dead and swollen face as he collapsed in the car. The sight of Dylan, psyching himself up to a killing rage, knives in both hands, as she swung down off the balcony. But even further back. The disapproval on her father's face. She remembered the looks he'd given her when she was young, but they'd never made any sense. The looks of slight disgust and solid disinterest. She remembered her mother's tears and protestations that they loved her.

Then why do you keep sending me away? Andrea had asked once. Three years ago? It was right before her thirteenth birthday, in June of 2010. *My birthday is in two weeks. Why are you sending me away?*

Her mother had sighed and said, *It's best, Andrea.*

She *hated* her mother. Her father she could understand—he was a cold bastard and rarely came out of his office to spend even five minutes with any of his children. But her mother? *Why?*

It had never made any sense. Until she discovered that Richard Thompson wasn't even her father. Then the ugly stares, the disinterest, the bitterness of her exile all made sense. Andrea was the evidence of her mother's infidelity. Richard was a bastard, but he was a bastard for a reason. Because of their mother.

Andrea started at a knock on the door. She sat up straight then grabbed for the long serrated kitchen knife Dylan had left with her. She didn't answer the door.

Another knock.

She tensed. Dylan was supposed to identify himself by voice if he came. So who the hell was at the door?

She slipped off the bed where she'd been sitting, and moved in a silent crouch to the door. The blackout curtains were ineffective, weak light slipping around them in all directions, but they were enough to block her view of the outside. She slowly came to her feet and put her eye to the peephole in the door.

She froze. Outside, standing in the oppressively dim light, was the hotel manager or desk clerk, a grizzled Indian or Pakistani with nearly white hair and beard. Next to the manager was a bored looking police officer. The hotel manager said something in words too quick to understand, and the cop said, "No, don't open it. What about the next one? That's where you said the noise was from?"

Shit! Andrea thought quickly. Someone, maybe the hotel manager, had called the cops reporting suspicious activity? Maybe reporting whatever was going on next door?

Did they think she was somehow involved in that?

A moment later she heard the thumping stop next door. A loud voice, the words unclear, then she heard the words clearly. "Open up. Police."

Shit. Shit. Shit. Andrea leaned close to the blackout curtain. Careful to not move it, she put her eye near the gap between the wall and the curtain, trying to get a view of whatever was happening next door.

Movement. Then a loud noise, and the door next door slammed. The cop moved into the room, and the manager stood outside. Loud voices. Shouting. A male voice, the john maybe, begging.

A moment later she saw a man come running out. Grey suit, his shirttail hanging out. He walked past the hotel manager, looked back, and then ran.

The door slammed. Andrea started to back away from the blackout curtain, but then she noticed that the manager hadn't moved. What the hell was going on? He stood, his back to the door, hands clasped behind his back. His right leg bounced a little. He swayed on the balls of his feet, turning slightly toward Andrea's room. She jerked back from the opening.

Then she realized exactly what was going on. Because she heard a female voice cry out. Loud. Someone *had* called the cops, and this was the result. Whoever that poor woman was next door, the cop had decided to exploit her too, instead of helping.

The rage that flooded through Andrea right then was nearly uncontrollable. She sank down, resting on her haunches, shaking with anger. She squeezed the knife in her hands tighter, wanting nothing more than to run next door and use it on the cop who was abusing his position.

Jesus Christ, what could she do about it?

And what would happen if Dylan came back right now? Would he blow his temper? Go next door? Would he get them caught?

Or was Dylan out drinking somewhere? She didn't know much at all about him, except that he was a war veteran. Sarah had said he was a reformed alcoholic who had started drinking again. Andrea knew about addicts and alcoholics, and the one thing she knew was they couldn't be trusted if they weren't in some kind of serious recovery.

The noise started again, the headboard of the flimsy bed banging into the flimsy wall of the crappy room next door, and Andrea realized that she had no choice.

None.

The bathroom had a small window that she could climb out. She stuffed her few things into her plastic shopping bag, then walked to the phone. She closed her eyes, then picked it up and dialed 9 for an outside line. Then 911.

"Prince George's County 911, what's your emergency?"

"I'm calling from the Annapolis Road Motor Inn. A girl was prostituting herself next door, and someone called the police. Now the police came and they're screwing her."

"Ma'am, what is your room number?"

"I'm in 112. They're next door, the door to the right of my room. The police officer is in there right now, screwing her. Do you hear me? Instead of helping her, he's fucking her while the hotel manager keeps watch."

"We're dispatching someone right now, can you tell me your name?"

"No. I have to go."

Andrea set the phone in its cradle and walked to the door. She set the chain on the door and turned the deadbolt. Then she ran for the back window. It was small, but she should be able to fit through. High above the toilet, the glass frosted. She slid the window back.

It stuck.

Damn it. What was she thinking? She should have checked the window first. But the rage, the thumping next door, all of it was just too much. She yanked at the window again, bracing her right leg against the corner of the wall. Slowly, she felt it beginning to separate. Finally, with a sudden crack, the window snapped back and she slipped off the toilet, falling to the floor and hitting her head on the wall. Her vision went white, for just a second.

Jesus. She had to move. Back on her feet, she stretched for the window, lifting herself up and through it with both arms.

Her window was directly above the bed of a white, dirty pick up truck. She let her body fold through the window, hanging on with both arms and flipping over, landing in the truck feet first. The truck was parked in a dirty alley behind the motel. A ten foot high chain link fence, tangled with weeds and brush, was about ten feet from the back wall, the space between worn and potholed concrete. Puddles of filthy looking water filled the potholes.

Andrea jumped to the ground from the back of the truck. Old crushed beer cans and condom wrappers scattered the alley. She ran to the end of the alley then calmly walked out from behind the building. The motel, a grey painted building that looked as if hadn't been maintained since the 1990s sat on a corner of a two lane road and a larger, six lane divided highway. Annapolis Road was lined on both sides by fast food places, mini-malls, check cashing places and pawnshops.

She walked, back erect, across the two-lane road and sat down at the bus stop. Dylan would be back soon—she could keep an eye out for him here.

Three police cars were already in the parking lot of the crappy little motel, lights flashing. She couldn't tell from here what was happening. But she knew she didn't want to be over there.

There was Dylan. He was walking up the street toward her, a new backpack slung over his shoulder and a large shopping bag in his hands. His eyes darted from her, to the hotel, then back to her. No change of expression. The police out front were obvious.

He sat down next to her at the bus stop and lit a cigarette. "What happened?"

With as few words as possible, she explained the situation. When she talked about the police officer exploiting the woman in the room next door, his fists clenched.

"You did the right thing," he finally said.

"We need to find a new place to stay," she replied.

"Yeah. Here, I got you some clothes. I hope they fit. Jacket, pair of jeans. Size six shoes. I thought we'd head to the public library, get on the Internet. I want to touch base with Alex, then we're going to have to disappear again."

Andrea nodded. "Okay, Dylan. It sounds like a good plan. But somewhere along the road, we stop running. I want to know who my father is, and why this stuff is happening."

"Yeah, me too," he said.

They stood up when a bus slowed down. "Let's take this one," he said. "If it goes to a train station, we can go from there."

She nodded, and they waited on the edge of the sidewalk as the bus came to a stop.

Andrea glanced over her shoulder toward the motel. An ambulance had arrived at the hotel, and a young woman was being led to it by two female police officers. She had a black eye.

The no-longer-bored police officer was handcuffed and being led by two of his fellow officers to a car. Andrea gave a grim, satisfied smile and stepped onto the bus.

Adelina. May 2. 6:55 am Pacific

"We have to get going, Jessica. Let's get you together, and then you can sleep again in the car, okay?"

Adelina felt her eyes water with frustration as she finally gave in and physically pulled Jessica up, pulling her legs forward until they dangled off the edge of the bed.

"Mmmmm, I'm okay," Jessica mumbled.

The exhaustion, if anything, was worse now than it had been the first few days after they'd arrived at the retreat. Sister Kiara had been clear about that. Ten to twenty days where Jessica would do very little other than sleep or eat. Six months where she would seem listless. Increased risk of heart trouble, strokes or brain aneurisms because of damage to the blood vessels.

Most meth addicts relapse, Adelina. She'll need a great deal of care and close attention.

Right now Jessica just sagged in place. At least she didn't curl up again. The sun would be up shortly, and she wanted to be out of here within the next few minutes. She couldn't trust that the manager of the campsite would keep his promise. He might realize he had fugitives on the property. He might call the police figuring a reward might be in the offing. He might do *anything*, and she wasn't willing to take a chance.

At the same time, she wasn't taking her daughter out looking like this. Jessica's face was smudged with what looked like dirt. Her t-shirt was rumpled and dirty, which was probably fine—she was a teenager after all—but her hair was also a snake's nest of tangles.

"Hold still," Adelina said. And in the dim light of the cabin in the northern California forest, she began to brush her daughters hair.

"It's okay … stop…" Jessica said, pushing Adelina's hand and the brush away.

"Hush," Adelina responded. She brought the brush back up and began to brush. Jessica's hair had always been lighter than her twin's, brown like Alexandra's—and Richard's. She could see his features clearly on Jessica's face. The squarer than was entirely feminine jaw, the thick, almost luscious eyebrows. Richard had been a handsome bastard, after all.

Of course, that was one of the saddest parts about their marriage. It's not like Richard couldn't have picked up a woman. For thirty years she'd seen a parade of unfortunate women throw themselves at her husband, though it had become less common as they'd grown older. She never cared. If he was busy with someone else, he was far less likely to bother her.

Right now, Richard wasn't her problem. Jessica, her eighteen-year-old daughter, was. Jessica was leaning forward now, her eyelids heavy, and Adelina said, "Come on, Jessica, sit up. We'll be in the car soon."

A few more swipes with the brush brought Jessica's hair into some kind of order. Not beautiful, because large amounts of it broke off every time it was disturbed. Her hair was far thinner than it had been a few months ago. Her whole body was far thinner. Once again, rage at her husband flooded through Adelina. He'd been with Jessica, in California, while Jessica fell apart from grief and addiction.

While Jessica went to parties with guys from school, Richard had been busy in his office doing God-knows-what. Adelina had never trusted him. She'd never loved him. He'd never been her *hus-band* in any way that mattered. But she'd believed that he'd watch after his own daughter, while she stayed in Washington to deal with the aftermath of Ray's murder and Sarah's injuries.

Instead, he'd just let her do whatever she wanted. She'd signed her own report card and erased messages from the home answering machine documenting her absences from school. While he stayed locked in his office, doing whatever the hell it was he did, Jessica had found their emergency cash fund—ten thousand dollars, sorted in a steel box in the attic—and spent all of it.

While he stayed locked away in his office, Jessica had become a slave. All it took was one night at a party.

Miriam said it was okay, Mom, Jessica had told her, tears running down her face. *She said it wasn't addictive. I didn't know it was meth.*

It was too late. When Adelina returned home from San Francisco, she knew there were problems, but not how serious. She knew Jessica was losing a frightening amount of weight, but briefly, her grades returned to normal. January and February crawled by, with Jessica attending weekly therapy sessions. Adelina began to believe they were home free, until Jessica snuck out on a Friday night in April, two days after her eighteenth birthday. She came home with her clothing torn and dirty and a nasty bruise on her face.

Emergency room. Waiting hours. Long discussions with the doctors and therapists.

Then the ugly news. No available beds for three more weeks.

Finally Adelina decided. She made the arrangements to take Jessica to a private Catholic retreat tucked amidst the redwoods, and hired a doctor and nurse to attend to Jessica during the worst of the withdrawals.

"Almost done," Adelina whispered, as she finished brushing Jessica's hair. She hadn't realized tears were flowing down her face. Almost angry with herself, she swiped at the tears and pulled Jessica to her.

"Can we get some breakfast?" slurred Jessica.

"Yes. Let's go," Adelina said.

She took her daughter's hand and they left the cabin. The sun wasn't quite up yet, but it was close, the sky a vivid rose and orange shimmering through the trees. Adelina led Jessica to the car, then walked around to the driver's side and got in. Once they were both buckled up, she slowly drove out of the campsite.

Adelina shivered when she saw the old man who managed the site. He was standing outside the cabin near the entrance, in a grubby t-shirt, with a suspicious expression on his face. She was grateful he'd let them stay, but it worried her for the future. She thought about his expression as she drove away from the campsite, pondering his suspicious demeanor, then abruptly pulled the car over.

"Whas wrong?" Jessica slurred. She was holding a hand up to her forehead, a pained expression on her face.

"Don't worry," Adelina said. Only she *was* worried. She got out of the car and walked in a circle around it. It was a green Dodge Caravan and looked little different than a million other minivans on the road. Mud splatters on the bottom showed they'd been near the campsite. Adelina walked over beside the road. Thick mud. She leaned over and picked up two fistfuls, then threw a mud clod at the license plate, obscuring three of the letters. It wasn't enough, but any more might look obvious. She shook as much of the mud off her hands as she could and walked back to the car.

Of course, now her hands were covered in mud. She ran her hands along the hood, getting them wet, then reached inside, searching for a napkin or paper towel. Jessica's eyes were wide, but she passed her mother a small stack of napkins.

Adelina wiped her hands as best she could, then got in and started driving. She switched on the radio, switching the satellite radio to the all-news channel. She needed to know what was going on, and if there was any kind of search happening.

Voices. She listened, the voices washing over, something irrelevant. A joint Justice Department and Internal Revenue Service investigation into—

She jerked in her seat just as Jessica muttered, "*What?* Turn it up."

Adelina reached for the dial.

"We're returning to Jim Bowers with WNN News, currently at the Justice Department. Jim, what can you tell us?"

"Hi Bill. Well, what we know so far is that the Justice Department apparently opened an investigation in response to tips received when Acting Secretary Thompson was nominated as the Defense Department head. According to Rory Armitage, this has been—"

"That's the Special Counsel?"

"Yes, Rory Armitage was appointed as an independent counsel by the Attorney General. He's in charge of the investigation."

"Okay. And Armitage felt there was enough information to bring in the IRS?"

"That's right. We don't know the details of their evidence, but the accusations are clear. They're accusing Richard Thompson of outright corruption, documenting bribes and money laundering activities as far back as the 1980s."

"And this somehow involved Crank and Julia Wilson?"

"That's what the IRS believes. And the most bizarre part, Bill, is the involvement of the children. There's speculation that Thompson got into a conflict with a drug cartel, because the family homes in San Francisco and in Bethesda, Maryland were attacked last night. His wife and two of his daughters are missing right now, and the rest are in protective custody."

"Can you tell us something about the search?"

Adelina sucked in a breath. She looked over at Jessica, who sat, eyes wide, confusion on her face.

"I don't have many details, Bill. I know nationwide alerts have been sent out, and an AMBER alert for Andrea Thompson, since she's sixteen years old. I don't think the FBI is holding out much hope of finding them."

Adelina sighed. Nationwide alert. She'd have to be very careful. The police would be looking everywhere for her. She needed to stop. Get hair dye or bleach, do everything she could to change their appearance before the alerts went out far enough that people started to recognize her.

Damn it.

"Mom?" Jessica said, her voice shaking.

"Yes, sweetie?"

"What the hell is going on?"

Adelina sighed. It was a long, painful story. It was a story none of her children knew. It was an ugly story. Everything about their lives had been lies. But wasn't it time to start telling the truth?

CHAPTER NINE
Adelina's daughter

Bear squeezed the steering wheel and said, "Have you met Senator Rainsley?" His expression was severe. Before they'd left the safe house, he'd drunk three cups of coffee, explaining that he had been up all night. Earlier he'd said he was going home, but after a brief phone call he'd changed his mind.

Carrie, who wore a simple, but elegant suit, said, "I don't think so. He and my father were political enemies for many years. I remember hearing his name spoken like a curse."

"Interesting," Bear said. "It would tend to back up the idea that he's your birth father. That's an incredibly long running affair, though. You were born, when, 1988?"

"Flattery will get you nowhere. I was born in January '85."

"Okay. So this affair was going on from at least, what, March or April '84 up through ... 1996?"

"It had to have been on again and off again. My parents were posted to different cities during those years. Washington, Brussels, Beijing."

Bear nodded. "That makes a little more sense. So, she meets Rainsley in DC sometime in '84. They have an affair. You're born.

Then she runs into him again years later. Where were your parents in '96?"

"China."

"Rainsley was in the Senate then. It'll be simple enough to check if he was in China at any point then."

"My dad said so … *shit!*" Tears suddenly welled up in Carrie's eyes. Her *dad*. She sometimes felt like someone had punched her in the face when the knowledge hit that the man she'd always believed was her father wasn't. And not just that he wasn't—but that both of her parents had lied about it.

Why? If her mother didn't love Richard Thompson, why didn't she leave him? Why the pretense? It was clear her mother had never been happy. She'd suffered from depression and anxiety and God only knew what else, and she'd taken that out on her daughters for years.

She sighed. "Julia said she had some news related to all this that she found in San Francisco. But she didn't want to talk about it on the phone and asked to wait until we could meet in person."

"She's on her way to DC?"

"Yes. Last we talked she was stuck in traffic near Fredericksburg."

"Christ," Bear said. "So we'll meet back up with her later."

Carrie sighed. "No news about Andrea? Or my mother?"

Bear shook his head. "No. We've got alerts out for both. Police in both states have pictures, details. But nothing for sure yet."

"And what do you know about Rory Armitage?"

"Armitage? He's the special prosecutor investigating your father—the Secretary of Defense."

"It seems like all of this is happening very quickly. I mean—you know a little about what happened with my husband, Ray, right?"

"A little. I read about it in the papers."

Mention of the newspapers made her stomach twitch. She and Ray had been smeared in the news. "Everything in the papers was wrong," she replied sharply.

"Okay, so tell me what happened."

Carrie swallowed. "Army platoon went off the deep end. They took a lot of casualties, then the platoon sergeant went crazy and shot a civilian kid. Ray reported it several months later, and his sergeant leveled counter charges saying Ray had pulled the trigger. They put him on trial."

"And he was murdered," Bear said.

The word always hurt. It was ugly, and bare, and truthful. It said nothing and it said everything. "That's right," she said. "By one of his fellow soldiers."

"Jesus," Bear said.

"Anyway," she said. "You've got to understand. I've already lost my soul mate. My husband. And ... all I have is my family. My sisters. My daughter. You understand? I can tell you this much: Andrea's not mixed up with money laundering or drugs or anything else. Neither is Julia. Whatever's going on with this prosecutor and investigation stinks."

Bear didn't answer. He kept his eyes on the highway as they got closer to the city.

"Why aren't you answering?" she asked. "You think they're guilty?"

Bear shrugged. "I don't have enough evidence to have an opinion. I know your sister took out two experienced killers with her bare hands. I know they found drugs and money in her room. A *lot* of both. I know my ex-wife got shot down trying to protect her, but instead of turning herself in for safety, Andrea disappeared."

"Wouldn't *you*? It's not like she didn't have reason to disappear. Three attacks, Bear. Three. In less than a week. The only conclusion is that *you* can't protect her. Especially when at least one of your own people was involved."

Bear nodded. "Yeah. Yeah, good point. Which is why I'm taking you to see Senator Rainsley. Because everything about this makes exactly no sense at all."

Bear was driving too fast for the wet road conditions as he sped through Arlington on I-66. The speed felt like death to Carrie, and finally she said, "Slow down. My daughter already lost one parent."

He slowed.

Traffic soon began to back up near the Roosevelt Bridge. Soon they were creeping along, cars all around. The Potomac River spread across before them; ahead, the Kennedy Center, the Lincoln Memorial, the US Institute of Peace.

Carrie had avoided this part of town religiously. She remembered the last time—walking with Dylan down 23rd Street to the edge of the National Mall, just a few blocks from George Washington University Hospital, where her husband had been laying. Dying.

It was still close sometimes. The moment the doctors told her she had to make a decision, that he was brain dead, that he would never recover, that there was nothing there but a husk, a body connected to life support.

She looked down at the floor of the car and went silent. It was easier than seeing those places, which for her would always ache with his memory.

Bear frowned and said, "Everything all right?"

She shrugged. "Ray died a few blocks from here. This part of town always reminds me."

Bear sighed. "Sorry, Carrie. For what it's worth, you both got a raw deal."

"You've got no idea."

She turned away from him, resting her chin on a fist and blocking her view of both Bear and the State Department building to their left.

She knew what Ray would have said. Always optimistic, always hopeful. *You just have to pick yourself back up, Carrie. I love you. You can do this.*

He would have encouraged her. To keep going. To do the right thing. To take care of herself and her sisters and especially her daughter. And she would. She'd do what he would have wanted, because that's what you do, right? You just pick up and keep going.

"Almost there," he said.

The Capitol building was in view, the giant cast iron dome with its dozens of columns and ironwork statues stark against the ashen sky. This had once been Carrie's favorite city. She remembered spending her first two years of high school here, before they left for Moscow. She'd come back briefly with Julia, Crank and Sean in 2003. Then finally, in 2013, she'd come here to live. The best and worst year of her life.

She sighed. Right now, she needed to set all of that aside. She needed to remind herself that Ray Sherman wouldn't have sat around sighing. And neither would she. Carrie Sherman was made of stronger stuff than that.

She cleared her throat and muttered, "Sorry about that. I'm good to go now."

"Good," he replied. "We're going to park at Union Station and walk over. That all right?"

"Of course," she said.

They didn't talk as Bear negotiated the traffic near the Capitol building and then parked behind the large marble structure of Union Station. Twenty minutes later they were walking down the sidewalk to the Russell Senate Office Building, where Senator

Rainsley had his office. All around them were people who felt at home here: Senate and House aides, lobbyists and lawyers, Senators and Congressmen. People from a thousand different walks of life— from the seven figure lobbyist-lawyers to the minimum wage deliverymen. It was overwhelming. She'd grown up around the Foreign Service; she knew the ins and outs of the government from an early age. There was something comforting about walking down a sidewalk filled with oblivious government functionaries, people who had a sense of purpose, people who believed their lives mattered.

She stared up as they approached the stone and marble Beaux-Arts Russell Building. White columns reached to the upper stories, the windows between them lined up in a row down the block.

It was almost intimidating, she thought, as they went through security and on to the elevators. Inside, past the interior rotunda, was a long marble hallway with twenty-five foot ceilings, imposing marble walls and floors. The entire structure was designed to make visitors feel small, insignificant. And perhaps they were, in the context of history. But she knew that right now, her focus needed to stay very solid.

Bear finally stopped outside Senator Rainsley's office. A large symbol, the state seal of Texas, was mounted next to the doorway.

"You've been here before," she said. "You knew the exact way to this office."

He nodded. "Day before yesterday, as a matter of fact."

She blinked. "In relation to *this* investigation?"

"That's right."

She frowned. "You're not telling me everything."

"Of course not, Carrie. I'm running this investigation. I brought you here as a favor. I'll tell you what I can later, but don't expect me to fill you in on all the details along the way."

She shook her head. "I suppose I should thank you." Instead, she opened the door and slipped into the office.

"Doctor Carrie Sherman," she said to the twenty-something girl behind the counter. "I have an appointment with the Senator."

The girl blinked, startled. "Yes, ma'am." She instantly picked up her phone and spoke into it. "Doctor Sherman is here, Senator."

"I think the Senator warned her to expect you," Bear murmured. "I'm gonna sit out here and send some emails and get caught up on the investigation."

"You don't want to come in?"

"For your reunion with your long-lost birth father? I think I'd rather pluck out my eyebrows. You two have fun."

The girl behind the counter followed the entire exchange; her eyes shifting back and forth like two undersized radar dishes. Carrie ignored her and turned toward the main office as the door opened.

A very tall, trim man stood in the doorway. At six-foot six-inches, he was Ray Sherman's height, and somewhat taller than Carrie. His hair was steel grey, but might have once been dark brown like hers. His eyes were hazel. He looked like he might have a normally ready smile, but right now he wasn't smiling. Instead, his expression was serious.

"Carrie Sherman," he said. "Come in." He stretched an arm out to invite her into his office.

She let out a breath, suddenly realizing that for the space of ten or more heartbeats, she hadn't breathed at all. She stepped forward into the office, her eyes darting around. One wall was covered in memorabilia. Senator Rainsley in a basketball uniform, on the deck of an aircraft carrier, in a Marine Corps Colonel's uniform.

One photograph caught her attention. Rainsley stood in the rain at a podium, the Founders Court at Rice University clearly visible behind him.

"I got my PhD at Rice," she said.

"So you're Adelina's daughter," he said, his voice low.

She turned toward him. His expression was unreadable, but it wasn't what she expected. He didn't show fear, as if he were concerned a fifteen-year affair was about to be revealed, or that she was going to demand blackmail or money. Nor did he look like he was about to welcome a long-lost daughter. She didn't know what his expression meant.

"So you're my father," she said.

His eyebrows scrunched together. "Have you discussed this with your mother?"

"She's missing."

Finally an expression. Rainsley was stunned. "Missing?"

"Yes. She was last seen leaving a Catholic retreat center with one of my sisters sometime yesterday afternoon. Then she and Jessica called, and she told us to run. I have no idea why, and I don't know whether she's alive or dead." Carrie's tone was devoid of emotion as she spoke.

"Christ," he said. "I didn't know."

"You should read the papers," Carrie said.

Rainsley said, "I knew about the attack on your condo. But I've been in meetings all morning. As you may or may not know, yours wasn't the only attack yesterday. The head of British intelligence was attacked in his home at the same time."

She raised her eyebrows then shrugged that off. "I can't even imagine what that has to do with me. But according to … according to *my mother's husband*, you've got some explaining to do."

"I'm not your father, Carrie."

Carrie staggered a little.

He reached out a hand and took her arm. "Come. Sit."

She did, sinking onto a long leather couch. He sat in the chair that cornered the couch.

"I don't believe you," she said. "Look at you."

He sighed. "Believe me. I'm happy to discreetly get a DNA or blood test or whatever to prove it to you, if you like."

"And my sister Andrea."

"Your mother and I were never involved, Carrie."

"Why does my father think you were?"

Rainsley sighed. Then he looked at her and said, "Are you sure you want to open this can of worms?"

Carrie laughed, a little hysterically. "You're kidding, right? Did you just ask me that?"

He chuckled. "I guess you're saying that ship has sailed."

"Just ... if you aren't my father, then why did ... *The Secretary of Defense* ... why did he tell me you were? If you aren't ... then who is?"

Rainsley stood, stretching his long, lanky body. "Okay, first of all, I need to tell you that I don't know all the details."

Carrie crossed her arms over her breasts and raised an eyebrow.

"Fine," he said, defensively. "I'll tell you everything I can. Your mother and I have known each other since ... oh ... 1984 or so. She had just come to Washington, and your father—Richard Thompson, rather—had just come back from his tour in Afghanistan."

"He was never stationed in Afghanistan. We didn't even have an Embassy there in the 1980s."

"Technically I'm breaking the law by telling you this. But Richard Thompson was a CIA covert operative and worked his entire career under diplomatic cover. He was a central figure in arming the Afghan resistance in the early 1980s."

Carrie stiffened. "That's the most ridiculous thing I've ever heard."

"It's true. Do you want to hear the story or do you want to argue with me?"

She snorted. "If you want to fill your office with bullshit, by all means, go right ahead."

He shook his head. "Adelina—your mother—was really quite amazing. I won't lie to you, I was taken with her enough that Brianna had words with me the night we met. She was nineteen, I found out later, but told everyone she was older. Spirited, and clearly afraid of Richard. For a while there, when your father was traveling—which was often—she spent a lot of time with Brianna. They grew to be close friends—or as close as anyone can get to Adelina."

"Wait," Carrie said. "What do you mean ... nineteen ... in '84?" She shook her head. "That's not possible. Julia was born in '81."

"Funny how that works, isn't it? Richard Thompson was on a tour in Spain that year—the year there was a right wing coup attempt. He marries a visibly pregnant sixteen-year-old, then whisks her back to the States and disappears for a tour in a backwater in Central Asia."

"Jesus Christ," Carrie said. "He would have been late twenties then? Early thirties?"

Rainsley shrugged and sank down into his seat. "Yeah. I felt bad for her. She was afraid of him, no question there. I never saw any signs of physical abuse, but who the hell knows? Her fear of him had to be based on *something*. Brianna saw it too, and insisted we have her over as often as possible."

Carrie's stomach turned. She couldn't reconcile that idea with the passionless, cold man who had raised her. But even though he was remote, controlling, she'd never seen him as cruel. She's always seen him as her father.

"I don't understand," she said. "Any of this."

"Yeah. Well ... I'll be honest with you. I was on a crusade then. Planning to run for the Senate. I'd seen my entire command wiped out in Beirut. Largely because of inept pencil necks from Washington like Richard Thompson. So I may have been a little too sympathetic to his wife."

"What happened?"

"She fell in love."

Carrie sat up straight. *"What? With you?"*

He shook his head. "No. Not me ... I don't know who. She never told me. But it was clear. She had a beautiful light in her eyes. And a lot of fear. So when she came to us—I guess it was January 1990—she told us she was in danger. And begged me that if Richard demanded to know—if he accused me of having an affair with her, of being your father—then I was to admit to it."

"Why?"

"I don't know. But I wasn't going to tell her no. I wasn't—look. I don't know how to explain it. She sounded desperate. Brianna and I both worried about her, but she clearly wasn't ready to leave him. She *begged me.* So when Richard called me about it—"

"He called you?"

"Yes. Mid February of 1990."

"Okay. What happened?"

"He called. He demanded that I stay away from his wife. He threatened me, and he threatened to hurt her. It was an ugly conversation. But I kept my promise."

Rainsley turned and stared out the window. His shoulders sagged.

Carrie whispered, "You loved her?"

Rainsley shrugged. "I'm happily married, Carrie. But Brianna and I both cared for her."

"Enough that you risked your career for her."

He kept his back to her and waved a hand in the air dismissively. "I'm a Marine. This Senate stuff is all bullshit. It's like retirement, but more interesting than golf. Brianna wasn't happy, but she agreed it was necessary."

Carrie sighed. Then she whispered, "I'm glad she had someone to love her."

He turned toward her. "She had somebody," he said. "I just don't know who it was."

"Who does?" Carrie asked.

"Her priest maybe? Or God. I wish I knew."

CHAPTER TEN
Shut Her Up

Jessica bit into her third burrito as Adelina carefully took another bite of her first. "How come we never drove up here before?" she asked. "It's beautiful."

She was right. They'd just passed over a river in coastal Oregon, and to their right was the exit for Rocky Point County Park. All morning, they'd been driving slowly up U.S. 101 along the coast. There were occasional flashes of ocean as the highway twisted and turned, following the Pacific Coast. Adelina had been following the gas station map she'd picked up somewhere north of Oakland—their cell phones were somewhere in the bottom of San Francisco Bay. That Jessica hadn't really noticed or objected to losing her phone was a sign of how profoundly depressed she was.

The heavy rain that fell overnight had passed, leaving the sky cloudless and blue.

Adelina sighed. "It's complicated."

"You've said that about every question I've asked you this morning."

Adelina sighed. "Can I be honest with you, Jessica?"

Her daughter blinked. "I don't understand."

"You're eighteen years old now. I've been keeping secrets since long before you were born. But this one—I'm afraid if I start to tell you, you'll panic on me. I'm afraid if I tell you too much, you'll go right back to the drugs."

Jessica flinched. She curled up a little in her seat, drawing her legs close to her, and she whispered, "I guess I deserved that."

"The only thing you deserved is love, Jessica. You deserved ... parents who weren't crazy." She shook her head, trying to shake off the regret clouding her vision. "I'm sorry I couldn't give you that."

Jessica shrugged and took another huge bite. Adelina had never seen anyone eat so much in her entire life. She hoped she had enough money to keep feeding her daughter. The cash she grabbed from the bank had to last indefinitely, but they were going through it far faster than she'd imagined.

Finally Jessica swallowed and said, "Tell me. Please. I don't care how bad it hurts. It won't hurt as bad as a lie."

Adelina sucked in a breath, trying to hold back a mix of grief and a sad, knee-jerk anger. The accusation was true enough. She had lied. She'd lied to her daughters, and she'd lied to herself.

"I need you to hear me, Jessica. I know you think it won't hurt as bad, but if I tell you the whole story, you're going to feel like someone died."

She looked to her right, meeting her daughter's eyes for just a moment. Jessica nodded, and Adelina looked back to the road.

"Well, then. The first thing you need to understand is that everything you know about your father, and how we met, is a lie, mixed with truth, and mixed with more lies."

"I don't understand."

Adelina sighed with relief when she saw a sign for a scenic overlook. She needed to stop and tell this story when she wasn't driving. She swallowed, took the exit, and two minutes later pulled to a stop in a parking lot overlooking the ocean. Below them, at the bottom of a long steep hill, was the ocean, spreading out before them.

"I was sixteen when I met your father, not eighteen."

"Oh..." Jessica said.

Adelina wished she could think of a way to soften the blow. But she was coming to realize that it was secrets that had poisoned all of her daughters in one way or another. It was lies that had kept them from having a whole mother. So, for the first time, she told the unvarnished truth.

"He raped and impregnated me. He may have killed my father. He certainly made me believe he had. And then my mother forced me to marry him."

Jessica sat, staring at Adelina. She shook her head slightly, dazed. "That's utter bullshit," she said.

"No, unfortunately. It's true."

"Why did you stay with him?"

"I was trapped, Jessica. He threatened to hurt me, and more importantly, he threatened to kill Luis."

"Your brother?"

Adelina nodded. "Luis was two at the time. And my father was dead. I ... I didn't have anywhere I could turn."

Abruptly, Jessica opened the passenger side door, flooding the car with a cool breeze and the scent of the sea, and dropped out of her seat to the ground, nearly staggering. Adelina sat. She'd just told her already fragile daughter that her father was a rapist and a liar. Should she have hidden it? Should she have kept her secrets longer?

Jessica sat down on the low stone wall that edged the parking lot. She pulled her legs up close and wrapped her arms around them, then lowered her face so she was resting it against her knees.

Adelina wanted to weep at the sight. She'd spent so many years trying to protect herself and her daughters, and she'd failed them one by one. Every single one of her daughters.

Slowly, she opened the van door and stood. Jessica's shoulders were shaking. A pit of anxiety in her stomach, Adelina walked to her daughter and sat on the wall next to her.

Without raising her face from her knees, Jessica said, "Either I believe you and lose my father, or I assume you're crazy, and I'm stuck in a car with a crazy person."

Adelina slowly nodded her head and picked at her fingertips, knowing that Jessica's accusations were deserved.

"Father was the only normality we had, you know. Carrie used to sneak us out of the house and take us to the zoo or the park or the pool or the movies or anywhere she could think of, just to get us out of your way. Because you were crazy. You were always screaming or crying or falling apart."

Adelina closed her eyes. Then she whispered, "It's true. Carrie was your mom because I couldn't be."

"Yeah, but who took care of her? Who took care of *Julia?*"

"I think maybe God protected them," Adelina said. "I couldn't. You're right. I was literally out of my mind with fear. All the time. I'm so sorry, Jessica. I'm sorry I failed you."

Jessica choked a sob. "Are you kidding me?" she spit out. "You're *sorry?* Do you know what it's like to not be able to bring your friends home because you think your mother might be having a freak out? Do you know what it's like to grow up in a house where everyone goes from cold to hateful in just a second?"

Adelina took Jessica's hands in hers. She looked her daughter in the eyes and whispered, "If I could take it all back, I would. If I could make it better, I would."

Jessica's eyes welled up, and tears began to run down her face. "Mama," she whispered, reaching out.

Adelina pulled her daughter close. Jessica began to cry. First a thin, reedy cry, but soon she was wailing in great open-throated sobs, her shoulders shaking, her face buried in her mother's shoulder. Adelina knew it wasn't just this revelation she was crying for. She was crying for her lost love. She was crying for her twin, still recovering from an accident thousands of miles away. She was crying for all of the lost moments, the isolation and the quiet cold in their home. She was crying for the father she was losing, the father she'd never had.

Adelina. February 12, 1984

The alarm blared in a grating, angry tone, startling Adelina awake. She rolled over, groggy. She'd been awakened twice the night before by a dream of choking. More specifically, it was a dream that Richard was choking her.

It wasn't the first time, not by any means. But she hadn't had the dream in some time. Partly, she thought, because he'd made no physical demands of her since their first night in Bethesda.

That night, he'd been insistent. He'd arrived home from Pakistan and made arrangements to purchase a brand new condominium in Bethesda, Maryland, right around the corner from the Metro station that was under construction.

"The location will be really valuable once the station is opened," he'd said, droning mindlessly about matters she'd cared little about.

She didn't care how his real estate investments did. She didn't care how his career did. She hated him and how he'd destroyed her life.

Her disinterest had antagonized him, and he'd forced himself on her that first night back, then not allowed her to leave the room, even when Julia's cries from down the hall indicated their daughter had wet her diaper.

Adelina thanked God she'd not had to deal with it since then. And that he hadn't managed to impregnate her that night.

After that night, they'd fallen into an uneasy truce. She promised to handle their social engagements flawlessly. He promised not to hurt her.

It was no way to live, and she needed to find a better answer.

That morning, though, she knew exactly why the dream had come. Normally, the dream was formless, and it always started the same way—Adelina, in the practice hall of the National Youth Orchestra. Richard walked in, always in the black jeans and black t-shirt he'd worn the day he raped her the first time. Smiling. Menacing.

Last night, the dream had been different. Because *he* had been there. The smiling twenty-one-year-old Prince George-Phillip.

You're a charming woman, Adelina, he'd said.

You're too kind, she had whispered.

Every time his eyes grazed over her, she felt herself flush. It wasn't that she hadn't felt desired before. After all, *Richard* had desired her. But it was different. George-Phillip was kind. He'd been interested in what she had to say about the Youth Orchestra and her opinions of international politics, which she'd spent considerable time studying in the last year. His expressive face and animated eyebrows demonstrated how closely he was paying attention to what she said. Adelina might have had to drop out of school, but she was a very intelligent woman. No more than five minutes into their conversation, George-Phillip and Colonel Rainsley both realized that. The conversation had naturally shifted, mostly to the circumstances of Colonel Rainsley's run for the Senate.

"The problem wasn't that the orders were badly thought out," Rainsley had said. "The problem was no one in the White House *cared enough* to think through the implications of putting us there with rules of engagement that wouldn't allow us to defend our-selves. Do you know that was the deadliest day for the Marine Corps since Iwo Jima? And here's the thing—the White House couldn't even decide on a response. Too much political infighting, so we pulled our guys out, used a battleship to bomb the crap out of the wrong people and left it at that. Every single one of those young lives was *wasted*."

Of course the discussion had circled around politics and inter-national affairs. Richard was a Foreign Service officer, and their guests included people who weren't high government officials yet, but likely would be one day.

Adelina found herself staying careful. Periodically Richard's eyes wandered to her, and it was important to maintain the pre-tense that she was entertaining their guests solely for his purposes.

In fact, she'd found herself more and more drawn in by George-Phillip. Rainsley, initially, was dismissive of George-Phillip's opinion of anything military. That lasted right up until George-Phillip described the British recapture of the Falkland Islands al-most two years before.

"You were part of the landing force?" Rainsley asked, disbelief on his face. "You're too young."

"I was nineteen at the time, sir. After my father passed, I served a two year tour with the 5th Infantry Brigade."

"Under General Moore?"

"Yes, sir, you know him?"

"I do, I was briefly assigned as Liaison to Royal College of Defense Studies in '77. General Moore was assigned there at the time."

Adelina watched George-Phillip, intrigued. At first she'd taken him as a fop. Royal, perhaps, but a fop. But apparently he had enough substance that he'd volunteered to serve in an infantry regiment and fought in the Falklands War, when he could have just as easily sat at home spending his inherited wealth.

Colonel Rainsley had turned his attention from George-Phillip to Adelina. "We should turn the conversation to other topics," he said, "so we don't bore Adelina."

At the opposite end of the table, Leslie Collins and Richard were leaning close to each other, nearly whispering. Prince Roshan seemed equally involved in whatever they were discussing, which left Brianna Rainsley and Myriam Roshan stewing in the two middle seats of the table.

"No need to worry about boring me, Colonel, I'm quite interested in the topic. Unless Brianna or Myriam would prefer we discussed something else?"

George-Phillip gave Adelina a warm look, a slight twinkle in his eye, one side of his mouth slightly upturned. Adelina felt a deep sense of satisfaction at Rainsley's clear look of discomfort.

Myriam Roshan took the opportunity to ask Rainsley a question about his experience in Beirut and to lament the damage caused by the civil war, and the conversation moved on.

That night, Adelina dreamt of George-Phillip. Dreams that slowly turned back to the familiar scene, dreams that ended the same way they always did. With Richard's hands around her throat.

Her eyes had popped open and she sat up instinctively, terror clogging her throat, her heart thumping in her chest. It was four in the morning when she awoke from the dream, and it took her a long time to get back to sleep. She got up and got a glass of water, then went back to her room and lay down alone. With the door locked behind her. When the alarm woke her at six am, she felt strung out. Exhausted.

All the same, she dragged herself out of bed. She didn't expect to see much of Richard, but Sunday mornings she attended Mass at the Saint Jane Frances de Chantal Catholic Church on Old Georgetown Road. Services. Communion. But since her arrival in the United States, she'd not attended confession. Maybe soon, she thought. She'd been telling herself that ever since the day almost exactly three years before when Richard had walked into her father's shop. The day of the coup. The day he raped her.

Adelina left her room cautiously, as always. She didn't know if Richard was home—he often wasn't—but she didn't want to take the chance. Julia would be awake any moment. Adelina wanted at least a few moments before she was. She walked down the hall, passing Richard's closed door on her way to the kitchen. At first he'd balked at the idea of separate rooms, but he'd finally given in, with the admonition that she was to never tell anyone.

People will think we don't love each other. Married couples don't sleep in separate rooms.

We don't love each other, she'd replied. *No amount of lies will change that.*

He'd snarled at her and she'd walked away, knowing that antagonizing him any further was a bad idea.

The coffee pot—a new one, with a built in clock—was already on with a fresh pot.

Thank God. She poured herself a cup, generously adding cream and sugar, and walked toward the sliding glass doors and the balcony. She passed the mantel, with its bizarre decorations, including a gigantic brass head he claimed to have bought in Indonesia. It was heavy. One day she wanted to use it to smash in *his* head.

She slid open the sliding glass door and slipped into one of the cast iron seats at the table overlooking Bethesda, Maryland, and in the distance, Washington, DC. She left the door cracked—Julia would be awake soon. This was the one compensation for living here instead of San Francisco—or, for that matter, Madrid or

Calella, or anywhere else on earth without Richard. She loved the view from this balcony, she loved sitting out here and drinking her coffee and relaxing. She rarely had moments of unguarded relaxation. Very rarely. She closed her eyes and leaned her head forward and whispered a prayer.

"Mummy?"

Adelina swallowed and opened her eyes.

Julia had awakened and was standing at the sliding glass door. Her brown hair was tousled, curling around her head, framing green eyes that looked alarmingly similar to Richard's. She wore a blue nightdress with white flowers.

Adelina smiled and stood, then slid the door open slightly.

"Come here, baby," she said. She sat down, and Julia scrambled up into her lap and stretched her arms around her.

Adelina stiffened for a moment, then fought that down and hugged her daughter back, cursing herself. It wasn't Julia's fault Richard had ... it just wasn't her fault. But all the same, every time, she had to fight back the initial reaction. She had to fight against her instinct to shy away, her instinct to not be touched, ever.

"I love you, baby," she whispered in Julia's ears. But she wondered if her daughter would someday wonder why Adelina recoiled against touch. She sat there, holding her arms around that precious baby, and promised herself that no matter what else happened, she'd take care of that little girl.

"I love you, Mummy," Julia said.

The phone inside rang. Adelina felt a flash of irritation as she stood up to go get it, swinging Julia around to rest on her hip. Was it the babysitter again? She was late last Sunday, and Adelina ended up being late for Mass, which was yet another sore point with Richard, because he'd insisted Julia be brought up as Protestant. Not that he would make arrangements for Julia to have any other religious instruction. Nor could he be bothered to take any interest in his daughter in any other way.

You're not even religious! Adelina had shouted. *You're only doing this to spite me!*

She'd lost that battle, and Adelina had learned long since that she simply *couldn't* win all of them. But she would teach her daughter in private, no matter what he said.

Adelina reached the phone and picked it up.

"Hello?" As she answered the phone, Julia began to squirm in her arms. Adelina held on tightly.

"Mrs. Thompson? It's Marcy Whitsun. I'm afraid I'm not going to be able to make it on time this morning."

"That's fine," Adelina snapped. "Don't bother. Don't bother coming back at all."

"Miss Thompson? Wait, it's just that—"

"I don't really care what it is. You've worked for me for three weeks, and this is the second time you've called to say you're late or not coming on Sunday morning." Julia began to kick in her arms, but Adelina held on. She continued speaking into the phone. "I have limited patience. You've reached the end of mine."

She slammed down the phone, hard. Unbidden tears sprang to her eyes. The only thing that tethered her to reality was going to Mass. That was all she had. She *needed* to go. She needed the time.

"Mummy?" Julia said. Her tiny arms were waving wildly. "Mummy? Mummy?"

"*What?*" Adelina shouted.

Julia's eyes seemed to double in size as they filled with tears. Her face began to get red, and Adelina said, "I'm sorry, baby, it's not..."

She didn't get a chance to finish the sentence. Julia's face turned red and she began to scream.

"Oh, for Christ's sake," she muttered. She slid Julia down to the floor, where the girl promptly collapsed and continued screaming. Adelina looked around, her head swiveling round as she searched for her coffee cup, which she'd only had maybe three sips from before Julia awoke.

Julia let out a piercing scream.

And *that* was when Richard's door opened and he shot out of his room.

"Can't you quiet that child?" he shouted. "I'm trying to sleep!"

"Why don't *you* quiet her?" Adelina shouted back. "The only time I *ever* get to myself is Sunday morning, and now I'm losing that too."

His face stiffened, his jaw working, and he reached forward and grabbed the sides of her face and began to squeeze. "I told you to shut. Her. Up. *Do it*."

His face was red as he said the words, his teeth clenched and his eyes bugged slightly. Adelina began to whimper, the pressure from his hands on the side of her face causing intense pain.

"Stop!" she shouted.

He let go and pushed. Adelina staggered back against the wall.

He sucked in another breath, his shoulders rising, and Julia let out another piercing scream.

He pointed. "That child. If you don't shut her up, *I* will."

Adelina slid down the wall, backing away from him. His words instantly quelled any argument or defiance. All she had to do was remember her father, run down by a truck on a narrow Madrid street, and he instantly gained her obedience. She had a little brother, Luis, to protect. She had a daughter to protect. It didn't matter that Richard was Julia's father. The longer she knew him, the more she realized he simply had no normal human feelings.

She kneeled down and picked up Julia, who screamed even louder. "Stay away from her."

Richard sneered at her. "Gladly. I'm going back to sleep. If you have to, take her outside, but shut her up."

"I'm going to Mass this morning."

He threw his hands up in the air. "Fine! Take her to your Mass! Just shut her up!" Richard turned and stomped off, then slammed the door to his room.

Adelina turned back into the kitchen. Her heart was beating rapidly, and she could feel sweat on her forehead. "Calm down, Julia. You must calm down. Don't disturb your father."

Julia hiccupped and began to whine again. Adelina was desperate. She knew how to take care of babies—after all, Luis had been younger than Julia was now when she married Richard. She'd changed plenty of diapers and fed plenty of babies, and she knew what to do to calm Julia down. But the hardest part was calming herself down, and Julia would not calm down until her mother did. All Adelina could see was Richard, reaching his hands around her throat, ripping her dress, harming the people she loved.

She closed her eyes, desperately trying to breathe as waves of nausea and fear swept through her. "Come on, sweetheart, let's get you something to eat."

Eventually, Julia began to calm, and they sat together on the balcony as Adelina fed her daughter. The sun was coming up now; great bands of red and orange stretching across the sky. Adelina reflected that despite herself, she'd won another victory against Richard this morning. She'd won an essential victory, the fight for her daughter's soul, the fight to bring her daughter up in the Church. The flip side of that was the bleak realization that she'd won that victory not through her own efforts, but through her daughter's.

***

It was well past one in the afternoon when Adelina returned to the condo. Julia was asleep in her stroller—the long walk back from the church had been peaceful. The sky was a little grey, but by the time she started the walk back home, the temperature had warmed to the low sixties.

Normally Adelina made the walk home regardless of the weather, but that would change if she took Julia with her every week. Adelina didn't mind walking in a raincoat with an umbrella in thirty degree weather, because it gave her time to think. But a two-year-old couldn't do that.

The need to go to confession had been stronger than ever today. The last time she'd gone to confession had been traumatic. She remembered being on her knees in the parish church of Santa Maria in Calella, her mother on one side and the priest on the other, as she sobbed out a half-true story. She was pregnant, and gave the name of the father—Richard Thompson. But she didn't describe the circumstances, because she was too afraid. Too afraid he would hurt her brother, or her mother.

Father Dennis, the priest at Saint Jane Frances de Chantal, seemed like a trustworthy man. She'd watched him over the last few weeks since her arrival in Bethesda. In his early thirties, he had deep brown hair and eyes and moved around the church with deliberate care and courtesy to everyone. He'd made a point of introducing himself at her first Mass, and then sought her out twice since to make sure she was settling in well.

She'd never had cause to doubt a confessor before. The bond between a penitent and confessor was supposed to be inviolate, but she'd learned the hard way that not all men were able or willing to uphold the trust of that sacred bond. After her experience in Calella, she needed to be sure. What would happen if she told Father Tom about her rape, about Richard, about her lies to her family, about all of it? She didn't know. Part of her was deeply afraid he would betray her the same way the parish priest in Calella had done. She couldn't imagine the consequences of Richard in a real rage. For example, if his position were threatened. He'd made it very clear to her that his ambition was both boundless and that she was to do everything she could to support it.

As Adelina rode up the elevator, she felt, rather than saw, Julia begin to stir. Adelina crooned a quiet tune in the elevator, hoping to keep her asleep long enough to take a nap. She decided to take the chance. Next weekend she would go to confession. Her soul was more important than any earthly consequences.

Inside, she stood still and breathed in the calm for a moment when Julia didn't stir. The concierge had let her know that Richard was out. She knew he wouldn't be back until late that evening—whatever Richard did with his free time didn't include her. Sometimes he spent long hours locked in his study, and sometimes he just stayed out. She didn't really care where, as long as she didn't have to deal with him often.

She rolled the stroller back to Julia's room and slowly lifted her out of the seat to the crib, then froze halfway up.

The phone was ringing. *Damn it.* Julia started to stir, but Adelina whispered calming words and slowly got her into her bed. She tucked the blanket around her then stepped back.

The girl didn't stir. Adelina stepped out and gently closed the door.

She reached the phone just in time to hear the answering machine pick up.

"Um ... hello," said the voice on the machine. A warm, upper class British accent. She instantly recognized George-Phillip's voice and felt an intense anxiety.

"I'm calling for uh ... Mr. Thompson. This is George-Phillip Windsor, you were kind enough to host me for dinner the other night—"

Adelina snatched up the phone.

"Hello? Hello?"

"Um..."

The awkward exchange went silent. Then George-Phillip said, "Is this Adelina Thompson? It's so pleasant to hear your voice."

Adelina felt her cheeks heat up at the same time she felt intense shame. Hate Richard she might, but she was *married* to him. But just hearing the sound of George-Phillip's voice on the phone sent her heart racing.

"This is Adelina," she whispered.

"I—I called to say thank you for hosting the dinner the other evening. It was a distinct pleasure."

Adelina started to answer and found herself stumbling over her words. Flustered, she said, "Thank you. Would you like me to pass a message to Richard?"

George-Phillip coughed. Then he said one word, a word that made Adelina's chest hurt a little.

"No."

She swallowed, waiting for him to speak again.

"Actually," he said, "it's really you I wanted to speak with, if that's all right. You see, I'm still fairly new in Washington, and..."

"Yes?"

"I suppose it would be improper of me to ask you to meet me for lunch."

Extremely improper. But she wanted him to ask her. She wanted it very badly.

"Perhaps," he continued, "you could bring along your lovely daughter. I genuinely do have the highest of motives. You see ... ironically, you're the first person I've really met in Washington my own age."

She wrinkled her forehead. Of course. That made much more sense. Julia would act as a tiny chaperone.

"Of course. I think that's a lovely idea," she said.

"Perhaps Monday?"

"Monday is good. I can meet..." She thought quickly. Nowhere near Embassy Row, of course, though that would be most convenient for George-Phillip. The State Department wasn't far from there, and Richard might well be in that part of town for meetings. "What about ... Matisse on Wisconsin Avenue?"

Matisse was sufficiently distant from the State Department. Richard would be unlikely to be in that part of town. Plus, he hated French food, except when he was trying to impress others.

"That sounds lovely," George-Phillip said.

"Monday then? At one?"

"I will see you then," he replied.

Quickly, before she could acknowledge what she was doing, Adelina hung up the phone. Thirty seconds later, she let out a gasp, and only then did she realize that she hadn't been breathing.

CHAPTER ELEVEN
The Prince of Penguins

Jessica Thompson sat on the stone wall overlooking the Pacific Ocean and wondered what it would be like to throw herself off the wall, to roll down the cliff, to die in the cold, heartless waves below. A brisk and cold wind blew a chill right through her soul as she wiped tears and stared out at the ocean, wondering if her mother was a liar or insane. She had a piercing headache; the kind that felt like someone had driven a nail right through her skull. The pain was centered just over her right eye.

Abruptly, she said, "Show me your driver's license."

Adelina didn't balk at the strange request. Instead, she stood and walked to the minivan and opened the door, then took out her purse.

A moment later Jessica was holding the California Driver's License in her hands.

Adelina Ramos Thompson. Birth date: March 21, 1964.

The math wasn't all that hard to work out. Julia was born in December of 1981.

"You were sixteen when you got pregnant."

Her mother nodded.

"But you always said you were two years older."

Adelina sighed. "Your father always wanted it that way. He didn't want to get married in the first place, I think. But leaving a pregnant teenage girl in Spain would have been detrimental to his career." Her face looked wistful as she said the words.

"Why did you marry him?" Jessica asked. "Who marries their rapist?"

Adelina shook her head. "You grew up in a different world, Jessica. A world where girls tweet and post on Facebook and Instagram and marry other girls if they want to. A world where people have heard the terms *date rape* and *sexual harassment* and it actually means something. When my mother realized I was pregnant, she dragged me to the priest to go to confession. They forced me to marry him."

"I don't understand," Jessica said.

"Of course not. To you, some level of freedom has always made sense. When I was growing up, divorce wasn't even legal in Spain."

Jessica shook her head slowly. Her mind was awash with thought, with confusion. Then she said, "Why did you have more children with him?" She felt a stab of pain and something akin to grief. "Why did you have *me*?"

Adelina sighed. "That's a long story. I hadn't planned to have any children after Julia."

"You must have loved him a little, right? To sleep with him again? Otherwise ... what about Carrie? If you didn't love him?"

"Dear, Carrie isn't Richard's child."

Jessica winced. "Am I?"

Adelina reached out and took Jessica's hand. "Yes, your father is Richard."

"My father is the man who raped you," Jessica said bitterly.

Adelina closed her eyes. "Yes. I'm sorry."

Jessica gave her mother a scornful look. "*You're* sorry? He's the one who should be sorry." She thought through so many things in the past that hadn't made sense. Her dad, always locked away in his study when he wasn't working. His long trips away from home. His cold demeanor.

Was that why—?

"Mom? Is that why Andrea left home? Is she also not his?"

Her mother nodded. "Yes. I tried. I hated him, but I still tried to—you can't imagine how hard I tried to ... to—"

As her Mom flailed around for the word, Jessica muttered, "You mean, you tried to stay faithful."

Adelina looked down, her face twisted with shame. "Yes. But I couldn't."

Why should she have? Jessica thought. She didn't say anything right away. So much of this made no sense. It was one thing to believe that her father had pushed Adelina. That it had been date rape maybe. That he was drunk or worse. But she couldn't believe the father Adelina described—a cold-hearted sociopath. A man who would murder to protect his secrets.

Who was Richard Thompson? What did she even know about him?

The answer was basically nothing. She knew nothing about her father. Nothing at all.

"Mom ... what happened? *Why?*"

Adelina took a deep breath then began to speak again.

Adelina. February 13, 1984

Adelina Thompson squeezed Julia's hand tightly as the taxi jerked away from the curb, pushing its way into the heavy traffic along Wisconsin Avenue. It was almost one in the afternoon, and grey drizzle chilled everything in the area.

"I'm coll," Julia said.

Adelina walked down the sidewalk and said, "Come along, Julia."

"But I coll!"

"Julia, the word is *cold*. Please enunciate."

"I coll!" She wasn't any clearer, but she was a lot louder.

"We'll be inside in just a moment."

Adelina's heart was racing as she walked to the entrance of Matisse. She didn't think she was likely to run into anyone she knew here, or for that matter, anyone Richard knew. But one couldn't be too careful. Washington, DC might be a large city, but the class of high level government workers her husband belonged to was a small town indeed.

Even if she did encounter someone, she had Julia beside her. She was having lunch with another recent arrival to the city, a *Prince* for God's sake, and no one had any right to question it.

As she entered the restaurant, a mustachioed man, arrogant and commanding, approached her. He wore a tailored Perry Ellis suit, which probably cost far too much for his position. His eyes scanned Adelina and Julia ruthlessly, probably tallying up the apparent value of their clothing and hair accessories, undoubtedly taking note of the diamond bracelet she wore. Richard might be a complete bastard, but he liked her to look the part.

"How may I help you, ladies?"

"I'm meeting a friend ... George-Phillip?"

The maître d' raised his eyebrows. "Indeed. Prince George-Phillip will be here shortly. Please, come this way."

She followed, surprised as he led her to a small room in the back. "Please forgive the presumption. A most noxious person has been here stalking the Prince."

"Oh no," Adelina said. "Not a criminal, I hope."

He chuckled. An unpleasant sound. "Not that I'm aware of. A young lady, as a matter of fact."

Adelina gave him a frozen look as he led her to the private dining room. "You are impertinent," she said.

He sniffed and walked away without taking her coat. Not her problem. She took off her raincoat, then Julia's, and threw them on the overstuffed chair in the corner.

"Have a seat, Julia," she commanded, pulling out one of the dining chairs.

The little girl's chin barely came over the top of the table. Her face was set and unhappy.

"It's all right, dear. We'll get something for you to eat in a moment."

"Hunngy," Julia said.

"I am too. What do you say we play a game?"

Julia smiled, a bright, happy smile, and clapped her hands together.

"We're going to guess who's coming in through the door next. You guess first."

Julia's lower lip puffed out. "Don' like this game."

"It's okay, Julia. Just take a guess."

"A penguin?"

Adelina raised her eyebrows. "It could be ... it could be indeed. What if it's ... a prince?"

Julia smiled. "A penguin prince!"

"Yes!" Adelina cried. "A penguin prince!"

And of course, at that very moment, George-Phillip walked in through the doorway.

"No penguin I'm afraid," he said.

Julia giggled. "You *are* penguin."

George-Phillip looked down. Adelina snickered. He wore a black suit with a white shirt.

"Hmmm," he said, raising his formidable eyebrows. "Perhaps I *am* the Prince of Penguins. But in disguise."

Julia giggled again.

The formerly rude maître d' lifted their coats from the chair, as a hostess pulled out seats for Adelina and George-Phillip.

"It's marvelous to see you, Adelina."

"And you too," she said.

"And Julia. You are, perhaps, the most beautiful little girl in the entire world. I could easily imagine that *you* are a princess. Tell me it's true."

Julia giggled and buried her face in her mother's lap.

"The maître d' told me you were having some trouble with a … uh … stalker?" Adelina said.

George-Phillip grunted. "A little. Do you really want to hear this story? It's dreary."

Adelina smiled. "I'm curious."

"Well, when I first arrived at the Embassy, the charge d'affaires had no idea what to do with me. So he arranged for me to meet with a young society columnist with the *Washington Post*. You might be familiar with her work? Maria Clawson?"

Adelina grimaced. "Horrid woman," she muttered. "I met her at a party two weeks ago. She's a terrible gossip."

George-Phillip grimaced. "Yes, indeed. We dated a few times before I realized how vindictive she was. I broke it off in fairly short order, but I'm afraid she took it hard."

"I'm sure she did," Adelina said.

She was fairly certain Maria had appeared in Washington from the recesses of some empty place in the middle of the country, Kansas or Ohio or Minnesota, and only had pretensions at society.

Which would make her doubly offended at being jilted by an actual prince.

"So, Adelina. You know my background. You know my father died, and that I became Duke at too young an age, and served in the Falklands. Yet, I know almost nothing of you."

She smiled and deflected his words by saying, "I'm just a simple woman, George-Phillip. No real story there at all."

"You're from Spain. And I heard you say that you played with the National Symphony? At such a young age?"

"Not the Symphony, the National Youth Orchestra. I played violin."

"Played? Past tense?"

A stab of sadness sliced through her chest. "Played. I've no time for such things in my life these days."

George-Phillip leaned his head slightly to the side. "So sad for one so young."

"I'm not much younger than you," she replied, laughing. "What are you, twenty-one? Two years is hardly *that* big of a difference."

George-Phillip frowned a little. "I thought *you* were twenty-one."

Adelina froze.

"Oh, dear," he said. "How old *are* you?"

"Nineteen," she whispered.

"Hmm," he said. "That rather changes things, doesn't it?"

"Not really. It's just—awkward to explain sometimes."

"There's no need for you to explain anything, my dear. Sometimes we do things when we're young that surprises others."

She didn't know why she said it. She didn't know why. Absolutely nothing forced her. Nothing in her history had given her any reason to trust anyone—much less yet another over-privileged upper class white male. George-Phillip and Richard were probably cousins.

Despite all of that, the words that came out of her mouth were, "And sometimes people do things to young people who have no control over it at all."

He frowned, and she instantly said, "Forgive me. So tell me ... what compelled you to ask me to lunch?"

George-Phillip coughed, then stumbled on his words. "I ... you see ... I needed to..."

Adelina couldn't help it. She felt her face begin to flush, the heat beginning at her cheekbones and working its way down her face to her neck and chest.

"Mamma turnded red," Julia said, helpfully.

"The word is *turned*, Julia," Adelina said.

"Nevertheless, you did turn red," George-Phillip murmured.

"I've no right to turn red," she whispered.

A second later a waitress entered the room, trailed by the maître d'. Within a minute, George had approved the wine and in fluent French, discussed their order.

Adelina's French was slightly rusty, but good enough. She joined in the conversation, and in a few moments they'd finished their order.

"Est ce qu'elle comprend Français?" asked George-Phillip, nodding toward Julia. *Does she understand any French?*

"Du tout," she said. *None at all.*

"Très bien," he replied. *Very good.* He continued in French. "You see, Adelina, I must admit I was intrigued and disturbed by the age difference between you and Richard, and even more so now that I know you're younger than you said the other evening. You were ... seventeen when Julia was conceived?"

"Sixteen," she whispered. "But not willingly. They forced me to marry him."

"*They?*" he asked.

"My mother. My priest. But you mustn't tell anyone. You mustn't do anything."

"Any man of honor would, and should."

She leaned forward. "*Not* if you would honor my wishes. Richard is dangerous. And I have a four-year-old brother in Spain to protect, along with Julia."

"Surely you don't mean—"

"I mean you must leave it alone."

He sighed and straightened his tie. "Well, then. I'm truly sorry, Adelina. I wish…"

"There's no point in wishing for anything," she said. "Enjoy lunch. That's all there is."

"*Oui,*" he replied, raising a glass of wine to her.

She steered the question away from the very dangerous ground they'd treaded on. "Tell me about your parents," she said.

"I've little to say about them," he said. "My father was a wastrel."

"I'm so sorry," she replied.

He took her hand and said, "It's quite all right. I do have a favorite aunt, the Princess Alexandra. Feisty woman. Her father died while defending his nation, unlike mine."

Adelina smiled. "My father spoke very warmly of her. They met at King Juan Carlos's wedding."

"Really? I believe I'm third cousins or some such with Queen Sophia. What took your father to the wedding?"

"It's a small world," she said. "Richard gets angry when I mention it, but my father was the Marquis of Cerverales, and second cousin to Juan Carlos. He met Princess Alexandra at the wedding, and told the story for years, among many others."

"What happened to your father?" he asked.

She sighed. "He lost everything to Franco. He had to start life over as a street vendor, but he succeeded. Then he was run down in the street. A truck *accident*." Her eyes pricked with tears. "I never had the opportunity to say goodbye to him."

He closed his eyes and reached out, taking her hand. "I'm so sorry, Adelina. Even my father ... even four years later ... I feel his loss keenly. I can only imagine your pain."

Julia said, "Mommy lost Daddy?" A line had formed between her eyebrows.

"No, sweetie," Adelina said. "I lost *my* daddy."

"Find new daddy?"

Adelina suppressed a sob. George-Phillip said, "Aren't you a sweet and kind little girl."

"Mommy say Jesus loves kindness."

George-Phillip smiled. "And so he does."

The conversation drifted from there to safer topics. The latest gossip from the diplomatic community. Fallout from the invasion of Grenada, the Falklands war, the attack on the Marine barracks in Beirut and the subsequent escalation of the war there, which had resulted in shelling of populated areas of the city in early February. The conviction of an Alabama Klansman who had randomly selected a black victim and hung him from a tree. And the topic which had dominated diplomatic circles for days: the selection of a new Soviet Premier following the death of Yuri Andropov. Politics was a far safer topic.

They moved on to entertainment, television and the media and *Spitting Image*, the satirical and somewhat scandalous puppet show, which had launched on the air the previous week in London. Among other things, the show lampooned the royal family.

"It's really funny," George-Phillip said. "Naturally, someone sent a film of it to the Embassy here. But all the old women running the Embassy were scandalized."

Adelina laughed as George-Phillip described the antics of the show, including the satirical show *The President's Brain is Missing!*

"Oh, how I wish I'd seen it," she said.

He sobered a little and said, "Maybe we can arrange for a showing at the Embassy—"

She reached out and touched his hand. "George-Phillip. No."

"But, it doesn't have to—"

She sighed. "Stop. We really can't see each other after today. This was sweet. And in a different life, things would be different."

His mouth quirked to the side. "Of course. And I'd never ask you to do anything dishonorable, Adelina."

"Gotta go potty," Julia said.

Adelina closed her eyes. She was closer to tears than she'd realized. She didn't need that. "Excuse me," she said, her voice at a near whisper. She lifted Julia out of her seat as Julia said the words, "Why Mommy sad?"

With Julia in her arms, she rushed out of the room. In her haste, she didn't see the young columnist from the Washington Post until she literally bumped her out of the way.

Maria Clawson gasped as Adelina stumbled back.

"I'm so sorry," Adelina said.

She kept moving, trying to bite back the tears. Inside the women's room, she sighed in frustration. She was too late—Julia had already soiled herself. Nearly crying in frustration, Adelina searched her purse for a diaper. She had one, tangled at the bottom with sundry other supplies.

"Mrs. Thompson." The voice was sickly sweet.

Twenty-three-year-old Maria Clawson was slightly taller than Adelina. Pale skin and blonde hair framed a classic Irish face with her upturned nose and apple red cheeks. Adelina wanted to pinch them until she cried.

"Maria. How pleasant to see you." There was no hiding the venom in her voice.

"Having a lunch out with friends?" Maria asked.

"I am. And you?" Adelina wanted to say, *Are you here stalking George-Phillip?* but she knew she couldn't.

"Yes, I'm here with Janna Farrington," Maria said.

Adelina raised an eyebrow, not recognizing the name.

"Oh, you wouldn't recognize her name," Maria said. "She's old Washington society."

Adelina snorted, unintentionally. She did *not* need to make an enemy of a *Washington Post* gossip columnist after all. But she couldn't help herself. "I suppose old Washington society means her money goes back more than ten years? Of course I wouldn't know her. *Society* in Europe goes back a bit further."

Maria froze. She sniffed and turned up her nose, then said, "I'm sure you're familiar with *all sorts* of society in Europe, aren't you Adelina? And really, you should be proud of yourself. Most homeless nobility wouldn't be caught dead marrying rich Americans. But you've done all right for yourself. And I bet Richard Thompson wasn't even as old as your father."

Julia began to cry, and Adelina realized she was holding her daughter's arm far too hard.

"*Excuse me,*" she said, forcefully.

A few minutes later she had Julia sorted and cleaned up. George-Phillip was sitting in the dining room, waiting for her.

"Adelina," he said.

"I really must go," she replied.

"Of course," he said, sadly.

For just a second, she let herself *see* him. He was her age, or close to it. Tall. He was a man, caring and considerate but strong. He was everything Richard wasn't.

He wasn't hers.

She sighed and set Julia on the floor beside her, then began getting her daughter into her coat. Two minutes later, she left the room, walking into the main dining room of the restaurant. Neither she nor George-Phillip had spoken another word.

As she walked out of the dining room, she spotted Maria Clawson, sitting with an older blonde woman near the window. Maria had her claws out as she spoke forcefully to her companion. Then she looked up, her eyes darting from Adelina to the door of the private dining room.

Adelina paused, then saw George-Phillip, standing in that doorway.

She looked at the floor and then walked out without meeting Clawson's eyes.

The entire ride home in the cab, Adelina thought about what Maria would say. If Maria, the gossip columnist, chose to write about seeing Adelina lunching with George-Phillip. It would make for an interesting piece, wouldn't it? Just enough innuendo to smear her and enrage Richard. She thought she might preempt the questions by telling Richard she'd had lunch with George-Phillip. After all, nothing inappropriate had happened. The two of them talked. Two-year-old Julia had been in the room with them the entire time.

But Richard wasn't home that afternoon, or that evening. When seven pm finally rolled around and she had Julia asleep, Adelina found herself staring at her closet.

Staring.

Finally she got up. She paced outside the closet door. Back and forth.

Then she opened it.

On top, on the shelf, in the back, was the dusty case of her violin. She pulled it down and reverently set it on the bed.

She'd loved that violin. It wasn't special. It wasn't an antique. There was nothing to make it stand out from a million other similar instruments. After all, her father might have claimed the title of Marquis, but in practice he was an impoverished shopkeeper, and no mere posturing could bring him into land or titles. He'd saved money for several months in order to buy this instrument.

She opened the case for the first time since her father had died. It was dusty, and she felt the dust against her fingertips with the cloying grip of grief. Slowly, she eased the instrument out. It would be badly out of tune, of course, but she'd forgotten nothing. She quickly tuned the instrument.

Then she began to play. A solitary, lonely note. Then another. And another. And before she knew it, she was playing. One note after another, the rapid-fire introduction to Antonio Vivaldi's *Winter*. Tears ran down her face as she played through the rhythm, a powerful, mournful movement.

The tears came faster and faster, just as the notes did, and she found herself swaying, playing louder and louder, quicker and quicker. The rising notes took over, and for just a second she felt herself close her eyes. She swayed with the music, and she wasn't standing in the prison of her life just outside Washington, DC. Instead, she was on the floor of the orchestra pit of the National Youth Orchestra, with two thousand people in the audience, her father in the seat of honor as tears ran down his face.

And then she cried out, because for just a second, her father's presence was so real. It was so real it hurt. So real she could smell his awful cologne, she could feel the roughness of his hands as he held hers, she could feel his beard as he kissed her cheek. His presence was so real it ripped her insides out. It turned her love into grief, her joy into hopelessness, her faith into dust.

In a sudden, jerking motion, she lowered the instrument from her shoulder, raised it by the neck, and swung it hard against the wall. The drywall cracked, and she swung it again, harder. This time the instrument itself cracked at the neck, and she cried out in pain.

She swung her violin a third time, as if it really were her past she was destroying. The wood of the instrument shattered, fragments and splinters flying everywhere.

Adelina let the remainder of the wood fall to the floor. Julia was stirring in her room next door, on the verge of crying. The noise. Adelina sank to her knees, gripping her head in her hands. Not meaning to, she found herself holding the sides of her head where Richard had the other day. Like him, she squeezed, as if causing herself pain could shut out the cries of her daughter, as if squeezing her own head could shut out her own cries of pain at the loss of everything.

She lay down on her side and wept.

Jessica. May 2. 11:00 am Pacific

A tear ran down Jessica's face as she listened to her mother's story.

"You smashed your violin?" she whispered.

"Yes," Adelina said. A tear ran down her face.

"Why did you tell George-Phillip you couldn't see him again?"

Adelina stared at the floor, and she whispered, "Because it's a sin, isn't it? I'm married. I was married then. I wanted to see him, so badly. But I knew, if I did, then ... well..."

"You were afraid you would love him?"

Adelina closed her eyes. Jessica leaned forward and touched her mother on the shoulder. And then she whispered, "I wish I'd known. Somehow."

"You weren't born yet. Not for a long time."

Jessica turned on the wall, looking out at the ocean. She felt numb inside. Confused. But also relieved. For the first time in her life, her mother made sense.

Her mother made sense. And the sense she made was so heartbreaking and full of grief and sadness and tragedy that Jessica wanted to throw herself off the wall. Instead, she leaned on her mother, and slipped her hand around her waist.

Her mother sighed.

"Did you get to see him again?" she whispered. "Is George-Phillip Carrie's father?"

Adelina took a deep breath and began to speak again.

CHAPTER TWELVE
Georgie, Indeed

George-Phillip. May 2.

"Sir?" Oswald O'Leary, George-Phillip's special assistant, had opened the door and leaned inside.

"Oh," said George-Phillip. "It's three o'clock, isn't it?"

"Yes, sir. The car is waiting."

George-Phillip stood and straightened his tie, then pulled on his jacket. He felt as if he were moving in slow motion. It was the afternoon of the second day since the assassination attempt, and he'd barely slept since. For one thing, security personnel had been in and out of his house since that night, installing bulletproof glass, armored doors and a safe room between his and Jane's bedrooms.

Moments like that made him question his choice of avocation. George-Phillip would have done just as well financially by following in his father's footsteps—serving on the board of several charities, concerning himself with hunting and drinking, and leaving the public service to men of lesser station. But something of his aunt Alexandra's example had settled in on him at a young age. Princess Alexandra had continued participating in hundreds of royal obligations every year right up until recently, when aging and arthritis had begun to slow her down. So instead of living a quiet life, he'd attended the military academy at Sandhurst. He'd served his time in the Royal Marines and the remainder of his career in the Special Intelligence Service.

The result? Some lunatic firing a rifle through his office window in the middle of the night from the woods in Belgrave Square.

Except, George-Phillip reflected, he knew full well that it wasn't some random lunatic. Whoever wanted to kill him had also placed a bomb in Adelina Thompson's home in San Francisco and attacked Andrea Thompson and her brother-in-law in the Thompson condominium in Bethesda, Maryland. Whoever it was had a long reach, a lot of resources, and a vendetta that appeared increasingly personal.

O'Leary walked silently beside George-Phillip as they made their way to the elevator. O'Leary was, in some ways, the perfect assistant. The two men had worked together for thirty years, and O'Leary was the *only* person who knew everything he'd worked on—including the Wakhan file, and of course, the links between George-Phillip and Adelina Thompson.

They stepped into the elevator. George-Phillip looked at O'Leary and said, "Any word on the whereabouts of Adelina? Or Andrea Thompson?"

O'Leary shrugged. "We've got people looking for both, but there's a lot of ground to cover. The best bet for Adelina will be when she uses her phone or credit cards, which is bound to happen at some point."

"Unless she threw them away. She must know there are people after her."

"I don't think she's that smart, sir."

George-Phillip grimaced. "She's a lot smarter than you'd think, O'Leary. You never gave her enough credit."

"We have trained agents looking for them, sir. They'll turn up."

"*Safely*," George-Phillip said. "I don't have to tell you that this is important to me on a personal level."

"That you don't, sir."

Two minutes later they were in a car, slogging through traffic to the bridge. It was only a mile and a half to 10 Downing Street, perhaps a twenty-five minute walk. On some days he might have walked it, but that was less of an option with people trying to kill him.

Who was he kidding? This wasn't new. At one time it would have been the Irish he was worried about killing him. Or the Arabs. Now it was ... who?

He didn't know. Likely someone inside the CIA. Rogues, perhaps, working for Leslie Collins. Nothing else made sense. Whoever it was, they would have answers soon enough. In the meantime, George-Phillip had other problems.

Once they cleared the guards, the car pulled to a stop in front of Number 10 Downing Street. George-Phillip took a deep breath, then stepped out of the car as the door was opened. A moment later the front door to the house opened.

"Your Grace," said the man who stood in the door, an aide to Prime Minister Duncan Howard. "Come in, please."

George-Phillip felt like a mouse walking into the house of a hungry cat. He smiled and approached the aide, who led him into the entrance hall.

"This way, sir," the aide said.

"Thank you," George-Phillip said. He'd first visited this house when Margaret Thatcher was still new in office. He remembered sitting across from the woman who would become known as the Iron Lady, the first—and still only—female Prime Minister.

I hope you'll be more of a credit to your nation that your father was, Miss Thatcher had said.

I plan to, George-Phillip had replied. *I'm seeking an enlisted po-sition in the Royal Marines, then appointment at Sandhurst.*

Good, she'd said. *I'll speak with General Moore.*

She'd been as good as her word—General Moore had found him a job, and not a desk job. George-Phillip had been trained and went ashore alongside the other Marines.

Duncan Howard, the current occupant of 10 Downing Street, was a mere shadow of Miss Thatcher. An arrogant buffoon who understood nothing of the needs of national security or of the economy, his only overriding goal was his own political preserva-tion.

That said, George-Phillip had to respect the position, though he had none for the man. A moment later, the aide stopped at the door, letting him in.

Duncan Howard stood as they entered the room. He gave George-Phillip a smarmy smile and held out a hand.

George-Phillip took the hand.

"Georgie," Howard said, and then waved vaguely to a scarlet brocade seat. "I'm so pleased to see you alive and well. That must have been quite a fright."

"Indeed," George-Phillip said. He took the proffered seat and waited for Howard to get to the point, doing his best to suppress his irritation at the nickname. *Georgie* indeed.

Howard sat down across from him and said, "Tea?"

"No, thank you."

Howard frowned then said, "Georgie, I called you over here because of a matter which has been brought to my attention. A matter which I'm not really—equipped—to deal with."

"Indeed?"

"How familiar are you with the Wakhan region of Afghanistan? And specifically—what happened during the Soviet occupation of that country?"

George-Phillip grimaced. "I'm intimately familiar with it. You may be aware MI6 conducted an investigation in the late 1980s. It was my first major assignment."

"I am aware. That's why I asked you."

George-Phillip nodded.

"I've received a disturbing report. Disturbing because it was brought to me directly. Disturbing because it involves you. I'd like to ask you to explain yourself?"

"I've no idea what you mean."

"Did you, in fact, find out who was responsible for the massacre at Wakhan?"

"The Afghan Mujahideen was responsible for the massacre, Mr. Howard. Specifically Ahmad Shah Massoud and his confidante Vasily Karatygin."

"The Soviet defector?"

"Yes. He's mainly a smuggler now."

"Where did they get the chemical weapons?"

George-Phillip didn't answer.

"Come now. This is what the report is about. I'm told that you found out who sold them the weapons."

"We did, sir. Richard Thompson, the new American Secretary of Defense, was the leader of the group that got the weapons into the country."

"Dear Lord. Why did we not take action then?"

George-Phillip rolled his eyes. "Ironically, I sat in this very office with your predecessor Mrs. Thatcher discussing this subject, Duncan. We didn't do anything about it for the same reason the American government didn't. Because at the highest levels, *no one cared* about the civilians who were murdered. I was ordered by Miss Thatcher to suppress my findings. We sealed the report in the interest of national security."

Howard looked at him and said, "That decision might still cost you."

"It's already cost me decades of sleep. Why are you raising this now?"

George-Phillip knew the answer. Of course he did. It must be one of the conspirators who had originally covered up the massacre. Perhaps because of Thompson's elevation to Secretary of Defense, perhaps because of the increasing likelihood that Carrie and Andrea Thompson would learn who their birth father was. Something had set this thing in motion and now who knew where it would end up?

Howard leaned forward. "We've been asked by the Guardian to comment on a story they are about to run."

"About Wakhan?"

"About what they are referring to as the cover-up at Wakhan."

"Do you wish me to comment?"

"We're considering pursuing them under section 2 of the Official Secrets Act."

George-Phillip grimaced and shook his head. "I don't recommend it. First, it will make the government look like clowns. We don't need another ABC affair. Second, it isn't even our secret."

Howard frowned at the mention of the ABC trials of 1978, when the government had aggressively prosecuted journalists Crispin Aubrey and Duncan Campbell for receiving official secrets. The trials were a credibility disaster for the government.

"Perhaps, but certainly it's classified information, even if it's not really *ours*."

"Who is *we* anyway?"

Howard frowned. "The Cabinet, Georgie. The Cabinet."

George-Phillip sat forward in his seat. "Duncan, I'm a member of the Cabinet. We've had no such meetings or discussions."

Howard waved a hand dismissively. "Informal."

"It's hardly a secret anymore, then. If you've discussed this ... informally ... with the Cabinet, then you might as well take out your own advertisement in the Guardian."

"George, really, that's not—"

"Would you like me to make an official statement?"

"Not yet. Actually I want you to stay quiet until we know which way the wind is going to blow."

George-Phillip sighed and closed his eyes. There were times he wished he'd never heard of Wakhan, Adelina and Richard Thompson, or their daughters. There were times, more and more lately, when he wondered why he hadn't followed in his father's footsteps. The lack of moral courage displayed in Duncan Howard's statement was appalling.

"Duncan, we can't avoid this or base our response on politics—"

Howard cut him off. "Everything is politics."

"Politics got us into this mess in the first place." George-Phillip stood up. *Not just politics*, he thought. *Politics and greed and lust for power.* "I really must go, Prime Minister."

George-Phillip. February 15, 1984.

"George-Phillip, can you come to my office for a moment?"

"Of course, sir."

George-Phillip laid the heavy black receiver in its cradle atop the rotary phone and stood up, stretching his back. He'd been at his desk for several hours, skipping lunch, as he studied the mind-numbing protocol standards required of Embassy personnel. While his goal was to serve in the military and possibly intelligence services, he knew that a brief stint in the diplomatic corps would help. Not to mention the fact that Mrs. Thatcher herself suggested it.

All the same, the minuscule details and gradations of the diplomatic world did not appeal to George-Phillip. Everything from the precise titles to be used when addressing the assistant chiefs of sub-Saharan villagers to the order of seating when meeting with deposed nobles was included. It was all precise, detailed, and utterly bloodless.

The phone call had come from the Ambassador, Sir Francis Galvin. Galvin, who reminded George-Phillip three times per week, without fail, that he was a *self-made* man. A boy who had grown up with a coarse East End accent, Galvin had distinguished himself in the Second World War and was awarded the Victoria Cross by King George VI. Subsequently, he'd traded on that for a career under the Foreign Office and the Diplomatic Service.

Despite his evident valor and the Victoria Cross he still wore daily, he was a monumental todger.

George-Phillip had to respond to his summons. He squeezed out from behind his desk in the tiny office in the basement of the Embassy and ducked his head to miss the large pipe that ran near the door. He stepped out of the door, rearranged his suit coat so that it was a little neater, and made his way down the hallway to the elevator.

George-Phillip was well aware that he was the only person on the Embassy staff who had an office in the basement. Somehow, the Ambassador managed to find homes for 200 diplomats and another 200 support staff, but the Embassy had been too full for George-Phillip.

Not for the first time, as George-Phillip rode up the elevator, he pondered the fact that being 46th from the throne was exalted enough to piss off egalitarians but not exalted enough to actually give him any privileges.

Nevertheless, he made it to Galvin's office in a hurry. George-Phillip was twenty-one years old, and he knew he had to earn his place here.

The Ambassador's secretary waved him in. She had crimped and poufed her newly blonde hair in a way that had become very stylish in the United States but was still a little too aggressive for the British Diplomatic Service. She opened the door for George-Phillip.

Inside the room the Ambassador sat, relaxed in his chair. A glass of bourbon sat untouched on his desk before him.

"George-Phillip. Come in. Have you met Oswald O'Leary?"

O'Leary was an aggressive looking man with the bunched shoulders and flattened nose of a prizefighter. A bulldog of a man.

"Nice to meet you," George-Phillip said.

"O'Leary, this is George-Phillip. Excuse me, *Prince* George-Phillip. Mrs. Thatcher has seen fit to foist him upon us."

O'Leary nodded at George-Phillip then gave him a sideways grin. "Pleased to meet you, sir. Oswald O'Leary. I work here and there."

"He's not allowed to tell you this, Georgie, but O'Leary works for MI6."

George-Phillip coughed politely. "What can I do for you, sir?"

Galvin said, "I presume you've read the gossip column in the *Post* this morning?"

George-Phillip answered very quickly. "Sir, I generally don't bother myself with gossip columnists."

O'Leary leaned forward and said, "How well are you acquainted with Mrs. Thompson?"

"We aren't close," George-Phillip said. "I was invited to a dinner at Richard Thompson's home last Saturday evening—I've written up my report."

Galvin leaned forward and said, "You didn't submit a report about your lunch with his wife on Monday."

"Well, sir, I..." George-Phillip sighed. He had no excuse. The rules were clear—contacts with foreign diplomatic personnel had to be reported. Including spouses. But he knew why he hadn't posted a report. He hadn't planned on telling anyone about lunch with Adelina, but that witch Maria Clawson had made it necessary. "Sir, you are correct. I did not."

"Tell us about your lunch," O'Leary said.

George-Phillip said, "I was quite taken with the young lady. She is ... not happy in her marriage."

"Maybe that's because he's old enough to be her father," O'Leary said.

"He is indeed. She's quite terrified of him—she seems to believe he's capable of harming her."

Galvin blanched. "Surely you can't be serious."

"I'm serious, sir. I felt bad for her. But she was clear we would not see each other again."

"And why was that?" Galvin responded.

George-Phillip sighed. "I believe the attraction was mutual, sir. She—she seemed quite torn and upset by the end of our meal."

O'Leary grunted. "So she doesn't want to see you?"

"I'm afraid not," George-Phillip said.

"We want you to see her."

"Whatever for?"

O'Leary said, "Have you ever heard of the Wakhan Corridor?"

"No—" George-Phillip said. Then he paused and held up a finger. "Wait ... I did hear the term mentioned Saturday night. In passing, and I didn't know what it was in reference to."

"You included that mention in your report," Galvin said.

"Yes, sir. But I think it was probably meaningless."

"It's not meaningless," O'Leary said.

"Well, what is it, then?"

Galvin leaned forward and said, "George-Phillip, first I must advise you, this discussion is classified under the Official Secrets Acts. Revealing anything we discuss here would be considered an act of treason to the Crown. You understand?"

George-Phillip stared at Galvin in shock, offended that Galvin felt the need to remind him. He stifled his anger and simply acknowledged the statement.

"I understand, sir."

"All right. Go ahead, O'Leary."

O'Leary leaned forward. "It's like this, sir. On December 12, Ahmad Massoud's militia swung through the Wakhan Corridor. It seemed that one of the local villages had been cooperating too closely with the Soviets. But instead of the typical retribution, they dropped two canisters of sarin into the village by helicopter."

"Good lord," George-Phillip said. "What ... what happened?"

"Everyone died. Women, men, children, it didn't matter. Even the sheep and donkeys died."

"So ... why are you telling me?"

"Unfortunately, we have reason to believe that the militia obtained the chemical weapons via the Central Intelligence Agency. We don't know if it was a rogue operation or not, but Richard Thompson was involved, along with Leslie Collins and Prince Roshan. I presume you know all three men?"

George-Phillip felt a chill. "Yes. Collins and Roshan were both at the dinner Saturday."

The Ambassador leaned forward and looked at George-Phillip closely. "Georgie, I realize you're still basically nothing more than a kid. But sometimes a nation asks something of its children as well. I trust we have your loyalty and discretion in this matter?"

George-Phillip looked Galvin in the eye. "Ambassador, my great-grandfather was George the Fifth. I know something of loyalty to the crown."

Galvin stared back at him, anger in his eyes. "Aye, well, I'm not interested in your grandfather, I'm interested in you. You're to make friends with Adelina Thompson and find out what you can of what happened in Wakhan. O'Leary will work with you. Am I clear?"

George-Phillip sighed. "Yes, sir. I'll do my best."

George-Phillip. May 2.

"Let me out," George-Phillip said.

"Sir?" said the driver and O'Leary simultaneously. The car was on Millbank, near the Riverside Walk Gardens. The Vauxhall Bridge crossing the Thames was still between them and the headquarters of the Secret Intelligence Service.

"You heard me," George-Phillip said. "Stop the car and let me out. I'll walk from here."

O'Leary leaned close. His voice was low and calm, as if he were speaking to a child. "Sir, someone tried to kill you two days ago."

"So they did. Now stop the car, and I'll walk. Keep nearby and watch over me if you're worried I'll be shot. But I need to be left alone for a few minutes."

"Stop the car," O'Leary called.

The driver brought the car to a stop. George-Phillip was irrationally irritated. The driver didn't stop when he gave the order, only when O'Leary did. But that's how it worked. The higher you went up the chain of command, the less direct influence you had over events. George had felt that frustration often enough before. But now it ached, because Adelina Ramos Thompson was out there somewhere, lost and alone and frightened, with people possibly trying to harm her and her daughters. It ached because *his* daughters were out there, unprotected and unknowing.

She'd never admitted it to him.

She'd never said a word. But he'd known ever since he first saw then twelve-year-old Carrie at a diplomatic function in Beijing, and later, when he saw both of his daughters together on the beach in Calella. It was obvious, because both of them looked so very much like him, and even more so like his cousin Eloise.

George-Phillip had respected Adelina's wishes for thirty years and not revealed himself to his daughters. But she was missing now, and they were all in danger, and now he had to keep his own counsel. No matter what it did to his career or his own personal aspirations.

He got out of the car and began to walk along the narrow plaza fronting the river, then along the Vauxhall Bridge. He was well aware this was the sort of behavior that would see him lambasted in the tabloids. *Giant Eyebrow covers the Thames*, or something equally offensive. But sometimes you simply had to get away. As he walked across the bridge, he studied the headquarters of the Secret Intelligence Service, towering over the bridge and the river. The green glass and stone building was oppressive, a pile of stone and glass straight out of Orwell's *1984*. What was truly astonishing was that the plaza between the SIS and the river was open to the public, access to the building and its grounds blocked by a high steel fence.

Inside, it was another story. Inside that building, George-Phillip barely kept control of the pulse of a hundred nations. Some people questioned the need for such an apparatus. Those people wondered why the SIS spied, why they had intelligence operatives operating in every nation on earth, why they worried about nuclear proliferation and terrorists and jihadists. But those people had never looked at the bodies of women and children scattered across a street, destroyed by the bombs of terrorists. People who questioned the need for SIS didn't understand that the purpose of an intelligence agency was nothing more than to protect.

All the same, sometimes the weight of this calling wore down on George-Phillip. The weight of constantly having guards. The weight of his daughter Jane being whisked from primary school to home to other locations with a full complement of guards, because his family was not safe.

The weight of his decisions was what wore him down. His decision to leave behind Adelina, even when he knew that she suffered at the hands of that son of a bitch Richard Thompson.

Adelina, he mused.

Sometimes he liked to play *what if* games. What if he'd gone to Spain instead of the Army the year after his father died? What if he'd been in Madrid the day of the coup? It wasn't *that* unlikely.

It was ridiculously unlikely. He'd been in school, determined to finish his final year before going into the Army. Struggling with his own identify after his father died in a drunken car accident. Adelina had been helpless that day, and ever since. Here it was thirty years later, and he'd never been able to help her.

What if, he sometimes thought. What if they'd said, *the hell with it,* and made a run for Brazil or Thailand or Burma or anywhere else far from the reach of CIA or SIS? What if he hadn't been such a coward?

He paused halfway across the bridge and looked out at the river. It was a grey, cold day.

What would Carrie or Andrea say? If they knew he was their father? If they knew he'd not been courageous enough to fight for them?

Well. It might be too late. It might wreck everything he thought of as a life now. But he was going to fight for his daughters. And … if she'd let him … for his love.

CHAPTER THIRTEEN
Witch, witch, witch, witch

Adelina. February 16, 1984.

"**N**o. I can't see you again."

"Adelina, I must see you."

At his words, she felt the blackness reaching out and grabbing her heart again. Because she *wanted* to see him. She wanted to so badly she could taste it.

She knew that could be nothing but disaster.

"I can't see you," she whispered.

Very slowly, she hung up the phone and closed her eyes, shutting out the darkness.

Jessica. May 2.

Jessica felt her stomach rumble. She hadn't eaten in almost an hour, and for days she'd been constantly ravenous. She hugged her legs tighter to herself and looked out at the water. The talk with her mother had been full of unwelcome revelations, not the least of which was that her father was a rapist.

Or Adelina *claimed* he was. After all, her mother was a lunatic. All of Adelina's daughters knew that. She took enough drugs to tranquilize an elephant. She had fits and breakdowns. She cried randomly and had panic attacks that terrified all of them. She'd more than once freaked out and injured her daughters with both her words and her slaps.

"Jessica?" her mother said.

"Leave me alone," Jessica whispered.

Adelina sighed and stood. Jessica didn't watch her walk away. Instead, she stared out at the ocean and fought to preserve her anger at her mother.

It wasn't that hard. All she had to do was remember too many incidents to count. Especially the worst one, the broken cello, the memory that had preserved for all time her memory of her sister Carrie as a saint and her mother as the devil.

Jessica had been six years old, and it had to have been late October, because she remembered she and Sarah had gone to the Halloween party at the Brewer's old Victorian up the street. Jessica had dressed as an angel, and Sarah as a witch. Black and white. They'd run around holding hands through most of the party and gorged on candy until Sarah threw up on Randy Brewer's Harry Potter and the Chamber of Secrets LEGO set. Randy, five years older than they were, punched Sarah. Sarah threw up again, while Jessica screamed, and their mother took the two of them and Alexandra home in a huff, complaining loudly the whole way that none of her daughters knew how to behave.

The next morning, everything in the house seemed ominous. Their father stayed locked in his office, not an unusual state of affairs, but Mother had been in the dining room the entire morning, sobbing. Jessica didn't remember where Alexandra had been that morning. Maybe she'd had a sleepover.

"Stay out of her way," Carrie whispered that morning. "Don't go downstairs, I'll bring you some breakfast."

"What's wrong?" Sarah asked. As always, Sarah had no sense of self-preservation. She'd constantly antagonized their mother.

"You wouldn't understand, it's something with Julia," Carrie had said.

"Who's Julia?" Jessica had asked.

"Sister, stupid," Sarah said.

"Don't call me stupid!" Jessica shouted. "She's hardly ever here. How would I know?"

"*Are* stupid," Sarah said. Then she reached out and pinched Jessica's arm.

"Stop it, both of you!" Carrie whispered urgently. "Mother's crazy today. *Don't* bother her!"

Sarah looked at the floor and said, "Sorry, Carrie." Her voice was low.

Jessica pinched her back. Sarah swiveled her wide open blue eyes to Jessica and stared. She didn't cry or say anything, but her lips curled up in a caricature of a smile.

"*Stop it!*" Carrie said again. "I'm going to call Julia, and then get you guys some breakfast. Stay up here and out of trouble, okay?"

So the twins stayed in Carrie's room playing with Andrea, who complained because she was hungry. But all three of them knew better than to go downstairs. It had been weeks, maybe even months, since their mother had a breakdown. But they knew.

It was a long twenty minutes later before Carrie came back upstairs. Andrea was crying. "I'm hungry," she cried.

"It's okay, Pooh Bear," Carrie whispered. She began handing out donuts and small cartons of apple juice.

"I wanted grape juice," Sarah said.

"It's all they had at the 7-11, Sarah. Maybe you can have some grape juice later?"

"Okay," Sarah whispered. Her eyes watered.

Now, at eighteen, Jessica understood just how awful it was that their older sister had to sneak out to the convenience store to get them breakfast, out of fear of disturbing their mother who was somewhere near the kitchen. But that was soon overshadowed.

They all froze at the sound of footsteps coming up the hardwood stairs.

"Carrie?" The voice was tremulous, shaky. It sent a chill down Jessica's spine. Their mother had been crying, and that was never good. "Carrie? Where are you? Who were you on the phone with?"

Carrie whispered, "Hide the food."

As the girls scrambled to push their donuts and juice boxes under the bed, Carrie stood up and walked toward the closed door. Stark terror filled Jessica as her big sister opened the door.

"In here, Mother," Carrie said.

Mother staggered into the room. Her face was puffy and red, and her hands were clenched, wringing each other. "Who were you on the phone with?"

"Um, a friend from school," Carrie said.

"*Which* friend?"

"*Witch friend*," Sarah said. Then she giggled.

"What did you say, young lady?" Their mother's eyes narrowed.

Sarah's eyes widened. Ridiculously so. Always defiant, she bared her teeth a little and rolled her eyes and said, "Witch witch witch witch."

"How *dare you?*" Mother shouted, raising her hand to slap Sarah.

That was the moment everything changed. Because seventeen-year-old Carrie grabbed her wrist.

"You're not hitting her," Carrie said. "Not anymore."

The response was instant. Adelina swung her other open hand and slapped Carrie across the face. "*You* don't tell me what to do! *You* don't touch me," she shouted, slapping Carrie a second time.

"Stop!" Carrie cried out as she stumbled back. "Stop, you crazy bitch!"

Mother screamed something unintelligible, and Sarah and Jessica grabbed Andrea and dragged her under the bed. The scuffle got louder, as their mother screamed, and Carrie screamed back, wordless sounds of rage. Then there was a loud crash, and Carrie was on the floor looking stunned next to her cello. Their mother had staggered back to the door, a look of horror and crazed grief on her face.

Mother swept out of the room without another word, and Jessica and Andrea swarmed out from under the bed. Carrie was on her back, her eyes closed in pain. Her cello was on the floor beside her, the neck snapped from where she'd fallen over it.

"I *hate* her," Carrie whispered, balling up into a fetal position. "*Hate.*"

Jessica didn't remember what happened after that, except that Sarah had hidden under the bed all morning, crying and refusing to come out and whispering, "I'm sorry, I'm sorry, I'm sorry, Carrie," over and over again.

The next fall Carrie had left for college, and Jessica never saw her play the cello again.

But she'd won one thing. Their mother never hit any of them again after that.

How was Jessica supposed to reconcile *that* with the image her mother painted of the wronged, raped woman struggling to survive a near psychotic husband? How was she supposed to ever, *ever* think of Adelina Thompson sympathetically?

"I hate you," she whispered, her words barely carrying over the sound of the surf crashing against the shore down below.

"What?" her mother said.

Jessica looked up from her knees and said, "I hate you. You weren't a mother to us. Ever. And now you're taking away my father too? I *hate* you."

Adelina flinched. "I deserve it," she whispered. "I don't expect you to forgive me."

"I don't know how you can even think of forgiveness," Jessica said. "You made our lives hell," she cursed. But as she said the words, tears ran freely down her face.

"I'm sorry," Adelina replied.

"I don't accept your apology. I never will."

Jessica turned away. Remembering Carrie's screams as she shielded her sisters from their crazy mother. Remembering Sarah sobbing under the bed for hours. She remembered Andrea packing to leave for Spain again, never knowing that the reason her parents didn't want her was because her mother had an affair. You couldn't tell a pretty story and apologize and expect everything to be better. You couldn't erase a lifetime of hurt.

Fuck her, Jessica thought.

Adelina. February 17, 1984.

"Come, Julia."

Julia wore a tiny blue dress with patent leather shoes and a matching belt. Lately whenever she moved it was at a dead run, slightly tilted forward with her arms behind her, as if smashing her head into a wall or the floor would be the most natural thing in the world. Completely in character, Julia ran forward at a dead run, straight toward the marble counter behind which sat the stunned concierge.

"Stop!" Adelina called out, reaching out with one hand while she simultaneously tried to balance the stroller, two bags of groceries, her purse and a cup of coffee. Something had to give, and it was the coffee, which fell on the floor and erupted in a brown explosion. Julia's feet slid in the sticky mess even as her arm stayed gripped with Adelina's, and she started to swing around in a great circle as the first bag of groceries fell to the floor.

Inside the bag, a bottle of something smashed open. Peanut butter, maybe, or apple sauce. God forbid it be the wine.

"Julia!" she shouted, even as the little girl's legs started to pump again.

In another moment, she had everything calmed down and her daughter stationary. The grocery bag and her coffee, however, were lost causes.

"We'll bring up the ... surviving groceries ... Mrs. Thompson."

"Thank you, Harold," she said.

The concierge said, "By the way, a courier delivered a letter for you earlier. From the British Embassy."

Her chest tightened suddenly, almost painfully. "Oh ... I'll take that," she said.

He handed over the letter. "I presume it's related to Mr. Thompson's birthday? The courier was very clear to deliver only to you."

Stunned, Adelina said, "Yes ... of course." She held a finger to her lips. "Our secret, please. We wouldn't want to spoil the surprise."

The only thing she wanted to give Richard for his birthday was a knife between the ribs. But that wasn't a realistic option. In a sharp voice, she said, "Stay still!" to Julia, then tore open the envelope.

An invitation on heavy cream-colored card stock with gold engraving, handwritten in delicate calligraphy: *You are cordially invited to lunch with His Grace Prince George-Phillip Windsor, the Duke of Kent, Wednesday, February 22, 1984 at Her Majesty's Embassy in Washington, The District of Columbia.*

She rolled her eyes. The invitation was intentionally vague, she supposed, in case Richard had taken delivery of it. *That* would be an ugly situation.

She wasn't having lunch with anyone.

She wasn't.

Especially not at the British Embassy. It was bad enough the Post had mentioned her lunch with George-Phillip at Matisse. Richard hadn't mentioned it yet. Would he? Would he know? Richard was no fool, and the diplomatic community itself was tiny. She couldn't imagine he hadn't heard. Richard was biding his time. Sometime, this afternoon or tonight or next week or next year, he would do something unspeakably cruel. That's how these things worked.

"Come, Julia!" she called, marching away.

The two-year-old ran after her, and grabbed Adelina's hand as they reached the elevator. She took her daughter's hand in hers and rode upstairs in silence. Adelina didn't notice that her other hand was clenched into a fist until she glanced down and saw the invitation was crumpled.

Adelina. May 2.

Adelina sat slouched in the driver's seat of the minivan. The day was beautiful, the sky free of clouds, and the view to the horizon unusually clear. A strong wind blew off the ocean and up into the hills, occasionally shaking the minivan.

Jessica still sat on the wall. Arms wrapped around her legs, face resting on her knees. She wasn't crying. Her shoulders didn't shake, though Adelina had no idea how her daughter sat out there without even shivering.

You weren't a mother to us.

It was true, and she knew it. Her oldest daughter was thirty-two years old, her youngest sixteen. Six daughters, and they all hated her. The worst part was, she knew she deserved it. Jessica sat there on the wall, refusing to talk to her, and she hadn't even been through the worst of it. She knew that it was Julia and Carrie who had borne the brunt of her unmanageable anxiety and fear, her panic attacks, her rage.

She'd have done anything to fix it. *Anything.*

For now, all she could do was help this one daughter. She slid out of the seat again and said, "You don't have to talk to me if you don't want to. But don't you think we should go get something to eat?"

Jessica's shoulders slumped. She nodded her head, and said, "I'm sorry. I don't understand you, but I don't hate you. I really don't."

Adelina sighed. "I wouldn't blame you if you did, you know."

Jessica grunted lightly and gave a tight shake of her head.

"Anyway, let's get moving."

"Where are we going from here?" Jessica asked.

"Well ... I'm concerned about being out on the road in the minivan, especially now that we know they're looking for us. It's a matter of time before we get caught. So I thought we'd stop at the next town and get a bus."

Jessica stared at her, her eyes unmoving, unblinking. Then she said, "To where?"

"Canada."

Stunned, Jessica said, "Why?"

Adelina said, "Haven't you been listening to the news? They're searching for us."

"Well, yeah. But ... Canada?"

"Yes. We need to get somewhere *safe*," Adelina said,

Jessica sighed. "I don't know how I can possibly trust you."

Adelina reached out and touched her daughter's hand. "I know. But nevertheless, we have to go."

"All right," Jessica whispered.

CHAPTER FOURTEEN
Cat got your tongue, Adelina?

In the week after Adelina's lunch with George-Phillip, she avoided Richard and avoided time alone with equal intensity. The day-times were easy enough to keep busy, as she went about interviewing possible full-time nannies, and took Julia around to meet with several different instructors for piano.

Richard had voiced some choice words about both topics. But Adelina had persuaded him, reminding him that most cultured children played an instrument. Julia was young, but Suzuki method training typically began between the ages of three and five.

I insist on her learning an instrument, she had said.

You should teach her on your violin, he had snarled back.

Of course he was aware of what she'd done to her violin. Richard missed little, but in order to drive it home she'd taken the shattered instrument and left it on his bed.

Richard responded by throwing the violin in the garbage and having a deadbolt installed on his door.

And so things continued. If Richard knew about her lunch with George-Phillip, he didn't say anything. But she was sure he knew. Of course he knew, thanks to that bitch Maria Clawson. There it was, the bottom paragraph in her column. *The Duke of Kent and current junior attaché at the British Embassy, Prince George-*

Phillip, was seen lunching with Adelina Thompson, the wife of a junior State Department official, at the exclusive eatery Matisse on Monday. Neither of them was available for comment, but this columnist wonders at opportunities for closer U.S. – British relations.

There was no way Richard didn't know. Maybe he was saving the knowledge for just the right moment. It would be like him, to sit on something for days and make her squirm in fear.

But the days went on with no mention of it, and no further contact from George-Phillip for nearly ten days.

When it came, it was like a bomb. The phone rang at 2:30 in the afternoon. Julia had been difficult that day—extremely difficult. When the new nanny arrived, Adelina made herself a drink and fled to the balcony. She was on her second drink when the phone rang.

She ignored it, choosing to enjoy the unusually warm weather instead.

The glass door slid open. "Mrs. Thompson?"

Jenny Sullivan, the new nanny, held out the phone. "It's Mr. Thompson."

Adelina closed her eyes. She didn't want to talk to Richard.

She had no choice. She reached for the cordless phone.

"Yes, Richard."

"Go get a new dress to wear. Something fancy. We're having dinner with the British Ambassador and guests tonight. It's a black tie affair, very formal."

"The British Ambassador?"

"Yes, and that boy you snuck off and had lunch with. Prince George-Phillip."

Adelina sucked in a breath, but didn't say a word.

"You didn't think I knew about that, did you, Adelina? You should know better by now."

Adelina's words were casual, but she couldn't stop her voice from shaking. "Don't be silly, Richard, it was just lunch. I even had Julia along."

"Of course it was just lunch. Even I know a British royal isn't going to be interested in some peasant slut from Spain. But I don't like being made a fool of in the papers, Adelina. This better be the *last* time Maria Clawson ever mentions my name in her column."

Adelina stiffened in rage. For nearly fifteen seconds she stood there, her teeth clenched, the phone gripped in her hand, unable to say a word.

"What? Cat got your tongue, Adelina?"

"I'll find a dress," she growled.

Then with a swift, smooth motion she slapped the cordless phone against the cast iron table. She hit the phone against the table three, four, then five more times, until the casing finally cracked with a snap and plastic bits went flying everywhere.

Then she burst into tears. She *hated* him. *Hate.*

She closed her eyes and slumped into her chair. Then she whispered a prayer, the words sweeping over her in a torrent. She had to get control of herself and her temper. Sometimes the rage seemed to wash over everything, to black out everything. This was new. As a child or a teen she'd never been prone to fits of anger.

She opened her eyes. Jenny was in the living room with Julia. Both of them stared at her.

Adelina stood and brushed her hands down the front of her shirt. Her temper terrified her sometimes. And embarrassed her. She slid the door open and said to the astonished nanny, "I'm going out."

"Why Mummy break phone?" Julia asked.

Neither Adelina nor Jenny answered the question. Adelina carefully buttoned her coat and walked out of the condo.

Hours later, she rode silently in the car with Richard to the British Embassy. It was dark out, traffic was heavy, and it was stifling hot inside Richard's Mercedes 500SE. She stared out the window, unaffected by the leather seats and polished wood dashboard. Her father had not owned a car for most of her life, and she'd have sooner lived with her daughter in a shack on a rock than in the shifting, often terrifying luxury Richard took for granted.

"You're quiet," he said.

Adelina shrugged. "I'm saving my energy for the dinner."

"Charm them, Adelina."

She rolled her eyes. "Anyone in particular?"

"Eugene Jackson."

"Who?"

Richard huffed in impatience. "I expect you to know these things, Adelina. We've reestablished diplomatic relations with the Vatican. Jackson is Reagan's envoy to the Vatican, and he's been nominated as the first Ambassador."

"Right," she said, holding a hand up. "His confirmation hearings are next week?"

"Exactly."

"Why didn't we have diplomatic relations in the first place?"

"Congress cut funding for the diplomatic mission in 1867, because the Pope banned Protestant services in the city."

"1867? Are you serious? And it took them more than a hundred years to fix it?"

Richard shrugged. "I don't know all the history. The Vatican was invaded and became part of the Kingdom of Italy or some such. Anyway, the British reestablished relations last year, and now we have."

"Okay. And why do you want me to charm Ambassador Jackson?"

His eyes narrowed and his fists tightened on the steering wheel as his face flushed red—dangerous signals for Richard. For a moment she thought he was going to say it was none of her business.

After a second, he relaxed, slightly, and said, "Along with being the new Ambassador, Eugene Jackson and his wife are close personal friends of the Reagans. A good word from him to the President could do a lot for my career."

Adelina nodded. "I see. What do we know about him?"

"He's seventy or so. Prominent businessman in California, he helped bankroll the President's campaign, and he was part of the Kitchen Cabinet." The Kitchen Cabinet was an informal group of conservative advisors to the President—political opponents had accused them of helping to select Reagan's actual Cabinet members.

Richard continued. "He goes *riding* with the President, and he and his wife hosted the Reagans for Nancy's birthday."

Adelina nodded. "Okay. So, charm him. What's his wife's name? Will she be there?"

"Elizabeth. They met at Stanford. And yes, she'll be there."

"Okay. Make nice. Charm him. Consider it done."

In a sharp tone, Richard said, "Don't be fresh with me."

"You're a sociopath and a complete bastard, Richard. Would I be stupid enough to antagonize you?"

Without a pause he reached over and pinched her thigh, hard, through her dress, twisting his fingers. She slid away from him, then grabbed his hand and tried to pull it off as the pain sharpened.

"*I hate you,*" she whispered.

"That's fine," he replied. "As long as you do what you're told."

She didn't respond, choosing instead to shut out the pain, staring out the window into the darkness. She reached a hand into her purse and clutched her rosary, tracing the beads with her fingers.

She knew well that saying the prayers out loud would evoke an immediate violent response from Richard. So she prayed in her heart, tracing the beads, starting with the Lord's Prayer. Sometimes she got stuck there, praying for protection from evil over and over again.

Twenty minutes later, Richard pulled the car to a stop. Guards at the Embassy gate checked his identification and waved him in. He parked, then came around the front of the car and opened her door. She slid out of her seat, letting the rosary fall back into her purse. He placed his hand on her arm and walked her toward the entrance.

Inside, it was clear this was to be an intimate affair. A dozen men of varying ages were in the room, many of them accompanied by wives or girlfriends. Adelina's eyes sought out George-Phillip.

He was across the room from her, talking with a slightly older woman in a mauve dress. Adelina felt a flash of jealousy, which was ridiculous. She had no claim on George-Phillip. The woman was shockingly tall, at least six feet. Her dark brown hair was cut in a reverse bob, and her green-blue eyes seemed unusually large.

Despite the fact she had no claim on him, he took the woman's arm and approached Richard and Adelina the moment he saw them.

"Mr. Thompson, I'm so pleased you could come," George-Phillip said. "And Mrs. Thompson." He turned to the woman beside him and said, "Eloise, please allow me to introduce Richard and Adelina Thompson. Richard is an American diplomat and graciously hosted me for dinner two weeks ago. Richard and Adelina, this is my cousin, the Lady Eloise Percy."

Cousin, Adelina thought, feeling oddly satisfied. It made sense. Eloise was tall, though not so tall as George-Phillip, and she was afflicted with the same hooked nose and eyebrows that looked powerful on a man but not so much on her.

"Charmed," Richard said. He sounded anything but charmed. The others didn't seem to notice, but Adelina's survival depended on knowing Richard and his moods, including the moments when he was lying or manipulating. His voice was laden with syrup as he continued speaking. "Lady Eloise, it's a pleasure to meet you. I don't believe we've met before. Have you been in Washington long?"

Eloise smiled, revealing two overhanging buck teeth. Adelina knew it was petty, but the teeth pleased her. "This is my first trip to Washington, actually."

"Welcome," Adelina said. "I'm actually new to the city myself."

"Oh really!" Eloise said. "I don't suppose you'd be interested in learning about the city with me, would you?"

Adelina smiled and tried to think of a way to politely beg off the invitation. She had no desire to spend days traipsing around the city escorting some over-privileged British—

"I think that's a delightful idea," Richard said, his voice still sickening. "Adelina was just saying the other day that she doesn't get out of the house often enough. We have a two-year-old daughter, and she's a very devoted mother."

George-Phillip said, "Adelina's father knew Alexandra."

Eloise's eyes lit up. "Oh, really? She's our favorite aunt. Your father is..."

"Juan Ramos, Lady, he was the Marquis of Cerverales."

"Oh, yes!" Eloise said. "I've heard of him. He had some political disagreement with Franco, yes?"

"I'm afraid so," Richard said. His voice no longer held a sickly sweet tone. "Adelina was the daughter of a shopkeeper when I plucked her out of Spain."

Adelina kept a death grip on her smile.

"Don't be so modest," Eloise said. "Our aunt spoke fondly of your father."

"He would have been delighted to know that," Adelina said.

"Oh dear," Eloise said, even as George-Phillip almost imperceptibly froze. "You speak of him in the past tense?"

"He passed away two years ago," Adelina replied. "An accident."

"So sad," Eloise replied.

"Tragic," Richard said in a dry voice. "Oh ... isn't that Eugene Jackson, the new Ambassador to the Vatican?"

He sounded like an idiot, Adelina thought. But he clearly wanted to exit any conversation having to do with Adelina's past.

"I believe so," George-Phillip said. "Oil man, right? Friend of your President?"

"I must go pay my respects," Richard replied. "Adelina?"

"Coming, dear," she said. "Please excuse us," she said at a near whisper to George-Phillip and Eloise.

"Of course," George-Phillip said, his voice low and troubled.

Adelina didn't have time to pay any more attention to George-Phillip, however. Richard had moved very quickly to Jackson, the new Ambassador to the Vatican, and was already speaking by the time Adelina caught up.

"May I present my wife, Adelina?"

"Pleased to meet you, Mrs. Thompson," Jackson said, his eyes dropping immediately to the cleavage at the front of Adelina's bodice. He was a kindly looking man, with salt and pepper hair swept back from his high forehead and deep wrinkles on either side of his mouth. "This is my wife, Elizabeth."

Adelina shook hands and smiled at the older woman. The Jacksons were probably seventy. Elizabeth was a trim woman with white hair just long enough to reach her shoulders.

"Congratulations on your appointment as Ambassador, sir."

"Thank you very much, young lady. Although it's not quite confirmed yet."

"Oh?" Adelina said, blinking her eyes innocently.

"There are a few old bigots still in the Senate," Jackson said. "They don't think we should reopen diplomatic relations at all."

"Oh, dear," Adelina said. "I'm so sorry."

Elizabeth Jackson smiled and said, "It's quite all right, dear. I'm certain Eugene is up to the challenge."

"I'm sure," Adelina said. "I didn't mean to imply otherwise."

"It's all right," Elizabeth said. "I will say, though, that I look forward to returning to Rome."

"How long have you lived there?"

"Two years," she replied. "We rent a townhouse in Celio. I'm trying to persuade Eugene to buy it and just stay there for retirement. It's a lovely neighborhood."

Jackson smiled. "It is. Crowded and dirty and loud, but lovely."

"It's *Rome,*" Elizabeth countered.

"True," Jackson said.

Adelina smiled at the older couple then felt a sense of real relief as Richard excused himself. "I always wanted to go to Rome," Adelina said. "I'd planned on going there after I graduated high school, but I got married instead."

"We love it," Elizabeth responded. "It's truly beautiful. Though I do miss California sometimes."

"Not Washington?" Jackson said, raising a bushy eyebrow.

"Pshaw," Elizabeth said, lightly smacking her husband on the shoulder. "Who could miss Washington?"

Adelina felt her lips curl up. "Not me," she said. "I haven't been here long, and I'll freely admit, it's taking a lot of adjustment."

Elizabeth spoke in a kindly tone, like a loving aunt. "Well, you're a very young woman, and I suspect with your husband in the

Foreign Service, you'll move a lot in the coming years. I'd suggest getting involved—local charities, or your church, or something. It can be a very lonely life following your husband's career."

"It hasn't been that lonely for you, has it, dear?" Eugene asked.

"You wouldn't know, you silly old man," Elizabeth said.

Adelina's eyes dropped to the floor.

"Thank you for the advice," she said quietly.

The last thing she ever wanted to do was follow her husband's career around the globe. But in her heart, she knew that unless she found a way to break from Richard soon, she might never escape.

Someone moved next to her. She drew in a deep breath and looked up, already knowing it was George-Phillip. She felt her cheeks warm and darted a glance at him, then back at Elizabeth.

"Elizabeth and Ambassador Jackson, may I introduce His Highness, George-Phillip, the Duke of Kent?"

George-Phillip grinned and held out a hand.

Jackson took it in his and said, "It's a pleasure to meet you. You go by George?"

"George-Phillip, generally," replied George-Phillip. "It's nice to meet you. Congratulations on your appointment as Ambassador."

Jackson grinned. "It's mostly ceremonial, to tell you the truth," he said. "As they say, the Pope doesn't have an Army, so as Ambassador I won't have earth shattering matters to attend to."

"Soul shattering, perhaps," George-Phillip said.

"You're a believer?"

"My mother was Catholic," George-Phillip said. "It caused quite a stir when she converted, actually. My father nearly had to abdicate. I'm loyal to the Church of England, as any good third cousin to the throne should be." As he said the words, his face had an endearing grin.

Jackson chuckled. "A diplomat despite your age."

"Forgive the lapse in this company," George-Phillip replied, "but sometimes I think *diplomatic* is a bad word. Perhaps world affairs would be better off and more straightforward if everyone said what they meant."

Jackson's grin actually grew wider. "Young and idealistic."

"You were young and idealistic once," Elizabeth said. "Don't knock him."

"I wouldn't," Jackson said. "Life will do that for him."

"I hope to always be an idealist," George-Phillip said.

His eyes were wide open, bright, and the slight flush on his cheeks seemed to indicate an intense awareness of Adelina. She looked away from him, searching out Richard.

Richard was thirty feet away, in a small knot of diplomats and wives. George-Phillip's cousin Eloise had moved to that group. He seemed unaware of her, but she knew better.

George-Phillip said, "And what about you, Mrs. Thompson? Are you also an idealist?"

For just a second she met George-Phillip's eyes—eyes that stabbed her, gripping her by the throat.

"One can't live on promises and hope," she said.

"I can't imagine what else you would live on," George-Phillip retorted.

"I'm afraid I have to step away," Elizabeth said. "It's been a delight talking with you both."

"I'll get you a drink for when you come back," Jackson said.

Both of them stepped away quickly, leaving Adelina and George-Phillip standing alone. Adelina felt as if a spotlight were on her.

"I must see you," George-Phillip said.

"I can't," she replied.

"I *must*," he said.

Adelina took a step back. She felt tears threatening, suppressed emotion welling up in her throat. She only barely remembered what it felt like to be cared for.

But she remembered all too well what it was like to be at Richard's mercy.

"I cannot," she whispered.

Then she walked away, to the safety of the crowd around Richard.

CHAPTER FIFTEEN
There's my little girl!

Adelina. February 26, 1984.

Julia had been difficult to get to sleep tonight—restless and irritable. Adelina finally gave up and lay down beside her daughter, lightly tapping her on the leg to soothe her. Julia's eyes dipped, opening and closing repeatedly as she fought sleep.

Finally, Julia's breathing evened out, her eyes closed, her cheeks slightly flushed. Adelina sagged against the bed and slowly released her daughter's hand. She desperately needed an hour to relax, uninterrupted. Now that Julia was down, she'd hopefully get it. It would be uncharacteristic of Richard to seek her out—she suspected he was finding some other source of sexual satisfaction than his captive wife, and nothing could make Adelina happier.

The last thing she wanted was Richard *touching* her. Unfortunately, she had to talk with him. She approached him as rarely as possible, but sometimes it was unavoidable.

Her mind kept returning to George-Phillip's words the night before.

"I must see you."

"I can't," she had replied.

"I must," he had said.

George-Phillip didn't understand. He must not believe her when she described the danger Richard represented. Or worse, he didn't care. He didn't care what risk *she* bore, what danger *she* was in.

It seemed likely, until she thought of his kindness, of the concern in his eyes. George-Phillip was not a man looking for an easy sexual liaison, and if he were, he could find much better targets for his lust than Adelina Thompson.

Which left her with one question. What *did* he want?

She was attracted to him. Intensely so. In their few meetings, it had become clear that her desire was mutual. It was also equally clear that it was impossible. Even if her husband weren't dangerous, the fact was, she was *married*. She didn't love Richard—in fact, she hated him. But she still had to live with herself, and no matter how much she hated Richard Thompson, she'd married him in the church. She was married in the eyes of God. Those were the only eyes that really mattered.

She stood, slowly, taking care to not disturb Julia. As she came to her feet beside the small bed, Julia's breath paused for just a moment. Adelina waited to see if her daughter would open her eyes—if she would clench her fists or turn red in the face or scream loud enough to draw Richard's anger. After a moment, Julia settled back into the bed a little deeper, her tiny chest expanding as she breathed in.

Adelina stepped into the quiet hallway. From Julia's room, she could see down the hallway: two more bedrooms on the right side of the hallway, three on the left. The master bedroom, Richard's, at the end of the hallway. Thank God this place was huge. Adelina had taken the furthest possible room from her husband.

His bedroom door was cracked several inches. She walked toward the door, feeling a sense of dread. His open door might mean he was careless, which occasionally he was. Or it might mean he was preparing to assault her. He'd only done that a couple of times since he'd returned to the United States, though.

As she got closer to the door, though, she realized that it was carelessness. And something else. He was on the phone with someone, his words falling out in an uncharacteristic rush.

"Christ," he said. "How was I supposed to know Karatygin was going to use it on civilians? I thought we were all done with this."

Silence. What was he talking about? What was used on civilians?

"Bullshit, Leslie," he said, his tone harsh.

Was he talking to his accountant friend? Leslie Collins?

Accountant, hell, she thought. She didn't know what Leslie Collins was, but he was most definitely not an accountant.

"Fine. I'll go and calm down Prince Roshan and then we'll move on, all right? I don't ever want to talk about this subject again."

He slammed the phone down, and Adelina's heart suddenly lurched. What if he realized she'd been standing here? What if—

It was too late. He stood in the doorway, still wearing his suit and tie. One eye narrowed slightly more than the other one and he demanded, "How long have you been standing there listening?"

"I didn't really hear anything—"

"Sure you did. I *know* you heard something. Tell me what." His eyes were cold as he said the words, his expression calm. Calculated.

She swallowed then tried to speak. But she found herself stammering, the words colliding at her lips and unable to come out except in a jumble.

"Let me help," he said, his open hand swinging at her.

She couldn't move away fast enough. His slap hit her on the ear, staggering her.

"*Stop*," she cried out.

"I'll stop when you answer my god damn question."

"All I heard was you say something about civilians, and that you need to calm down Prince Roshan. I don't have a clue what it's about."

Another slap knocked her back against the wall.

Against her will, tears ran down her face. He placed his palms against the wall on either side of her head and pressed his face in close to hers.

She cringed, turning her face away from him.

"Let me be clear about one thing, Miss Adelina. Make no mistake that my daughter would be far better off with a white woman as her mother."

She froze.

"You just remember that. You *never* talk to anyone about anything I say, do you hear me?"

She nodded, trying to suppress the tears.

He shouted. "Do you understand me? Answer me!"

"Yes," she whispered.

Down the hallway, she heard the sound of Julia sputtering in her bed. *Damn it.*

"Please don't wake the baby," Adelina whispered.

"I'll do whatever the hell I want," he whispered back.

"Mama?" The word rang out from down the hall. Julia stood in her doorway, a hand stretched out to steady her. "Mmmm wet."

"Right here, Julia," Adelina said, her voice shaking.

Richard grimaced, and then in a display of frightening calculation, he winked at Adelina. He broke into a broad smile and turned toward their daughter.

"There's my little girl!" he nearly shouted in a cheerful, warm voice.

Julia broke into a smile, her cheeks puffing out.

Richard lifted Julia high in the air and she giggled.

"Da!" she said, a smile on her face.

Adelina. February 27, 1984.

When Adelina awoke the next morning, Richard was gone.

He'd scrawled a note on a small sheet of paper, torn off of a pad with the heading, "From the Desk of Richard Thompson."

The note read:

Dearest Adelina, I must travel to Saudi Arabia and possibly Pakistan in the next few days. I'll be in touch.

She sagged in relief when she read the note.

Dearest Adelina. As if. He must have thought the nanny would see the note. Or he was truly a sociopath. She didn't know which, and right now she didn't care. What she knew was that his absence meant an unexpected reprieve from the daily grinding fear that she didn't realize had overwhelmed her for the last month.

Month, she thought. It had only been a month since he'd returned to the United States. Only a month since she'd left San Francisco to occupy this condominium on the edge of the nation's capital.

As she stood there, tears running down her face, she tried to picture how she was possibly going to survive her marriage to Richard. During his assignment in Pakistan, it had seemed bearable. She'd been alone with her daughter in San Francisco. She'd made friends, gotten involved in the church. She'd begun to have a life again.

His return had swept all that away. Again. And he might be gone today, but she knew he'd return, tomorrow or next week or next month, and his return would spell the return of instability, of fear, of the lies and twisted behavior. As she thought about it, her breath sped up, and she could feel the tightening in her chest, the constricting threads of fear tugging at her neck.

She forced herself to breathe, but even her breathing became ragged.

As the wave of panic swept over her, she began to pray, head bowed, until she fell to her knees. She didn't realize she had tears pouring down her cheeks. She didn't realize her shoulders were shaking.

She didn't realize that she was coming apart at the seams.

She sank down into her prayers, her fingers unconsciously running along the beads of her rosary, her lips moving silently, trying to calm the terror.

"Mama?"

Julia's voice didn't initially break into her consciousness.

"Mama? I'm hunngy."

This time she heard Julia, the high-pitched whining voice breaking over her prayers.

"Hunngy. I'm hunngy."

God damn it, couldn't she see—

Adelina froze. Of course she couldn't see the condition Adelina was in. Julia wasn't even three yet.

She took a deep breath and opened her eyes and said in a shaking voice, "Okay, Julia. Want to come pray with me first?"

"I hunngy," Julia said. Her eyes were huge.

Adelina let out a staggered, broken breath and stood up. The fear wasn't gone. It felt like a huge welt on her chest. She furiously wiped at the tears that had fallen down her face and lifted Julia to the sit on the counter.

"I'll make you some breakfast," Adelina said.

"Some cereal?" she asked, words coming out automatically. Heart still thumping rapidly in her chest, she turned to get the cereal, but Julia said, "Wan' ice cream."

"No ice cream, Julia. You can have cereal or yogurt."

"Ice cream!" Julia demanded. "Wan' chocolate!"

Adelina closed her eyes. "I don't have chocolate ice cream."

She took down the cereal and poured it in a plastic bowl, then added milk. In three weeks she'd be twenty years old. The thought made tears run down her face again. She was twenty, and her father was dead, and her life was hopeless.

She set the bowl on the highchair tray then lifted Julia into the chair. Julia began to scream. "Ice cream! Ice cream!"

Adelina wanted to scream too. She readjusted the tray after bucking Julia in. Julia was full out crying now, and Adelina was desperate just to get her to *shut up*. The pain in her chest was getting worse, and all she could think of was the fact that she wasn't even twenty years old yet and she wanted out. She wanted her mother. She wanted her father. She wanted her life back, and she couldn't have it.

She sank back against the counter, the screaming from Julia unabated. Julia hit her bowl with a fist and it went flying, spattering milk and cereal on the wall.

For just a second Adelina felt rage flood her again. She turned away, walking into the living room and clenched her fists at the side of her head. She fought down the urge to scream, to yell at Julia, to throw something, to *break* something. She fought it down, but as she did so, she felt the tightening in her chest worsen.

The knock on the door startled her.

Oh, thank God! That would be Jenny, the nanny. Adelina rushed to the door and opened it in a rush.

Jenny was twenty-two—three years older than her employer—and a student at University of the District of Columbia. She was smart and pretty.

Adelina was envious. Jenny might be dirt poor, taking on this job to help buy her books for her night courses, but she was making choices for her own life. Choices that had been taken from Adelina.

"Bless you," Adelina whispered urgently. "She's a terror this morning. Come in."

Jenny's eyes widened at the sight of the screaming Julia in her highchair and the mess of cereal and milk splattered on the wall.

At the sight of Jenny, Julia screamed even louder. "Mommy! Don' go! Don' go! Mommmmyyyyy!"

Adelina swallowed the pain in her chest. "It's all right, Julia. I'll be back soon." She gave her daughter a kiss on the cheek and rushed back to her room to change. With luck, she'd have time to stop for a cup of coffee in relative peace, outside the house, before she went to the church.

Adelina. February 27, 1984.

"Bless me, Father, for I have sinned," Adelina whispered as she made the sign of the cross. Father Dennis waved his hand and muttered a blessing, and she felt a shudder as she said the next words. "Lord, you know all things. You know that I love you. It has been three years since my last confession."

Father Dennis shifted his position. Though the church had confessionals, Adelina had requested they meet in his office. She kneeled across from him, and occasionally her eyes darted to the purple stole he wore. On one level, it was calming, reminding her of the presence of God and of Father Dennis's authority.

On another level, it terrified her. After all, it was the Parish priest in Calella, acting under the authority of God, who had ordered her to marry Richard. If only she hadn't had to move to her mother's home in Calella. If only her father hadn't died.

If only she'd never met Richard Thompson.

She took a deep breath, not knowing where to start.

"You may begin," Father Dennis said.

Her voice tiny, her body full of shame, Adelina said, "I don't know how to."

He reached out and rested a hand on her shoulder. "The Lord knows the story already, Adelina. If you're penitent, then just tell it however you can."

She nodded, and, horrified, choked back a sob. Sniffing, she said, "These are my sins."

She squeezed her eyes closed, tightly, and whispered, "For three years I've lied to everyone around me to protect my brother."

"What have you lied about?"

"My age. My husband."

"Tell me the truth now."

She choked on the words. Then she spit them out. "I was sixteen, and he raped me. I hate him. Father, I know he's my husband, but I *hate* him. Sometimes I imagine him rotting in jail. Or in hell. I think of the most dreadful things."

Father Dennis paled. "Your husband raped you? Before you were married?"

She nodded. The tears were streaming rapidly down her face now, and she shook, terrified.

"I'm so sorry, Adelina, I had no idea. Did you report it to the police? Wait, now you … how did you end up married?"

She struggled to get her mouth around the words. But then she told the story, of how her mother had dragged her to the parish priest in Calella.

He muttered to himself, then said, "I'm so sorry, Adelina."

"That's not the worst of it," she said. She looked up, looking in his eyes, and she said, "Father, I've fantasized—about killing him. About … about running away. Sometimes I get so angry I'm afraid I'll hurt my daughter."

"You must learn to control your anger, Adelina."

"I pray for that every day," she whispered.

"Continue to do so. You mustn't hurt your daughter. Or your husband. I believe—Adelina, I believe you should report this to the police. Or allow me to do so."

Terror flooded Adelina. She jerked back, and said, "You wouldn't!"

He smiled reassuringly. "I wouldn't, unless you gave me permission. You remember the story of Saint John of Nepomuk?"

She shook her head. "I … no."

"Saint John was the confessor to the Queen of Bohemia. It seemed that Wenceslaus, the King, thought the Queen was committing adultery, and ordered John to divulge the secrets of the confessional. When he refused, the King had him tortured and murdered, then thrown in the river."

Adelina shivered, imagining with horror what it must have been like for the priest. "And he didn't tell?"

"No, Adelina. He went to his death to protect the Seal of the Confessional."

"My priest didn't. He told my mother when I learned I was pregnant."

Father Dennis closed his eyes. "He committed a grave crime in doing so. I assure you, God will deal with him. But I can promise you, no such thing will happen now."

She looked at Father Dennis and said, "Is it a sin to hate my husband?"

He sighed. "Perhaps not so uncommon a sin, and given your circumstance—the fact is, if you are truly contrite, you shall be forgiven. I would urge you to consider what I've suggested to you. Your husband committed a crime, and against a child."

"I can't," she whispered. "He'll hurt my brother. He's threatened to before, and I believe him."

Dennis sighed. "Then I suggest you pray. Perhaps you can be a moderating influence on Richard. And you can still raise your daughter. Do you intend to have any further children?"

Adelina shivered. Then she whispered, "I'd rather die."

"I must advise you against artificial contraception."

Adelina nodded. Birth control was the least of her worries.

"Finally—though I know this is hard given the circumstances of your marriage—you must remember that Richard is your husband. Cleave to him, and perhaps you can somehow bring him back into the path of God. Is he Catholic?"

She shook her head. "Anglican," she said. "But not devout. The only thing he believes in is himself."

"Teach him as best you can. Perhaps through your daughter."

Adelina knew the advice was sound, but all the same, it made her want to vomit. She felt more desperate than ever.

"I will," she whispered. "What is my penance?"

"I'd like you to read First Peter, chapter three, and think on the instructions given within. Not just of wives, but also of husbands. You're subject to him, but you can also set an example, and bring him to the Lord."

She nearly recoiled from him. She would read the verses. But they frightened her.

"Yes, Father."

He brought her the book and they read it together. As they read the words, she felt fresh tears begin to stream down her face.

Wives, in the same way, accept the authority of your husbands, so that, even if some of them do not obey the word, they may be won over without a word by their wives' conduct when they see the purity and reverence in their lives.

The words made her angry. She felt her fists clench, and her first thoughts were rebellious. She didn't want to be an example to Richard. She wanted to *hurt* him. She wanted to walk away. She wanted him to go to hell.

She closed her eyes. Mary hadn't taken the easy way out. When she realized the fullness of God's plans for her child, she didn't run away. She didn't hide her child. She let him be raised up, exalted, hammered to the Cross in shame and disgrace and terror and pain.

Adelina didn't have that sort of courage. She could admire it. She could wish for it. But how was she to live it?

Father Dennis began to pray. "God, the Father of mercies, through the death and resurrection of His Son has reconciled the world to Himself and sent the Holy Spirit among us for the forgiveness of sins. Through the ministry of the Church, may God give you pardon and peace, and I absolve you from your sins in the name of the Father, and the Son, and of the Holy Spirit."

Adelina bowed her head and choked out the word, "Amen."

As she left the church, she kept thinking to herself that she felt no relief. She felt no guidance. God and the Church expected her to simply be submissive, to let Richard continue to do whatever he wanted.

It was wrong. It was *so* wrong. She found herself running as she exited the front door and rushed down the front steps. It was cold again, winter returning with fierceness, a chill biting right through her inadequate clothes. The sky was nearly black with dark, roiling clouds. Her heels clicked on the front steps as she ran down them, barely paying attention to what she was doing. Tears ran down her face, and she began to sob as she started to sprint.

But then she came to a sudden stop. Because a car stood next to the curb, and standing next to it, blocking her way with an open and hopeful expression on his face, was George-Phillip Windsor.

PART TWO

CHAPTER SIXTEEN
Calling in a favor.

"**I**'m getting kind of hungry," Andrea said.

"Yeah, me too," Dylan said. "We'll get something after this."

As he spoke, his eyes scanned the desks where the library patrons sat at the computers. Just to be on the safe side, they'd taken the Washington Metro out to the Virginia suburbs. The library was busy, and the dozen computers lined up on three long tables were all in use. The library was well lit by long lines of overhead fluorescent lights, and the place was crowded. At the opposite end of the building, a large crowd of children sat in a circle around the librarian, who was reading a story. Young mothers stood nearby, some of them chatting, others reading, all of them looking relieved to have a few minutes' break from their children during story-time.

"There," Dylan muttered.

A woman at one of the computer tables stood and shouldered her bag, then walked away.

Andrea breathed a sigh of relief when she saw the woman hadn't logged out. They'd been surprised to learn that access to the computers in the library required a current library card—which neither of them had.

She followed Dylan as he slumped into the seat and opened up a web browser. He started with *The Washington Post.*

"Jesus," he muttered.

Andrea felt her eyes widen. The entire front page of the website was devoted to the attack on the Thompsons, underneath a huge headline.

Secretary of Defense Elect's Family Homes Attacked Adelina Thompson, Two Children Missing: Sources Speculate Drug Connection

Underneath the headline were smaller stories and photographs, including individual photos of her mother, Jessica, Dylan, and Andrea. Andrea felt her breath accelerate as she squeezed in beside Dylan and looked at the story. The newspaper also had photos of the entrance to the Bethesda condo and the burned out house in San Francisco.

"Jesus," Dylan muttered again. His voice was low. "I talked to your mother last night. Just for a second—that's when the shooting started."

"Do you think she's hurt?" Andrea whispered.

"Probably on the run," he said. "She called to warn us to get you out. It was just too late."

"What the hell is going on?"

He shook his head. "Beats me. All I know is, we're staying under the radar until we know more. Check this out." He pointed.

One of the several articles described a press conference that morning. It didn't make any sense. Richard Thompson was accused of corruption and money laundering. The feds had put out a warrant for her *arrest* as a conspirator.

"That's what the drugs were about," he said, "and the money." He looked at her. "I bet the bills we have are marked somehow."

She nodded. "Maybe we can go ... I don't know ... buy a bunch of prepaid credit cards?"

"Not too many in any one place. If the money gets tracked—say through a bank—it might link back to the card. We'll buy a few at a time in several different places, I think. And ... new clothes. Haircuts."

"You could use a shave," Andrea said.

Dylan grinned, his teeth showing up white in the midst of a darkening beard. "That's what Alex always says. But that photo shows me clean shaven, so I'm gonna let it grow."

"We can't go back to the hotel."

"Nope," he said. "Pretty soon they'll match up the fingerprints, if not today, then tomorrow. And then the surveillance cameras will show up on the Metro."

She grimaced. "What do we do?"

"Hold on. I'm not out of options yet. But once we're finished here, we've got to book."

He turned back to the computer and opened up Facebook, then logged in. Then he typed in a name: Christopher Mendoza.

The page that came up showed a grinning man with short-cropped black hair and a five o'clock shadow, wearing a grey sweat-shirt with the word ARMY on it. The *About* section on the page said, "US Army, Arlington, Virginia."

"Who is that?" Andrea asked.

"Old friend," Dylan replied. He opened up a message box and typed in the message: What's up, Border Bunny?

The response was nearly immediate: Redneck motherfucker. What do you want?

Andrea sucked in a breath. What did *Border Bunny* mean? *Motherfucker* she could figure out.

Dylan: Calling in a favor. Priority 1. Need help now.

Mendoza: Wut u need?

Dylan: Place to sleep. And a ride. I'll explain later, but if you help me you could go to jail.

Mendoza: Sick. Where?

Dylan: Clarendon Metro. 3 pm.

Mendoza: See you, Bacon Bits.

Dylan laughed silently, then typed in the search bar. Alex Paris. Andrea's sister's profile showed up immediately. Dylan pulled up the message box and typed in: Andrea and I are alive and well. In hiding. I'll be back in touch as soon as possible. Stay low. Keep your status updated so I know you're okay. Love u.

Then he logged out without waiting for an answer. He looked over his shoulder, then pulled up the drop down menu. Delete cookies. Delete history. Then he logged out of the computer.

"All right. Let's go." He stood, and Andrea followed. Both of them walked as casually as possible toward the door of the library. Andrea could see Dylan was nervous. Like he thought someone was watching them, or they were in danger. His back was tense, muscles in his arms bunched up, his neck tightly wound.

She touched his arm and he froze. "Is something wrong?" she whispered.

He shook his head. "Come on," he said. His voice was curt, almost rude.

She didn't understand why he was always such a prick. What did Alexandra see in him?

She followed him anyway. What choice did she have? Once they were outside, he turned quickly to the right and walked down the sidewalk. A cool wind was beginning to blow, and since they'd been in the library, the sky had become much more cloudy.

Lips compressed tightly, he walked. His right leg was a little stiff—the leg that had been nearly destroyed during the war.

"One of the librarians was watching us as she talked on the phone. She was sweating."

"You think she recognized us?"

"Yeah. We gotta get to the Metro right now. Cops might be on their way already."

She nodded. They were less than half a block from the station entrance.

That's when she heard the sirens.

"Shit," he muttered. He didn't falter, his legs moving, one step in front of the other. "Mess up your hair," he said conversationally. "In your face a little."

He turned and walked backward, casually lighting a cigarette. A police car rounded the corner, drove past the Metro station, and then passed them. Another sped past. Both police cars had their blue lights flashing, but no siren.

He took a deep drag from the cigarette and turned around again. "Come on." He ducked into the entrance to the Metro station, tossed his cigarette to the ground, and swiped the Metro card he'd purchased from a machine earlier that day. She followed.

The inside of the station was crowded. It wasn't quite time for rush hour, but there were far more people in the station than they'd seen when they arrived an hour before. Dylan led her down the escalator to the platform, then stood leaning against a pillar. She leaned against it too, facing him.

"I'm worried, Dylan," she whispered.

He grimaced. "It's going to be okay."

He said the words, but she could see his eyes, and Dylan was a terrible liar.

"You don't look like you mean it."

He shrugged. "Maybe I don't. Ray used to say that shit to me. It's gonna be okay. Don't worry, he'd say. It's all good. But sometimes it's not." He looked away.

Andrea sighed. First rule of being on the run with Dylan: don't tell him when you're feeling anxious. Because he can't help.

"What happened to you?" she asked.

He rolled his eyes. "I'm fine."

Yeah, right. She turned away from him. She could feel wind blowing from the tunnel, and a moment later saw headlights. With a loud roar of brakes and a rush of wind, the train entered the station.

She turned to him as the train was coming to a stop. "I know you lost your friend, Dylan. But you need to get yourself together. You've got a lot more you *could* lose."

His mouth opened, but he didn't say any words. She walked away and stepped on board the train. He followed a moment later. A loud ringing peal burst from the overhead speakers, and the doors closed with a thumb. She scanned the car. No seats, so she wrapped her left hand around one of the stainless steel poles. Dylan took the pole opposite the car from her and glared.

As the train pulled out, he said, "What exactly does that mean?"

She sighed. "I'm worried. I'm worried because you sound like a pessimist and you look like a drunk and my life depends on you. That's what it means."

"I'm the guy who took those killers on with a knife to protect you," he muttered.

"I know that, Dylan. Don't think I'm ungrateful. I'm telling you, I'm worried about you. You know my sisters said it too. Carrie said you haven't been the same since Ray died."

He looked as if she'd punched him between the eyes. "He was my best friend."

She leaned close as the train car swayed, a loud screeching sound from the tracks below. "You should honor his memory, then."

Dylan's eyes widened. He shifted his position and turned away from her, looking out the windows of the car into the blackness of the tunnel.

He sighed, then said, "You're right. I know it. It's been almost nine months since he died. I'm stuck. All I can remember is seeing him in that hospital bed, with his body all screwed up, then the funeral. He had a lot of life left in him."

She reached out with her right hand, the one that wasn't wrapped around the steel pole, and took his arm. "It's going to be okay, Dylan."

He gave a small laugh. "You *do* look like you mean it."

She shrugged. "I do. Some things we can do something about. We can run and protect ourselves. We can do our best for the people we love, for the people around us. We can push for—for truth. For doing the right thing. But some things we *can't* control. And that stuff—it's out of our hands. All I know is I've got family I love. Uncle Luis and Abuelita, and my sisters. You, even."

He nodded. He didn't say any words. Just nodded.

"All right, then. What's next?"

He gave her a soft grin. "We go see Mendoza."

"Who is this Mendoza? He's Spanish?"

"Guatemalan, I think. Or Texan. I don't know. Anyway, he's wired, and he owes me some favors."

"*Wired?*" she asked.

"Wired in. I think he can get us fake IDs. Give us a place to stay. And he feels like he owes me a favor."

"What sort of favor?"

"I knew him in Afghanistan. He broke an ankle two months into our deployment, so he basically missed all the fun."

What sort of fun? she wondered. Her impression had been that Dylan was very bitter about his experience in Afghanistan. Sometimes the things he said made no sense. Or maybe she just didn't grasp his bizarre language.

"Can you trust him?"

He shrugged. "Yeah, I can trust him. I told you, we served in Afghanistan together."

Andrea said, "I thought Ray was falsely accused. By his Sergeant."

Dylan froze, stricken. He stared at her, his mouth open for a minute, then he nodded. "Yeah," he whispered. "That's true."

"Dylan..."

"Just leave me alone. We trust Mendoza because right now we don't have any other choice."

She stared at him. "All right."

Ten minutes later the train came to a stop at Clarendon Station. Dylan bent his knees as the train pulled into the station, peering out the window, looking for police. When the doors opened, he said, "Come on."

The platform was uncomfortably hot, air blowing from the tunnel. The train on the opposite track pulled in and disgorged its passengers. Andrea was suddenly crowded in, people on all sides, elbows and briefcases and backpacks. Dylan grabbed her arm and pulled her along with the crowd.

Conversationally, he said, "Look over there, near the station manager."

Andrea's eyes darted to the small office encased in glass near the turnstiles. Two police officers stood there, scanning the crowd.

Her heart began to pound, and she shook her head, letting her hair fall partly over her face. Dylan scanned the crowd, then made a snap decision. He walked over to a teenager, a boy with spiked hair. He whispered something, urgently, as the crowd rushed past them. Another inbound train pulled in. Dylan stuffed something in the teenager's pockets, then turned and took her arm again. "Head low," he said.

They walked toward the turnstiles. The cops were still scanning the crowd carefully. There was no way they were going to make it by.

Until the teenage boy suddenly shouted at the opposite end of the platform, letting out a loud *whoop, whoop, whoop!* and waving his arms in the air. One cop, then the other, looked toward the teenager.

"I WANT TO FUCK SOMEBODY!" shouted the teenager.

Someone in the crowd tittered, and the cops shook their heads simultaneously, then began to push their way through the crowd.

Andrea and Dylan had reached the turnstiles. They swiped their cards and went through just as the cops reached the other end of the platform. Andrea took one last look—the teenager stood between the two police officers, a grin on his face.

They rode up the escalators and reached the top right in the middle of the crowd.

"Over there across the street. That's Mendoza in the green car."

The car was an Oldsmobile, probably thirty or more years old. It was twice the length of most of the other cars on the block, and it wasn't just green, it was a loud, fluorescent green that probably stood out in satellite photos. A twenty-something man—Christopher Mendoza—sat behind the wheel.

Mendoza saw them in the crowd, but Dylan didn't acknowledge him, instead turning down the sidewalk away from the station.

At the end of the block, Dylan said, "Here he comes."

She could tell, because the rumbling of the engine underneath the hood of the Oldsmobile was shaking the newspaper stands half a block away. The car pulled to a stop at the corner. Dylan opened the back door for her, then ran around to the passenger side and got in the front passenger seat.

The back seat had been leather once, but now consisted largely of grey duct tape. The seat was large enough she could have laid down lengthwise and almost slept comfortably. As it was, she slid to the center of the seat.

"Chris Mendoza," said the driver, holding a hand back to shake. "I used to hang out with this jerk."

She smiled and shook. "Andrea Thompson."

Mendoza put the car in drive and sped away when the light turned green. He turned to Dylan and said, "I saw cops going in the station—how'd you get past 'em?"

Dylan smirked. "Paid a teenager to make an ass of himself."

Mendoza chuckled. "Well, let's get out of here. I went online and checked out the news after we talked. You got some big guns after you. What the hell for?"

Dylan looked over his shoulder at Andrea. Then he shrugged. "Don't know. But whoever it is, they're serious."

"Yeah, you aren't kidding," Mendoza responded. "Anyway, we'll get you under cover. You need anything?"

"New clothes. Haircuts. I've got a ton of cash—I want to buy some prepaid credit card and disposable phones."

Mendoza nodded. "Can do all that. What about ID?"

Andrea said, "The police have my passport. Everything, really."

Mendoza looked in the mirror and met her eyes. Then he looked back to the road. "We can cover that. I know a guy. He's good."

"How long?"

"Rush job? I don't know. Usually he takes a week or two. Sometimes I help arrange some IDs for the local high school kids."

Dylan snorted. He turned in his seat and said to Andrea, "Mendoza had a whole operation going. Buying and selling shit we couldn't get through the PX. I swear to God guys all over the FOB were crying when he broke his ankle."

Mendoza chuckled as he slowed the car at a red light. Andrea half listened. She didn't know what a lot of the words Dylan said meant. Was the PX some kind of supply shop? Store? What was a fob? She didn't know, and somehow she didn't think the details mattered. What mattered was Dylan's manner. As he talked, he seemed animated, his eyes wide, a light and easy tone of voice.

Andrea had only met Dylan twice before: at his wedding with her sister Alexandra, and a few months later after the accident, when Ray was still hanging onto life, then the days they'd spent around each other over the last week. Dylan seemed to be unstable. Humorless. But in Mendoza's presence, a different Dylan emerged. He laughed and seemed less grim.

Was it merely the presence of an old Army buddy? And if so, why didn't Alexandra affect him that way? After all, as Alexandra had said no less than 99 *thousand* times, she and Dylan were soul mates.

Whatever that meant. Instead of speculating any further, she sat back in her seat and tried to relax as Dylan told their story to Mendoza. He went into a lot of detail, taking his time.

When he'd finished, Mendoza looked in the rearview mirror and caught her eyes again. "You seriously went up against those guys in the car and took them out? *Then* jumped off a twenty-story building?"

She swallowed, but didn't answer.

Mendoza had pulled up to a driveway, in front of an old town-house. It was brick, surrounded by yellowing grass, and toys were scattered around the front porch. He twisted around in his seat, and raised a hand to her, fist closed.

"Respect," he said.

She touched his closed fist with her own. And didn't say a word as they got out of the car.

CHAPTER SEVENTEEN
What's your plan, Paris?

"**Mama!** This is my friend, Dylan Paris, and his sister, Andrea."

Dylan breathed a sigh of relief as Mendoza said the word. From then on, if anyone asked, Andrea was his sister.

Mendoza's mother was not what Dylan expected. She wore a black dress with a cowl-neck collar and a strand of unusually large pearls. When they walked in, she was sitting at a table with three other women, all of them elegantly dressed and with cards in their hands. Dylan looked at the cards—they were unlike any he'd seen before. Colorful, with swords and cups and coins instead of the suits he was used to.

"Dylan and Andrea? I'm Sofia. It's nice to meet you." She set her cards face down on the table and stood, then muttered, "And don't you card sharks touch mine."

She walked over and took Dylan's and Andrea's hands.

"Nice to meet you," Dylan said. "I don't see how such a beautiful woman ended up with *him* as a son, though."

Mendoza punched Dylan in the shoulder even as his mother blushed.

"Thank you, dear. Are you just visiting? Do you live around here?"

She was a nice lady. But Dylan wasn't planning to tell anyone the truth about anything right now. "We're from Raleigh, ma'am. North Carolina." His accent wasn't exactly North Carolina, but only a Raleigh native would be able to tell the difference.

"Oh, isn't that nice. I got a speeding ticket in North Carolina once," she said.

Dylan chuckled. "Most people can't get away fast enough," he said.

"Ma, we're gonna grab some lunch, all right? Then we've got some errands to run."

"You go ahead, I've got to get back to my game," Sophia said.

Mendoza led Dylan and Andrea into the kitchen.

Andrea said, "It was pleasant to meet you," as they left the room, and Dylan thought he might have to come up with a better cover story. *He* could pass off North Carolina. Andrea couldn't, not with that Spanish accent.

"So what's the plan?" Mendoza asked.

Dylan looked at Andrea. She looked back at him, her expression not giving him a clue. He spoke. "Can we hole up here for a couple days? And then we'll make ourselves scarce. I don't want to put you in any danger."

"Danger is my middle name," Mendoza said, pushing his chest out.

"Yeah, well, maybe it's yours, but I don't think it's your mom's."

Mendoza nodded. "Truth. All right. I'm thinking we go for a completely new look, right?"

"Yeah," Dylan said.

"Let me get that rolling, then. I gotta ask you one question though—you got enough cash for all this? The IDs are gonna cost. I can spot you some … I still got a little in the bank from Afghanistan."

"Nah," Dylan said. Mendoza didn't have to offer, but in some ways it relieved Dylan that he did. "We're good."

For the next several minutes Mendoza puttered around the kitchen like an old woman. Dylan and Andrea stood there in uncomfortable silence—Andrea sipping a glass of water and Dylan just watching. Mendoza seemed different. They'd been friends at Fort Drum, then deployed to Afghanistan together. Just a few weeks into their deployment, Mendoza had broken his ankle, a nasty compound fracture, during a firefight.

He used to joke and laugh a lot more, Dylan thought. Now, Mendoza had a haunted look. He didn't talk as much, and he certainly didn't laugh as much.

It worried Dylan. He didn't say anything right away, letting Mendoza finish putting together a salad.

"All right," Mendoza said. "Hope you guys don't mind some greens. They're good for you, make you live longer."

"That looks wonderful," Andrea said.

"Rabbit food," Dylan muttered. "Ah, well."

Mendoza grinned. "We'll take it out on the porch, and if you don't like it you can throw it to the rabbits, all right? Some live in the neighborhood."

Outside, Dylan sat on a cast iron seat and soaked in the sunshine. The backyard was simple, with neatly cut grass and a wooden fence surrounding it. Toys were scattered here and there.

"You got a little sister, right?" Dylan asked.

"Two. Twelve and seven. They'll be home from school soonish."

"And you doing okay?"

Mendoza met his eyes. "Why do you ask?"

Dylan shrugged. "You don't seem yourself is all. You don't laugh."

Mendoza chuckled a little. "You should look at yourself, *amigo*. You look like someone died."

Dylan shrugged. "Someone did."

Mendoza's lips tightened in a straight line. "That's right. A lot of someones."

Andrea looked confused. Mendoza leaned forward and said to her, "Bunch of our guys got killed in Afghanistan. Or after, with Sherman and Hicks."

"Hicks is the man who killed Ray?" she asked.

Dylan nodded. "Yeah. He was—just really messed up."

"Everyone was, except me," Mendoza said. "I broke my ankle and went home and missed out."

"Good thing," Dylan said.

Half an hour later they were back out in the car. Mendoza drove them first to a stylist on Columbia Pike.

It wasn't anything like the barbershops Dylan usually frequented. For one thing, the pictures on the walls showed a wide variety of hairstyles, not a single one of which looked normal. Spikes and mohawks in a thousand variations. He watched as Andrea walked around. Her eyes narrowed in, finally pointing.

By the time they left, Andrea didn't look like herself. Her hair, mostly dark brown, was now completely black, except a wide alternating turquoise and violet streak across the front and down the left side of her face. Her hair had been cut into a reverse bob, and both eyebrows had been plucked and shaped, giving a significantly different look to her face. Older, narrower, with her cheekbones far more prominent than before. Dylan thought there was no mistaking that she was sister to Sarah Thompson, but she looked nothing like before.

Dylan's hair and eyebrows were three shades lighter, a blondish brown, and his unshaven beard was neatened up and trimmed. He looked at himself in the mirror for a long time—the change in appearance had an odd effect on his mood. Even as a teen he'd never paid much attention to his personal appearance other than trying to stay generally neat. But this was an intentional look, and that felt strange.

"Ladies man," Mendoza muttered, half sarcastically, when Dylan finished.

"You should get yours done," Dylan replied.

"Nah," Mendoza said, running his fingers through his thick black hair. "Nobody touches the locks."

Andrea giggled, and Dylan smiled. It was the first time he'd seen her really laugh.

"All right," Mendoza said. "Time to complete the look."

Dylan muttered curses to himself, but followed.

An hour later, they had discarded their clothes. Dylan had shifted from his typical khakis and flannel shirts to more business-like pants and a button down shirt. Andrea wore a red and black flannel dress.

"You look like the 1990s," Mendoza said to Dylan.

"Shut up." Dylan chuckled. Then he adjusted the plastic-rimmed rectangular sunglasses he'd bought. "These are hideous," he said.

"No," Andrea said. "They look good. And the point isn't for you to be fancy. It's for you to be hidden."

Dylan nodded. "Yeah, yeah, that's easy for you to say. You don't suddenly look thirty."

She smiled. "What's next?"

Dylan thought a moment. Before leaving the condo the night before, he'd reached into the bag and randomly stuffed stacks of bills into his own bag. Once he'd finally counted the stacks of money, he'd been stunned. He'd barely scratched the surface of the bag full of money they'd found in Andrea's room. But that scratch had contained 32 stacks of bills totaling 80,000 dollars.

He didn't know where the money had come from. Or why they'd been attacked. But he knew that right now they needed to stay hidden, and the money was going to help.

"Mendoza, how much time do you have?"

"I'm all yours, man."

"I want to buy some pre-paid Visa cards. Bunch of them. But you can't just walk into one place and buy a lot ... so I'm thinking half a dozen stops. And then I want to pick up some burner phones. Four phones, a dozen SIM cards."

"All right."

"Okay ... I got one last thing for you."

"Yeah?"

"How much is that piece of shit car worth?"

"I don't know ... two thousand?"

"I'll give you six for it. We're gonna need wheels."

"Done. And I got a text back from my guy—he's gonna meet us to do the IDs."

Andrea. May 2. 6:00 pm.

Andrea sank into the booth, exhausted and with aching feet. Dylan, looking equally exhausted, shrank into the faux-leather upholstery across from her. He had a bleak expression on his face as he looked around the diner.

"What's up, man? You look like someone pissed in your Cheerios." Mendoza was sitting next to Andrea, and was far more alert than he had any right to be. Of course, he hadn't spent the night being attacked by assassins, then holed up in a shitty hotel in the worst neighborhood in suburban Maryland.

"Nothing," Dylan said, shaking his head absently. "Missing Alex a little—we usually eat at this diner down the street from campus. Looks kind of like this place."

Mendoza shrugged. "She'll be all right, man. Don't fret. It's you two I'm worried about."

Dylan just looked away from Mendoza, his eyes tracking the approaching waitress. Mendoza shifted position, unhappily. Dylan knew he didn't like not being the center of attention, and he didn't at all like Dylan ignoring him.

"What's your plan, Paris?"

Dylan looked back at Mendoza. "We crash at your place tonight. I think we're all set to fly under the radar now, so in the morning we start searching for Andrea's father."

Andrea sat up. "Where are you going to start?"

"We start with our burner phones. I want to ask some questions of your oldest sisters. Find out what they remember. Carrie was in Spain with you when you were a baby, right?"

Andrea nodded. She thought about that album, and the damnably out of focus photographs. She opened her mouth to speak, but the waitress arrived, and they hurriedly placed their orders.

Who *was* the man in those photos? She wished she'd had more of an opportunity to look at them. It seemed like it was an eternity ago that she'd sat down with her sister Carrie, looking at the album from Spain. That was only on Tuesday. She closed her eyes, picturing the man in those two photos again. His face had been slightly blurred, but it was clear enough to see his eye color matched hers, as did his slightly aquiline nose. The man in the photo was easily six-five.

But she had no idea who he was, and Carrie didn't remember either. Maybe Luis or Abuelita would know. She needed to call them both anyway. They'd have heard about the attack by now and would be terrified. She felt awful she hadn't gotten in touch already, but there had hardly been an opportunity.

She could tell her voice sounded tired when she said, "I think we should ask Luis."

Dylan looked confused. Andrea said, "My uncle—Mother's younger brother. He's *much* younger. I think she was sixteen when he was born. He might know who the man at the beach was. Or other details I don't know about."

Dylan started nodding as she spoke. "Okay. We got something there. Do you know if Carrie has those photos on her Facebook page?"

Andrea shook her head. "I don't think so. I'd never seen them before."

"Okay," he said. "We need to get her to post them. I want to do image searches on all the people in the photos. Everyone you don't know. Who knows what might turn up there?"

"Julia might know more," Andrea said. "She's the oldest. I mean—I was born in China. She was already a teenager. She must have seen something, right?"

"She's never really talked about it with me much, but I get the impression she saw way too much in China," Dylan said.

Their waitress was already on the way out, carrying a heavy tray of food. "Food's coming," Andrea said.

"About time," Mendoza said. "I got a question. What if this isn't about the blood tests at all?"

"What do you mean?" Andrea said.

"Well, look—I get it. Your dad isn't your dad. And you got attacked. But no one attacked—what's your other sister's name? Carrie? Right?"

Dylan raised an eyebrow. "It was her condo we were in," he said.

"Yeah, yeah, I know. I'm just saying—don't close off possibilities. If your dad is into bad shit," he said, nodding at Andrea, "there could be all kinds of possibilities. Plus, it's not like this is the first time. I mean, Ray was murdered."

Dylan frowned. "That's not happening to anyone else."

"Good luck controlling that, Dylan. No wonder you look like crap if you think you could have done anything to save Ray. You were in New York when it happened, right?"

Dylan grunted. "Yeah, I know. I tend to blame myself for stuff that's—"

"Stuff you couldn't do nothin' about. I get it, Dylan."

"Yeah, yeah. I can at least protect *this one*," he said, pointing at Andrea.

The statement, and the fierce look on his face, sent shivers down her spine. She couldn't get her mind around the fact that less than twenty-four hours before, he had fought gunmen *with a knife*. To protect her.

"Good. There you go. Something you can do," Mendoza said.

"Leave him alone," Andrea said.

"Do *what?*" Mendoza replied.

"Dylan's had a rough time. Let him alone."

"You don't need to protect me," Dylan said. His tone was harsh.

"You don't need to protect *me*," Andrea replied.

Dylan rolled his eyes. "People are trying to kill you."

"Yeah, I know that, Dylan."

He closed his eyes. And then he said, "I'm so tired I could collapse right here. I can't eat a bite."

"Go get some rest," Mendoza said.

"Yeah," Dylan replied. "But do me a favor. Is there some place busy, like a mall, not close to where you live?"

"We could go up to Tysons, maybe. It's a big mall. Crowded. But we gotta be back at my place by 9, so you can get your IDs."

"Yeah ... let's do that. We'll call Alex and Carrie, then toss the first SIM card in the garbage and head to your place. And get some sleep. I don't know about you, but I'm desperate."

"Let's go," Andrea replied, heart suddenly beating faster at the thought of talking with her sisters.

CHAPTER EIGHTEEN
One of the little people

Anthony Walker felt a wave of exhaustion slip over him as he slid into the chair in front of his desk at the offices of the *Washington Post*. Spread in every direction across the floor around him was the staff of the entertainment section—a dozen reporters, editors and photographers, two research assistants, and his boss, Linda Halloran.

Linda wasn't exactly a friend. In fact, the day he'd shown up at her desk, she'd looked up at him with scorn. "I know you think you're better than the rest of us, Walker. But foreign correspondents put their pants on the same way as everyone else. While you're working for me, you're one of the little people. Understand?"

Her attitude was unjust. Anthony might have been a foreign correspondent, but he had professional respect for everyone at the paper.

Personal respect—now that was something different. In the few short months he'd been in exile at the entertainment desk, Linda had gone out of her way to assign him to the crappiest possible stories. He'd covered the free weekly plays for toddlers at the National Theater. He'd interviewed Efua Lawal, the Nigerian pop singer who'd been arrested in New York with two prostitutes and fourteen grams of cocaine. He'd spent *two entire weeks* in January covering Justin Bieber's arrest in Miami.

Prior to January 24th, he'd never even heard of Justin Bieber.

Only a few weeks left and he'd be out of this hell. But then the call came early last week. *Morbid Obesity* was recording a new album. Would he do a profile of the headliner, Crank Wilson, and his wife, Julia? As an added incentive, Julia Wilson was the eldest daughter of the newly nominated Secretary of Defense.

Anthony jumped at the chance. It would be far more interesting than any other stories he was likely to get.

Julia and Crank had presented far more of a story than he'd bargained for. First, Julia's youngest sister had been kidnapped the day she arrived in the States, setting off a media firestorm. Now someone had blown up their house, the IRS had shut down their business, and Julia's father was under investigation.

Not your typical entertainment desk story.

Anthony logged into his computer, then picked up the handset for his phone and dialed into his voicemail. He opened up a notebook and began writing down the messages. Two from Linda Halloran, sometime yesterday evening. A call from his mother. Bill Lieby, his best friend and a foreign correspondent for the *Post*. The final message was from Jackson Barlow, the executive editor. *That* message had been left at 12:30, only half an hour ago.

Anthony pulled the phone to him and dialed.

"Jackson Barlow's office." A pleasant voice, but an unfamiliar one. Did Barlow have a new assistant? He was notoriously grumpy and went through executive assistants at a pace of two or three per year. It was a miracle the paper had never been sued—or at least, as far as Anthony knew it hadn't. That didn't rule out the possibility that something had been hushed up. Anthony had wondered more than once if Barlow was a womanizer in addition to being so grumpy. It would explain the continuous parade of new pretty young girls working for him. Over the phone, at least, this one sounded young.

"Is Jackson in? This is Anthony Walker, I just got back in the office."

"Oh! Mr. Walker! Mr. Barlow's in conference room A. He told me if you called to send you right there. The meeting just started."

"On my way," Anthony said, already rising to his feet and grabbing his laptop.

As he did, his eyes fell on one of the several monitors mounted not far from his desk. The screen showed a CNN news feed. Prince George-Phillip, the head of the SIS, was standing in front of a podium speaking into a microphone as reporters waved their arms. The headline flashing across the bottom of the screen read: *Terrorists attempt to assassinate British Intelligence head.*

Anthony shook his head as he turned away, heading toward the elevator. He'd interviewed the tall, gangly George-Phillip four years before, when the Prince became the first head of the Secret Intelligence Service to ever give a public address. The London newspapers liked to make fun of George-Phillip's admittedly ridiculous eyebrows, which were constantly in motion whenever he talked. But it was clear enough to Anthony that the newspapers missed his most important features—the intelligence behind those cool blue-green eyes was fierce. George-Phillip Windsor was a worthy head of the Intelligence Service.

As he walked from the elevator to the conference room, Anthony thought he'd have much preferred to be covering the story of George-Phillip's assassination attempt instead of whatever was going on with the Thompson family.

Then he froze, his hand on the door to the conference room.

Wasn't it an odd coincidence that someone had attempted to assassinate the head of British intelligence at the same time the children of the US Secretary of Defense were attacked?

Anthony's mind raced as he opened the door, and he didn't really pay attention to the dozen or so people in the room as he entered. He thought about the photographs he'd seen of Carrie Sherman and her sister, Andrea. Two remarkably tall women with very dark hair and blue-green eyes. *Was it possible?* What an incredible scandal that would have been: the wife of an American diplomat, pregnant not once, but *twice*, with children of a member of the British royal family.

Jackson Barlow stood at the head of the table. "Welcome back to Washington, Anthony. Nice of you to join us."

"Uh ... thanks, Jackson."

Anthony forced his attention back to the present. He glanced around the room, taking note of the occupants.

Jackson Barlow, the executive editor of the paper. David Samuel, the National Desk editor, plus four reporters from his team. Jim Hsu, Anthony's old boss on the World Desk. Bill Leiby, and several other foreign correspondents. Two legal reporters and a politics reporter.

From the people in the room, it was easy enough to deduce which story *this* meeting was about.

"Have a seat," Barlow said. "I understand you spent yesterday and this morning with Julia Wilson?"

"And her husband, Crank," Anthony said, giving Barlow an insincere smile. "He's got a new album coming out soon."

Barlow met Anthony's eyes. "Understood. You still have access to them?"

Anthony nodded. "Yes. They want their side of the story out there."

"Okay. I want to hear your take."

Anthony looked around the room. He didn't know what anyone else in here had. Some of them would undoubtedly be buying the special prosecutor's story—that somehow Richard Thompson was involved in money laundering and more, and had enlisted his daughter's aid. Anthony didn't buy it.

He looked Barlow in the eyes and said, "We don't have enough information. But the idea that Richard Thompson somehow enlisted his children in a giant money laundering scheme is doubtful. Honestly, I don't think Julia Wilson is that stupid."

Barlow nodded, then said, "Okay—if that's the case, what's the real story?"

Anthony looked around the room. Why the hell was Barlow putting him on the spot like this?

"I don't know, Jackson. I've been stuck in moving vehicles since early this morning. But I think that's what we need to find out. What's the real story?"

Barlow shook his head and smiled. "All right. Here's what we're going to do. Legal team—I want you guys to concentrate on the actual investigation. What does the independent prosecutor know, or what does he think he knows? What's the IRS doing? Why did they seize Julia and Crank Wilson's assets? National desk—you guys follow up on the political side. What's going on with the Pentagon? Is Richard Thompson going to step down? Is Congress getting involved? What else?"

Anthony said, "I want to know if there's a link to the assassination attempt on the head of SIS."

Barlow's eyes nearly bugged out. "*What?* There's no link there, Anthony."

"Probably not. But the timing is curious."

"There was probably an earthquake in Mumbai last night too. That doesn't mean it's linked to Richard Thompson."

"No ... but this is different. How often are there attacks on multiple people at high levels of intelligence agencies of different countries on the same day?"

"Richard Thompson isn't—"

"He's CIA. Not State Department."

"Bullshit. Where do you get that?"

"From his own files. When Julia and Crank Wilson busted into his office last night they had me along for the ride. There's more here than meets the eye, Barlow."

Barlow gave Anthony a cool look. Then he took a deep breath and closed his eyes.

"Fine, Anthony. You're off the entertainment desk. I want you in charge of the team for this story."

Anthony tried to fight back a grin. And failed. He was going to be back in his element. As he stood up, Linda Halloran stirred in her seat.

"Jackson," said Linda. "Anthony's got live assignments on the entertainment desk. He needs to finish those."

Barlow dismissed her with a casual hand wave. "This is priority, Linda. Anthony—your show. What do you have?"

Anthony felt remarkably little tension in his stomach. This was a chance to get his life back. He was going for it. He walked around the conference table, picked up a dry erase marker, and wrote in large bold letters:

Same-day assassination attempt
Wakhan massacre?
R. Thompson - sexual assault of his wife 1991?

The others in the room stirred as he wrote the second and third line. To Anthony's right, Jackson Barlow frowned.

Links between GP and R. Thompson?
R. Thompson - CIA career
Missing: Adelina Thompson, Dylan Paris, Andrea Thompson, Jessica Thompson

He stood back and looked at the white board.

"What am I missing?" he asked.

"What the hell is that about Wakhan? And sexual assault?" Barlow's voice was harsh as he asked the question.

Anthony said, "What we found in Thompson's office was ... serious. First, Adelina Thompson was only sixteen when she conceived her first daughter. Richard Thompson married her when she was seventeen and already pregnant."

"Holy shit," someone muttered.

"Second—we found a report of a paternity test, determining that Carrie Sherman was not Thompson's daughter. The very next day, after the report was written, we have a police report. Adelina Thompson was assaulted and raped in February 1990. She refused to press charges, but according to the San Francisco Police, her husband was the prime suspect."

Silence had fallen across the room. "Finally—and this is the most confusing part for me—Thompson had a file with information about the Wakhan massacre in his office. Nothing classified there, everyone knows the massacre took place. What I want to know is this: did he know about it when it took place? Richard Thompson was assigned to the US Embassy in Pakistan in 1983."

"Motherfucker," Jackson said.

"I'll look into the Pakistan stuff," said Bill Leiby. "And the links with Prince George-Phillip. That's really interesting. Did you know he was involved with the SIS investigation into Wakhan?"

Anthony's eyes widened. "Are you serious?"

Leiby nodded. "My timing may be off—it was, I don't know— '84 maybe? The results never made the light of day, but I remember George-Phillip asking questions one day—"

Leiby's eyes widened and met Anthony's.

"What?" Anthony said.

"Understand, he was a kid then. Twenty-one maybe? I was on the diplomatic beat at the time. And there was some fuss—the British Embassy made a formal complaint to the paper."

"About?"

"Our society page columnist wrote something about George-Phillip and Adelina Thompson being seen having a private lunch together."

Barlow nodded. "Yeah, that happened. Maria Clawson wrote the story, I think."

Anthony frowned in distaste. Maria Clawson was a gossip blogger, specializing in destroying people's lives. "Clawson worked for the *Post*?"

"Until the late 90s," Barlow said.

Anthony shook his head. "Jesus. Before my time. So—George-Phillip and Adelina Thompson had lunch in the 1980s. Anything more?"

Barlow shrugged. "No idea."

"We'll find out," Leiby said.

"All right. We need to find out what the British concluded in their investigation of Wakhan. And I think we need to do our own investigation again."

Linda Halloran said, "What about the political implications? Does anyone know if the President will keep backing Thompson's nomination?"

Barlow shook his head. "I'll be stunned if he does. And that's going to get ugly."

Anthony responded, "Everyone else will be covering the political angle. Does it hurt the President? How will this affect polling numbers? They'll all miss the real story."

Barlow pointed a finger at Anthony. "You better get the real story for us."

Anthony nodded. "I'm on it."

Julia. May 2. 2 pm.

The phone rang four times. Five. Six. Then it cut over to voicemail.

"You've reached the personal line of Richard Thompson. I can't take your call right now. Please leave a clear message and a phone number."

Julia clicked disconnect. She'd left messages already. Several of them, in fact. Her father wasn't answering his phone.

Of course, he was the Secretary of Defense. *Plus*, he'd gotten news that morning that the Justice Department was investigating him under charges that were clearly ridiculous.

But he still needed to answer his damn phone.

She put her cell down and looked around the suite they'd checked into in Arlington. She needed to *do* something. She needed something to fix, something concrete to put her hands on. Carrie was back at the safe house, but neither she nor Julia knew the address. Her lawyer was meeting with the Internal Revenue Service, and there was absolutely nothing Julia could do to help that situation.

She'd spent an hour on the phone with employees, both reassuring them and making sure their immediate needs were taken care of. But she felt a pit in her stomach. Payroll was in a few days, and the corporate accounts had been frozen, along with her and Crank's savings and investment accounts. Their cash account had a lot of money in it, but not enough to cover payroll for any length of time.

Julia stood and paced. In the next room, behind a closed door, she could hear Crank practicing. He had the volume low, which was good. He'd been working on several new songs, and she'd been pushing. Pushing, because in some ways, the most recent songs he'd written seemed like rote. Morbid Obesity had been together more than a dozen years, and had released 8 albums. They'd done so many tours that the hotel rooms and suites across the globe had long since merged together into a hazy mess. But the music had always been cutting edge, emotional, deeply connected to who they were as people. Lately, though, it felt like they were following a formula.

She stood for just a second, tilting her head and listening to the tones of the guitar through the closed door. Hard to hear, but whatever Crank was working on, it had an odd, catchy, syncopated beat.

She reached for her phone again. Maybe Carrie had gotten clearance to meet.

It rang before she could touch it. She froze. The word "Dad" appeared across the front of her phone.

Answer. Decline. The two choices felt like the choice between good and evil, and she didn't know which was which.

She stared at it. Her tongue felt like copper. She picked the phone up, tapped on the "answer" button and spoke without a pause for thought or breath, her words as much of a surprise to her as they would be to her father.

"Where's my mother?"

Stunned silence at the other end. Then he said, in a perfectly calm, placating voice, "I don't know, Julia. I don't know where she is."

A cold rage wrapped around her heart. "Why did the IRS close my offices this morning? What the hell is happening to our family, *Father?*"

"Julia, I am returning your call. I did not expect to be spoken to this way."

"I didn't expect to find out that—that..." She couldn't say the words.

"Find out what?"

"I read the police report."

"What police report? I have no idea what you are talking about." His voice sounded damnably reasonable.

"Let me refresh your memory, Father." Her voice was cutting and sarcastic and bore thirty years of lies and hurt. "The day after you found out Carrie wasn't your daughter, Mom was beaten half to death and raped. Does that ring a bell?"

"Julia, where did you—"

"In your office, Father. You don't even deny it?"

His response was unexpected, both harsh and insistent. "*In my office? When?*"

"Yesterday. Right before two thugs broke into the house, tried to kill us, then set off a bomb."

Silence. After a few seconds, he said, "There's a great deal more to this than you realize, Julia. You mustn't jump to conclusions."

The bedroom door opened, and Crank appeared in the doorway. "Hey," he said. "You won't believe this song—" He froze and stopped talking when he saw her expression.

"What else can I do, Father? Apparently neither of my parents can be bothered to tell me the truth about anything. What else am I supposed to do other than come to my own conclusions?"

"I've never lied to you, Julia."

"What?" she shouted. "You've never lied to me? What about the affairs in China? What about my sister not being my sister? What about you raping my mother? What about the fact that she was a *child* when she got pregnant with me? You've never lied to me?"

As she cried out the words, she saw it. Julia had been—eight years old? She had run downstairs that day, holding hands with Carrie. They had been giggling, free. It must have been a Saturday, and they both had Valentine's candy from school. They'd been playing and laughing, but she remembered wondering why Mary, the nanny, looked so distressed.

That morning, she and Carrie had run into the family room and jumped on the couch together, then Carrie said, "Why Mommy cry? Mommy? Why Mommy sad?"

Her face had been bruised, and she'd lay curled on the couch, eyes red with tears, reading a book. Her arm was in a sling.

"I'm not sad," their mother had said. Then she tried to smile. "I'm just a little sick."

"Sick make you purple?" Carrie said. Then she giggled and ran to their mother and wrapped her arms around her, and Adelina winced. Carrie said, "Kiss make Mommy better," and leaned up and kissed her.

Valentine's, Julia thought. She hadn't thought about that day in years. But she'd seen the police report last night. Her mother hadn't been sick. She'd been beaten and raped.

I'm not sad. I'm just a little sick.

Just a little sick. That was a couple days after Valentine's, a couple days after the police report indicated she'd had cracked ribs.

A surge of rage swept over Julia. In a low voice she whispered into the phone, "You've never done anything *but* lie to me."

Then she put the phone down. Bright sunlight poured into the hotel room, but she felt dead inside.

"Babe?" Crank said in a low voice.

Julia turned to her husband. She opened her mouth, but couldn't speak. There were no words. Nothing. She thought of all the times she'd been at war with her mother. The cruel things her mother had said. The constant warfare.

Why? Why had her mother been so hateful? Was it all fear of her father? Why had she had the affair? Her mother had been sixteen when she became pregnant with Julia.

And fifteen years later, Julia got pregnant, and aborted the child. A child who would have been Andrea's age now.

A child she'd never be able to hold or kiss or love.

She knew it wasn't logical. She knew it didn't make any sense at all. But suddenly tears were running down her face, and Julia let out a low growl. Crank instantly moved to her, putting his arms around her.

"It's okay, babe," he whispered.

"No," she said. "It's not. It'll never be okay." Then a wave of agony hit. Not physical pain, but spiritual agony, remorse and grief and loss for the thing she'd always wanted but never had. "I have to call Carrie," she whispered.

He broke away from her and she dialed Carrie's number.

"Where are you?" she asked as soon as Carrie answered. "Did you get the address?"

Carrie gave her an address. "Call me when you're less than five minutes away. I'm not supposed to tell anyone where we are, so we won't tell our security until the moment you drive up."

"Perfect," Julia said. "I'll call. We need to talk."

Julia turned to her husband. He had a concerned expression on his face, his eyes wide, eyebrows raised. "Let's go?" she asked.

Five minutes later they were in a rental car. Crank drove while Julia fidgeted with her phone.

"Talk to me," he said.

"I keep thinking about Belgium. I remember being so alone. I don't ... I mean, I get it that she must have been afraid of him. She must have been crazy sometimes. But why didn't she just leave him?"

She closed her eyes, not expecting an answer from Crank. Julia didn't remember the flight to Belgium, but she did remember being angry they had to leave San Francisco and her friends.

The last day in San Francisco.

Her mother had been in rare form that day, trying to herd three children, get the house packed and arrange everything by herself. For several weeks Mother's patience had been short, as she became alternately inconsolable and angry.

Where had her father been? Julia had a vague memory that he'd met them in Brussels—for most of the three years before leaving for Belgium, he'd only been home for brief visits.

Julia clearly remembered the meltdown right before they left for the airport. The cab had been waiting at the front steps for several minutes as Adelina corralled three children and half a dozen bags. Julia had already seen the signs, the stress lines appearing around her mother's eyes, the thinning lips stretching across her mouth.

They had been standing on the front steps as her mother panicked, searching around.

"Julia, watch your sisters, I left one of my bags." She ducked in the front door.

Julia took six-year-old Carrie's hand in her left, and Alexandra's in her right. Alexandra immediately began to pull away, and Carrie shouted, "Stop, you're holding my hand too tight!"

Carrie had reached over and pinched Julia's arm. Julia spun toward her sister, and Alexandra's hand got loose, sending the toddler spilling down the steps.

Carrie screamed and Julia felt her heart in her throat. Alexandra had been—maybe fourteen months? She hadn't been walking long, and when she fell it was like watching a limp doll just fall end over end.

Her tiny face instantly turned bright red and she began to scream. The cab driver got out of the car and shouted, "Is she okay?" just as their mother came back outside.

Adelina had let out a cry and rushed to Alexandra, yanking her out of Julia's arms. "I can't trust you alone for *five seconds*!"

Julia remembered feeling—injured? Hurt? Her mother's words dug deep.

"Is okay, Mommy," Carrie said. "She not broken."

Adelina had sniffed. "No, she's not broken."

"I want to go see *Daddy*," Julia had said.

Her mother had looked at her with weary, incredibly sad eyes, and said, "Well, you're going to get your wish, Julia. Go get in the car."

The bitterness made her choke. Thinking back now, Julia found herself questioning everything she'd ever believed about her mother and father.

She said to Crank in a broken, strained voice, "Everything I've ever believed is upside down."

Crank nodded, but didn't say anything. He reached over with his right hand and intertwined his fingers with hers.

"Things were good in San Francisco. I remember that. Mostly. Not always—I remember my mom being sick and hurt after Valentine's the year Alexandra was born. When he beat her up and ... and..."

Her voice trailed off. She couldn't say the words.

"It's okay," Crank said.

Julia forced the words out. "When he raped her. I remember it, but I didn't know what it meant. I just knew she was sick, and I was mad because she couldn't do anything for a few days and we were stuck with the nanny. And then she got so sad when we went to Belgium." Julia moaned a little. "Oh, God, she was so sad. And I was mad at her. Because we were going to see Daddy, and I didn't know why she was sad."

Crank turned the car onto the highway. "No way you could have known what was going on with her."

"True," she said, "but still. I keep thinking about those three years in Belgium. Barry looked after Carrie and me sometimes. Alexandra had a governess. I barely remember seeing Dad. They were already sleeping in separate rooms. I guess they always did and I just didn't think anything of it."

"You were so lonely," Crank murmured.

"I was," Julia said. "But I never realized—what must it have been like for her? Did they hate each other? Dad—I don't get ... I don't get any of it. I mean—do you know how many years of therapy I've gone through, thanks to her?"

It was a rhetorical question of course—he'd been right there with her through it all. He knew all about her therapists.

She closed her eyes. She remembered the day she'd confronted her mother right before leaving for Germany. Julia had spit out bitter words. *Why wouldn't you help me? Why weren't you there when I needed you?*

Even then, during that confrontation, her mother had hidden her father's secrets. And during the drive to the airport the next day, her father had calmly and smoothly lied to Julia. He'd lied to her about when and how he'd met her mother. He'd lied to her about his posting after that. He'd lied to her about being in therapy. He'd lied about *everything*.

But so had her mother.

Julia shook her head. She didn't understand any of it. She looked at the cars ahead of them on the highway, an empty feeling settling over her. Her company had been shut down by the IRS. Two of her sisters and her mother were missing. Nothing made sense any more.

She sat straight and slowly closed her eyes. She was not going to cry. Not now. She had too much to do, too many problems to deal with, too many people depending on her, not the least of which was Carrie and the tiny little baby who was going to need help to live.

CHAPTER NINETEEN

Suspended.

"**Yeah,**" Bear muttered into his phone, fighting to force his eyes open. He groaned and shifted position, sitting up, disoriented. Light flooded his eyes and he squinted them, realizing where he was.

The hospital. He'd spent the afternoon with the kids after dropping Carrie Sherman back at the safe house, then slept for two hours, then he'd come here. Leah was in intensive care, and Gary, her giant pug of a husband, was pacing at the other end of the waiting area.

Bear sat up, when he heard the voice on the phone. It was the Secretary.

"Bear, I need you to come in."

"Yes, sir," Bear said, desperately suppressing a burp, his entire chest rumbling. "What ... sorry, sir ... I'm a bit groggy."

"Be in my office in an hour."

"Yes, sir."

Shit. Bear took the phone away from his ear as Secretary Perry hung up. He looked at his phone, uncomprehendingly. It was 8 pm. He'd been asleep for two hours. Not enough to feel rested, but plenty to make him feel desperate.

He stood up, staggering a little, wishing he hadn't quit smoking. Jesus, he needed to get some coffee. And a shower. Did he have time for a shower? Maybe, if he booked it right now. He walked to the other end of the waiting room.

"Gary," he said.

"Motherfucker," Gary said.

"How is she?"

"Not awake yet. But she's in recovery."

Bear sagged. "The kids?"

"Your mom's with them."

"Okay," Bear said. He looked at his phone and said, "The Secretary just called me. I gotta go in."

"Yeah, whatever."

Bear shrugged. He and Gary were never gonna be pals.

"Call me if anything changes."

"Yeah, all right."

Bear put a hand out and briefly rested it on Gary's shoulder. Gary froze.

"Gary. She's gonna be okay."

Initially Gary didn't respond. He just stood there, his entire body a jumbled mass of tensed muscles. Bear felt him shaking, all 220 pounds of packed muscle vibrating like a well-tuned instrument. For just a second, he thought Gary was going to slug him. Instead, he sagged.

"Yeah."

Bear stepped back and let his hand drop. He didn't want to push his luck, nor did he feel much appreciation for the irony of comforting the husband of his ex-wife. Miss Manners didn't give out any scripts for *that*.

He left the hospital as quickly as he could. At 8 pm he could count on a long wait at the subway station, or an equally long wait for a cab. Or he could just walk or run it. It was twelve long city blocks back to his apartment, probably a fifteen-minute run. Far quicker than waiting for a cab.

He opted to run. Maybe that would help wake him up some.

Bear hadn't counted on the heat. Washington, DC—the entire East Coast really—had just been through an unusually long and cold winter. Bear hadn't fully adjusted to the sudden change from winter to summer with barely any transition at all. The air was soupy, thick with humidity and street smells. And, instead of sneakers, he was running in business shoes.

Asshat. Sometimes Bear's internal monologue was less than diplomatic.

He was soaked with sweat by the time he reached his tiny apartment. For just a second, when he walked in, he was disoriented. Twenty-six hours had passed since he'd gotten the phone call from Leah.

Bear, is there supposed to be a relief team here?

No. No relief team.

It was an ambush, an ambush by at least one person who was supposed to be on their team. A betrayal by a long time DSS agent, and Bear still had exactly nothing to go on.

Bear left a trail of dirty clothing from the door to the shower, and washed his hair and body in record time, the water turned all the way up, pounding his sore and exhausted body with the hottest water possible. He was red faced and relaxed when he stepped out and began to dry himself off, only to discover that he'd failed to wash his armpits, which still smelled pretty dodgy. Whatever. He sprayed himself with deodorant and got dressed quickly, wearing the thickest socks he had because he'd developed a blister on the back of his ankle on the run over.

He picked up his shoes and started to put them on. They were scuffed all to hell. 8:32, and he had twenty-eight minutes left before he had to report to the secretary's office. He took thirty seconds to apply polish to his shoes, ninety seconds to chug a Red Bull and fifteen seconds to reach in the drawer for his laptop so he could check his email.

Then Bear froze. The laptop wasn't in the drawer.

His kitchen table was completely clear.

Oh, shit. When he'd left the apartment twenty-six and a half hours ago, he'd left at a dead run. Shots had been fired at the Thompson condominium, his ex-wife was in the line of fire, and he didn't take a minute to lock up the classified documents that had been sitting on his kitchen table. Classified documents, which included the personnel file of the former spy turned diplomat turned Secretary of Defense-elect Richard Thompson.

He could see it in his mind's eye. The file, carefully opened on the table, where he'd been reading it.

He traced his movements the night before. He'd left the office a few minutes after 5:30. The classified documents desk had called him after receiving the fax from the San Francisco police. The police report.

It still made no sense. Adelina Thompson sexually assaulted, and her husband the suspect, more than twenty years ago. She'd refused to testify and the case had been closed with what looked to Bear to be unusual dispatch. Bear put the file, along with Thompson's personnel file and background documents on Wakhan and Pakistan in the 1980s, into a bag and walked out of the building.

He'd walked out of the building with a bag full of improperly secured classified documents. Then, when he found out his ex-wife had been shot at, he'd left them out on the table.

Shit. Shit. Shit.

He was shaking. He looked at the clock. 8:38. Twenty-two minutes. It was a twenty-minute walk from here to Main State, and typically four minutes from the entrance to the elevator and then up to the 7th floor.

He needed to leave right now. Instead, he walked over to his closet and kneeled at the floor safe. Maybe he'd forgotten. Bear had slept a total of three hours out of the last forty-eight. He was functioning on empty. Maybe he'd just forgotten.

He dialed the combination, but got it wrong and cursed in frustration. Then he tried again, and opened the safe.

It was empty.

No classified documents.

No nothing. His passport, birth certificate, a thousand dollars in cash, and other documents were gone, including the three surviving photos of his and Leah's wedding, which he'd locked in the safe to ensure he didn't burn them while drunk. Everything was gone.

Shaking, Bear shook his head, then stood up. He had to get to the Secretary now. He had nineteen minutes. He ran out the door, letting it slam shut behind him, and hit the down elevator button.

Then he stood there. The left elevator was on 18, the right on L. Neither moved.

Christ.

He shifted his weight back and forth from one foot to the other, limbering up. He was going to have to run. It wasn't far, straight down New Hampshire Avenue to 23rd Street, then left, through the George Washington University campus and there it was. He walked it every day.

He didn't run it twice a day. He wished he'd worn sneakers. Finally. The elevator was moving.

"Oh, there you are. Mister Bear!"

Christ. It was Millie McPherson, the widow who lived two doors down from him. Millie was a blue-haired old woman who had, from her patterns of speech, probably grown up on an antebellum plantation in central Georgia. She had on a sixty-year-old yellow sundress, patent leather shoes and a bow in her hair, for Christ's sake, and her smile revealed a full set of unnaturally straight teeth.

"Oh, hey there, Miss Millie."

"Do you have time to chat for just a moment, Bear?"

The elevator was moving now, coming up, floor 7, 8, now 9.

"I don't, really, I'm kind of on an emergency call, if the freaking elevator ever gets here."

"It won't take but a moment, sugah, I promise."

"Maybe you could ride the elevator down with me, Miss Millie." He wanted to be polite. He really did. But the elevator dinged and the doors opened and he stepped inside. He stabbed the L with his index finger as she tottered over toward the door.

"Wait…" she called.

He pretended to reach for the door to stop it and said, insincerely, "Oh no," as the door closed.

The elevator started moving and he prepared to run.

Two minutes later he was out the front door of the building and on his way. It was 8:47, and he had thirteen minutes to make a twenty-minute walk. He ran as quickly as he could.

It was a warm Friday night in Washington, DC near DuPont Circle. The crowds were out in force, people spilling onto the sidewalk and traffic jammed up, nobody moving in their cars except the cabs who drove recklessly in between other lanes and sometimes narrowly missing bumping onto the sidewalk. Bear ran through a crowd of twenty-something college students who crowded the sidewalk, all skinny jeans and halter tops and skin everywhere, an appalling display of youth and beauty and crushing envy which Bear might have normally enjoyed. Tonight he had no time and no inclination, pushing past the kids aggressively, his passage evoking cries and curses.

Finally he was free, headed down New Hampshire Avenue. He dodged traffic at the intersections, only having to stop when he finally hit K Street with its wall-to-wall traffic. He checked his phone. 8:55. *Damn it.* There was no way he'd make it in time.

No matter. The moment the light changed he launched himself across the street, hearing the screech of tires as an overly aggressive cabbie had to suddenly stop. Down 23rd Street, past George Washington University Hospital where Leah was recovering from the gunshot wounds, and on toward Main State.

It was five minutes after nine when he arrived, breathless and sweaty, at the Secretary's door.

He knocked, sucking back breaths. He had to compose himself before that door opened. He took a last shuddering breath, then tried to hold himself calm as the door opened.

It was the Secretary himself at the door. A tall and gaunt man, James Perry had once been a naval riverboat captain in Vietnam, and later a United States Senator. His runs for the Presidency had ended in failure—Republicans labeled him as too wonky, too intellectual, too weak-kneed, to be President. Bear admired him, though in general his attitude about Democrats was to be appalled at their lack of fortitude or patriotism. But in Bear's eyes, no one could question Perry's courage or his patriotism.

"Bear, come in. I was starting to worry."

"Sorry about that, sir," Bear gasped out.

"Bear ... you all right?"

Bear followed Perry into the dimmed office. "Yes, sir," he said.

The Secretary's office was large, with a sizable sitting area marked with ornate couches and tables. His working space, a large mahogany desk, was at the opposite end. Wide planked hardwood floors stained a deep reddish brown stretched across the broad space, contrasting with the white walls, elegant wainscoting and elaborate molding.

"Have a seat, then," Perry said, walking over to the desk and indicating a chair that sat at an angle to the desk. Bear took a seat, sucking in another shuddering gasp of air as he did so, trying to be discreet.

"Are you *sure* you're all right?" Perry asked. "Breathe, man."

"I'm fine. I was running late so I actually ran over here from DuPont Circle. I live over that way."

Perry raised his eyebrows. Bear noticed for the first time that the eyebrows were shot through with white. Perry must dye his hair.

"I see," Perry said. "First, how's Leah Simpson?"

"She's out of surgery, sir, and in recovery. The last news we got was that her prognosis was good."

"Good, good," Perry said, nodding. "And the Thompson daughters. They're still at our safe house?"

"Yeah," Bear said. "Though Carrie Sherman blew the location earlier, with one of the other sisters."

Perry frowned. "How did she do that? You didn't take their phones?"

"They aren't prisoners, sir."

"True. All right, that's what it is. Tell me what else you have?"

Bear sighed. Then he said the first thing that came out of his mouth. "Nothing, sir. Or—very little."

Perry bit his lip. Jesus. He was *personally* interested in this, not just professionally.

Bear said, "We know that Adelina Thompson lied about her age. Not on official documents, but socially. She was actually sixteen when Richard Thompson knocked her up."

"Okay. What else?"

"She had an affair. Who with we don't know, but two of the daughters aren't his. And we know that when he found out, he beat her up and raped her."

Perry blanched. "What? Are you serious?"

"Yeah, unfortunately. It happened in 1990."

"I didn't know about that. What's your conclusion about Richard Thompson's original employment?"

"Thompson was CIA."

"Right. You saw that Henry Kissinger signed his recommendation. He was National Security Advisor then. Richard Thompson was CIA."

"But CIA puts people in diplomatic cover all the time."

"Of course they do, Wyden. Tell me how that works."

Bear nodded. Of course. When CIA needed to place someone, they created a cover *with the cooperation* of State.

"He was some kind of a long term plant," Bear said. "But for what purpose?"

"Think about the crew running CIA then. George Bush and William Colby and Kissinger. Those guys thought they could do anything. The CIA was running assassination programs and drugs and all kinds of stuff. I think Thompson was a recruit, and they placed him at State. Then Kissinger came over here too, as Secretary."

"What does all this have to do with *now?*"

"I don't know yet. But I can tell you this—Thompson's got some enemies. They're trying to take him down, and they don't care who goes down with him. Things are changing very rapidly right now."

Bear's mind turned to the missing files.

"Right. I get that," Bear said. "Sir, we may have one problem. I suppose I'm reporting myself. I had Thompson's personnel file along with some other classified documents about Wakhan and Pakistan at my apartment. I didn't properly secure the documents last night when the shooting was reported. And when I finally got back tonight—they were gone."

Perry sat back and rubbed his eyes. Then he said, "We *do* have a problem, then."

Bear waited. It was a problem all right. DSS sacked people for far less. People *went to jail* for less.

Perry looked up and said, "You should know, the reason I called you in—I got a call from the White House about an hour before I called you."

"Yes, sir?"

"Thompson's nomination is being withdrawn by the President. He's going to hang him out to dry, which I think is well deserved."

Bear nodded. That was good news. But not if they took down his daughters with him. Bear didn't know the oldest daughter Julia, but he knew Carrie had been through too much already.

"I was ordered to hand over the investigation to the independent prosecutor and the FBI. They're doing a joint investigation with the IRS and Secret Service. We're out of it."

"Yes, sir," Bear muttered. He didn't want to be out of it. He wanted to know who had shot Leah.

"The thing is," Perry said, his voice quiet. "There's something that isn't right here. Something just doesn't make sense. Richard Thompson is a snake. But drug money laundering? I don't buy it. Not at all."

Bear was confused. He looked at Perry and said, "So ... what happens now?"

"Well, obviously I have to take you off the case," Perry said. "We'll have your team here turn over whatever they have, which isn't much from what you've led me to believe. And—given what you've reported to me, I may have to temporarily suspend you, with pay, while I investigate."

Suspended. That was a blow. Bear sat back, nodding. Then he realized Perry was staring closely at him.

"Now, Bear, I can't tell you what to do with your free time, if you're suspended. But I'd expect you'd be careful."

Huh. What was he saying? Go investigate on your own? Was he saying he'd cover for him? Or was this one of those situations that happened sometimes, where people just got hung out to dry? He'd be out there with no professional backing, no actual business being on the case. He wouldn't have a budget, or a right to carry a weapon except for self-defense, with no jurisdiction to do anything at all.

Did it even matter? He thought for just a second about his ex-wife, fighting for her life in the hospital. About Andrea Thompson, on the run and not even knowing who her father was. He thought about Carrie Sherman, fighting for the life of her daughter.

He nodded slowly. "Sir, I apologize. I suppose I'll have to accept the suspension. How long will I be suspended, sir?"

"I'd say indefinitely. Until I can complete an investigation. Right now I'm a little busy, though."

"Yes, sir. I understand." Bear stood. Then he let an uncharacteristic grin appear on his face. "You know, sir, for a Democrat, you're all right."

Perry winked. "You are too, Wyden. You know what to do now."

CHAPTER TWENTY
I haven't
been honest

The text message came in first, and Carrie looked at her phone. Her eyes narrowed, and she looked at Sarah.

"Sarah, do me a favor," Carrie whispered.

Sarah's eyes narrowed. In the months since the accident, she'd gotten to know her much older sister a lot better. And right now Carrie's posture radiated tension. Her back was unusually straight, and Rachel, normally a fairly docile baby, was starting to squirm.

"What's up?"

"Go over to the front door. I want you to watch. In a couple of minutes a car's going to pull up. Julia and Crank. Make sure they let them through."

"I thought Bear said we couldn't give anyone the address," Sarah whispered.

"It's Julia," Carrie replied, even as Sarah stood.

On door duty was Lucas Steelman, a twenty-four-year-old uniformed agent of the Diplomatic Security Service. Sarah was sure he'd changed his name, or just made it up, or found it in a puddle of pure testosterone. No one was actually named anything so stupid.

On the other hand, he *was* easy on the eyes. The name might be stupid, but it fit. An obvious weightlifter, his biceps bulged underneath his sleeves, which looked tailored for someone just slightly smaller. Extremely muscular. In fact, Sarah thought, he looked like a lunk. A delicious lunk, but a lunk nonetheless.

She was pretty sure Eddie could take him in a fight. Eddie was a pretty big guy too, but more importantly, he was smart as hell.

Right now Steelman—she couldn't think of his name without wanting to chuckle—leaned against the wall near the front door, whistling in a low tone.

She leaned against the opposite wall. "Hey."

He looked at her with impassive eyes. "You aren't supposed to be at the door." But his eyes grazed slightly down to her chest, as she knew they would. She leaned back against the wall a little more, her back arching slightly, probably setting off every serotonin receptor in the poor guard's brain. His eyes widened slightly, but she thought it was unconscious.

"This job must get boring for you," she said in a low tone. Her voice laid out a lure at the end of a not very long line. He wouldn't take long before he started nibbling.

"Sometimes. You do a lot of waiting, but then when the chips are down, you gotta man up." Now his eyes were fully on her. Predictable. He was hooked. Already.

"Have you done that sort of thing often? Where you had to um ... man up?" She let one side of her mouth curl up a little, and parted her lips just slightly. This was ridiculous.

He shrugged, failing to appear modest. "I'm a federal agent. You do what you gotta do. Say, how old are you, anyway?"

"I turned eighteen three weeks ago," she said, intentionally making her voice a little husky. She crossed her legs at the ankles.

Agent Steelman blushed, his ears turning bright red. Sarah almost burst into laughter, but she needed to keep him occupied for at least another minute or so. Instead, she licked her lips.

That was when the grey rental car turned into the driveway. Steelman instantly tensed, reaching for his sidearm.

"Stop," Sarah said. "That's my sister Julia and her husband."

"What the hell?" he shouted. Four agents ran up to the car, weapons out, shouting.

"Stop them! That's my sister."

"Son of a bitch!" he muttered. He opened the door and snarled, "Stay here!" She watched him as he charged out the front door, shouting to the other agents, who quickly lowered their weapons.

A pale faced Crank and Julia Wilson emerged from the car. Immediately, the four agents hustled them into the safe house, where a tense Ben Crosby confronted Carrie.

"Someone want to explain what the hell just happened here?" he demanded.

"I think the answer to that is obvious," Julia replied.

Crosby ignored Julia, facing Carrie. "We explicitly told you not to tell *anyone* where you were."

Carrie shifted Rachel in her lap. The baby, whose arms were flailing around, began to burble as Crosby spoke.

"I'll thank you to not shout at me," Carrie said. "You'll scare my daughter."

"What the hell were you thinking, Carrie?" Crosby's face was red as he spoke.

The baby chuckled, a deep gurgling sound, and began waving her arms at Crosby.

Sarah leaned against the wall and snickered. Crosby's angry face looked funny anyway, almost like a caricature, but the laughing baby just topped off her sense of the ridiculous. His face worked in indescribable antics, his jaw twisting a little, and finally Carrie spoke, since he'd apparently lost his capacity to do so.

"We're not prisoners, Crosby. This is my sister, and she's as much a part of this as the rest of us. And since you weren't telling us anything, I took it in my own hands. End of discussion."

Crosby shook his head. "I'll be reporting this to Bear."

Scorn filled Carrie's face. "Report it to the *President*, for all I care. I understand you're trying to protect us, and I'm grateful. But I'm not keeping my sister away."

He sighed and walked away. Lucas walked by Sarah, diverting his eyes from her. He knew he'd been had.

As the agents walked away, Carrie stood, holding Rachel in the crook of one arm, and reached for Julia. "Thank God you're here," she whispered and they embraced.

The two eldest sisters held each other for a long time. Crank walked over to Sarah and said, "Hey, kiddo," then pulled her into a hug. "You hanging in there?"

"Yeah," Sarah said. "You?"

"Julia's carrying the brunt of all this. I don't even know what's going on, really."

Sarah shrugged. Of course Julia would. Her oldest sister had left home when Sarah was little more than a toddler. She was confident, assertive, and competent. She managed the band and ran her own company and never seemed entirely human to Sarah. She remembered times when she was younger, when Julia would visit, or they would meet her. The house would fill with tension, their mother sometimes angry and inconsistent. But those visits were few and far between, and became less and less frequent over the years as Julia's career became more and more successful.

It wasn't exactly that Sarah didn't love her eldest sister. She did. It was more that she just didn't know her that well. A long gap of years and experience left them distant, and she didn't know how to bridge that gap.

At the opposite side of the room from Sarah, Alexandra stood in the doorway, looking just as unsure as Sarah felt. Of course, she'd been a gigantic bitch to Carrie earlier, and Carrie would undoubtedly tell Julia about it. The two of them were very close. Sarah looked at Alexandra. She loved her sister, but didn't always like her. Alexandra was the middle sister, and never seemed quite sure of who she was. It was as if her older sisters had taken all the talent, leaving Alexandra nothing but sheer determination to push through.

She at least had that in spades. Sarah met Alexandra's eyes for just a second. As if they'd shared an invisible signal, both of them moved to the center of the room and hugged Julia.

When they parted, Julia said, "Listen—we need to catch up. On a lot of stuff. But in particular—Crank and I found some stuff in Dad's office you need to know about."

"In Dad's office?" Carrie asked, a frown pulling down the corners of her mouth.

Julia nodded. Her eyes darted to Crank, and she described the scene they'd found at the house in San Francisco last night. Sarah's eyes widened at the details. Jessica and their mom were gone. Vomit on the floor in the dining room, and a spoiled gallon of milk in the middle of the kitchen floor. The *diary.*

Julia handed the diary to Carrie as she spoke. She spoke words that Sarah barely comprehended. Their mother was sixteen when she got pregnant with Julia. *Sixteen.* Julia looked at Alexandra with what Sarah would have sworn was a pitying look, then showed them the police report.

Sarah blanched at the pictures, but froze, keeping her reaction to herself. Alexandra was pale, a hand covering her open mouth. She began to shake violently, and Carrie said, "Alex, it's—"

"Leave me alone," Alexandra said. "That's not possible. You're *lying*."

"Alexandra," Julia whispered. "I know this is hard..." Her voice trailed off.

Sarah looked at Alexandra, her mind calculating the months back from Alexandra's birth to the assault.

There was no question. If their father had raped their mother, and the police report and documentation of the assault was accurate, then Alexandra had been conceived in that rape.

Horrified, Alexandra stood. "Leave me *alone*," she demanded. Then she stumbled off to her room, slamming the door shut behind her.

Alexandra. May 2. 8 pm.

When Alexandra's cell phone rang three hours later, she almost declined the call. It was from an unfamiliar number with a 571 area code, and she didn't even know where that was. She was groggy from crying until she fell asleep. She'd ignored Carrie's entreaties to open the door earlier—she just couldn't face it. After the third ring, she picked it up, suddenly in a panic.

"Hello?" Her voice was urgent and cracked a little.

"Hey, babe, it's me."

Panic and elation ran simultaneously through Alex and she urgently whispered, "*Oh my God, are you okay?*" As she did it, she found herself looking around. Was Ben Crosby around? Or one of the other guards from State Department? They'd report Dylan in an instant.

She looked out in the hallway, then hurried down the hall to the bathroom and closed the door behind her. As Dylan spoke, she turned on the shower, letting the water run.

"I'm okay," he said. "Andrea's okay. We're hiding out for now."

She closed her eyes, pressing a hand to her chest. She knew she couldn't ask where he was. But she ached to know.

"Are you safe?" she whispered. Tears formed up in her eyes, involuntary tears that she couldn't do anything to stop, and they began to run down her cheeks.

"We're okay for now. You'll probably get some questions at some point. But there was a bunch of cash in the apartment."

"Bear told us," Alexandra said. "He said they found drugs too."

"Yeah. And I don't know where they came from. Andrea doesn't either. Alex, someone set us up."

Alexandra whispered, "Bear said you killed the intruders to protect Andrea."

Silence. Breathing on the other end. Then he said, "I don't want to talk about that. Not now. I've got too much to focus on."

Oh, Dylan. She couldn't even imagine what he was going through. "You know I love you," she whispered. "No matter what."

"I know," he said. "And I love you. Now talk to me. What's going on? I've tried to check the news but it's all bullshit."

She sighed. "We're at a safe house. State Department security picked us up during dinner last night. Right after ... right after ... you were attacked."

"You're safe there?" he asked.

"We've got guards. A bunch. Julia and Crank are here now, at least for tonight."

"They've got trouble," he said.

"Yeah. You read about it?"

"It's all over the place. It's bullshit."

"That's not the worst of it. Carrie went to see Senator Rainsley. He's not her father. But ... Dylan..." Her voice began to shake. The bathroom was beginning to steam up, and she sat on the closed toilet seat and wrapped one arm across her stomach.

"What is it, babe?"

"See, my dad found out Carrie wasn't his. Julia had ... she had a report from some testing place. It was from February 1990. And ... the next day my Mom got beat up. Like ... badly. Assaulted and raped, and the police thought it was my dad. Everyone thinks it was my dad. My sisters do."

"Yeah? It wouldn't surprise me."

She flinched. She knew Dylan and her dad had never gotten along. Her over controlling father had run a background check on Dylan when they were still in high school. She still didn't know exactly what had occurred when Dylan and her father had talked back then, and she didn't really want to know. Dad was overprotective. But he couldn't be—evil.

"Dylan, it's ... you don't understand. It was ... it was almost exactly nine months before ... before ... I was born."

She closed her eyes. She couldn't say the words, even to herself. That her mother had been *raped*. That she was the product of a rape. Unwanted. Just a ... a thing.

"Jesus, babe," Dylan muttered. "Are you serious?"

She closed her eyes. "It can't have been my dad. He would never do that."

Dylan was silent for a few seconds. Then he took a deep breath and said, "I love you, babe."

"I love you," she whispered back. "Dylan..."

"Yes?"

"When can you come home? When will it be safe?"

"I don't know," he said. "But I promise I'll be careful, and I'll take care of your sister."

"Will you stay in touch?"

"Yeah. I'll be calling from different numbers, and at random times, okay? So keep an eye out. I don't know who is after us, so we're keeping a really low profile. And I want you to be careful too. Stay in the safe house, or wherever you can that's safe."

"I will," she whispered.

"And Alex ... I need you to hear me for a second."

"I'm listening."

He exhaled slowly. Then he said, "I haven't been much good since Ray died. I know that."

Her voice cracked as she spoke. "Dylan, you don't have to—"

"Yes, I do." His interruption was forceful. But then he paused a moment and said, "I've been a disaster. I've been a lousy husband. And I haven't been honest with you."

"Dylan..." She felt her heart twist at his words.

"Stop interrupting and listen to me. The thing is ... I ... shit. I can't say it."

"You can," she said.

He groaned. Then said, almost whispering, "I've been drinking again."

"I know," she replied.

"I'll get help. I promise."

She leaned her head back against the wall, letting the steam envelop her. Then she whispered, "You know I'm proud of you. And I love you. I'm here, Dylan."

"I know. I won't screw it up anymore."

"Maybe you should consider AA like your mom?"

He sighed. "I—I can't do all that God stuff. You know that."

"Will you just think about it? You've been trying to do everything on your own, Dylan."

He didn't answer right away, but after a few seconds of silence, he said, "Yeah. Yeah, I'll think about it."

She sighed, then said, "Thank you for telling me, Dylan. You know I love you."

"And I love you," he responded. "Listen—keep watching your Facebook. I'll call or message when I can. And I want you to keep your status updated and message me so I know where you are. Okay?"

"I will. And Dylan?"

"Yeah," he said.

"I love you. No matter what. Just come home."

"I will," he said. And then he hung up the phone.

CHAPTER TWENTY-ONE
Why is he still alive?

"**R**eally, sir, I don't see how I'm going to be able to continue in this work if you cannot keep regular hours. It's past midnight. Poor Jane nearly cried herself to sleep when you didn't come home. I should tender my resignation right now."

George-Phillip sighed. Jane's nanny, Adriana Poole, stood erect in the doorway of his office, color on her cheeks, as he sagged into his chair. She was right, of course, and normally George-Phillip fought to ensure that he was home at a reasonable hour, even if it meant working late into the night after Jane was in bed.

"Miss Poole, I'm going to ask you to bear with me for a little while on this. Unfortunately we have a crisis developing."

"What crisis?" Her voice was high pitched and loud enough to be heard at Whitehall.

"Please, Miss Poole, lower your voice." His tone was urgent as he spoke. Jane's room was right down the hall, and she'd already been disturbed enough.

"The only crisis I see is a daughter missing her father."

"It seems likely I'll have a great deal more time soon enough," he said. The words escaped from his mouth before he could do anything about them.

"Whatever are you talking about, sir?"

"I just told you we have a crisis brewing. There's a possibility I'll be forced to resign. In the meantime, I've just found out I must travel to Washington in the morning, and I need you to look after Jane. You simply cannot quit now."

"You're leaving! Now? After some lunatic shot at the house just last night? I think you've lost your senses, sir."

George-Phillip groaned. He might be a Prince and a Duke and a member of the Prime Minister's Cabinet, but this twenty-four-year-old girl routinely dressed him down, and he couldn't do anything about it *because she was right*. He couldn't leave his daughter now, when she was terrified after the attack on the house.

He thought it through for five seconds, then said, "Well, you'll both have to come with me, then."

"To America?" Adriana screeched.

"Yes, to Washington, DC. I don't know how long we'll be gone—perhaps a week."

"I couldn't. I don't have anything to wear."

George-Phillip closed his eyes and took a deep breath. Then he counted slowly to ten. And then ten more, just for good measure.

When he opened his eyes, she still stood there. "Miss Poole, I'm asking you to please accompany my daughter to Washington, DC. It's urgent, and at least for the next few days, I will not be able to spare the time to find someone else. I'm begging you. It's a matter of national security. I must go."

She was silent for just a moment. Then said, "All right, then, sir. If it's a matter of national security, you should just say so. I'll get my things packed."

"We'll leave for the airport at six in the morning."

"Yes, sir."

Adriana bustled away, thank God. George-Phillip turned to his desk and sighed. He was exhausted. Not long after he had returned to his office after the meeting with the Prime Minister, the call had come in. Richard Thompson was facing indictment in the United States. The political wheels in Washington were spinning, and no one knew where they were going to end up.

George-Phillip's eyes fell to his desk. Inside, the file. He knew that if the contents of that file were to be made public, Richard Thompson's career would be over, and his wouldn't be the only one. Over the years, he'd often revisited the decision to bury what had happened, to bury it right alongside the bodies of the civilians who had died there. A generation had passed, governments had risen and fallen, the Cold War had come to an end and yet the secrets of three decades ago still lingered, poisoning the well of the present.

George-Phillip reached in his desk and took out the file. The original report of his own investigation. Interviews and documents. Records meticulously kept for three decades. He carefully slipped the file into his steel walled briefcase and secured the briefcase itself to his desk. He checked the time, then dialed O'Leary.

The phone rang only once before a curt voice said, "O'Leary, sir."

"It's C," George-Phillip said. The nickname, just the letter C, had been the traditional name for the Chief since Sir Mansfield Cumming, the first Chief of MI6, had signed his papers that way. "Any updates?"

"None, sir, but our investigators seem to think she went south. We're watching the border crossings in San Diego, among others. But if she's using cash, we might not be able to track her."

"All right, then. And Andrea Thompson?"

"Last known location was a motel in suburban Maryland, sir, just outside Washington, DC. Seems she heard something suspicious in the room next door and called the police. They found her fingerprints all over the place. Sir—the hotel was a nasty one. Prostitutes and drug dealers."

George-Phillip winced. "Keep looking," he said.

"We will, sir. I've got my best people on it."

"Good, good. I know I can trust you with this. Any leads on who attacked the Thompsons?"

"None, sir. They were professionals. I'm guessing Middle East."

"All right. I'll be on a seven am flight. Just keep me informed."

He disconnected the phone. Four more hours and he'd have to be back up and getting ready for the flight. Time to get some sleep. He stood and let his eyes fall on the window, now covered with a steel plate until the window was replaced with bullet-resistant glass. The shots had narrowly missed him last night—it was pure dumb luck he hadn't been killed. But he still didn't understand *why*. Was it the Wakhan file? Or something else entirely?

Leslie Collins. May 2.

Leslie Collins tried to remind himself to pause every day when he entered the lobby of the original headquarters building at Langley. There, against the north wall of the lobby, was the Memorial Wall. 102 stars carved in the wall, each of them representing an agent who had died in the line of duty. More than a third of those agents were unnamed—represented *only* by a star. Their names, their operations and their deaths were still a matter of national security.

Collins reminded himself once again, as he exited the building, that he had a responsibility to those 102 men and women. A responsibility to protect the integrity of the agency, to protect its secrets, to protect the nation the agency protected. Sometimes, however, meeting that responsibility required sacrifices—sacrifices that he found personally distasteful, and in some cases immoral. But one didn't just decide to do what one wanted, after all. The purpose of having government agencies, the purpose of having checks and balances, all of it was built to ensure safety and security. As a part of that system, Collins felt that sometimes you had to set aside your personal desires and beliefs.

His feet echoed off the floors of the lobby as he walked toward the front door. Even in an agency that ran 24 hours a day, 365 days a year, it was quiet in the late evening. Watch officers and other essential personnel worked late into the night, but the bulk of the agency's personnel commuted to the office just like any other government employee in Washington. He stopped at the door, looking out across the vast parking lot. He could hear crickets and frogs and God only knew what else from the woods around the two hundred fifty acres of land occupied by the agency.

He jumped a little, startled, when his cell phone rang. Only a dozen or so people had his personal phone number. The dozen included his wife, his pastor, and the President, among others.

He sighed when he saw the name on the phone.

Richard Thompson.

His car let out two loud beeps as he pressed the unlock button on his keyfob and disarmed the alarm. He answered the phone.

"This is Leslie Collins."

"Leslie. *What the hell?*"

"Richard, this is not a secure line, as I'm sure you're aware."

Richard's reply was ragged, angry. "I don't really care, Leslie. Can I make that more clear? I do not care."

Leslie sighed and opened the door of his 2014 Volvo S60. Initially Leslie had objected on political grounds to buying a European vehicle. But Meredith had driven one owned by one of her silly friends, and had convinced him to take a test drive. The handling and leather seats convinced him. He passed his old 2010 Cadillac to her and took the new car.

He always felt calm when he sat in the leather seat.

"Richard, you may not care, but I do."

"What do you know about this investigation?"

The voice automatically spilled over to the car speakers as he cranked the car. Hearing Richard Thompson's disembodied voice surrounding him was more than a little bit disturbing.

"I don't know anything about it, Richard. But I would take it seriously, if I were you."

"Bullshit you don't know anything, Leslie. You went to school with that son of a bitch, Armitage."

Rory Armitage was the special counsel investigating Thompson. He had also been Collins' college roommate. Not that it mattered.

"Armitage is just doing his job. I can't imagine where he came up with such a wild theory. *Drug money laundering?* Really? I can't imagine there's any truth to it, Richard. Unless..." Leslie's voice trailed off with a suggestive silence.

"You son of a bitch. You planted this, didn't you?"

Collins sighed. "Richard, I'm finding your wild accusations a little disconcerting. I know you are under some stress right now. Maybe you should consider taking a step back—or even seeing a therapist. I'm concerned about you."

Thompson didn't respond. The silence at the other end of the line troubled Collins. Thompson, when calm and organized, was a formidable enemy.

After a moment, Collins said, "Richard, are you there?"

"I'm here," Thompson replied. "Leslie, I want you to be careful. You don't want to mess with my life."

Collins raised an eyebrow. He put the car in reverse and backed out of his reserved parking space, then turned, heading into the darkness toward the checkpoint at the entrance to the headquarters. For just a second, his headlights illuminated three pairs of glowing eyes—deer on the edge of the parking lot, just on the other side of the fence. Sometimes they played hell with the motion sensors on the edge of the property.

He thought it was curious Thompson didn't talk about his wife or daughters. Or was he so self-absorbed and narcissistic that he didn't worry about them at all when his own position was at risk? That was kind of sad, wasn't it?

"Richard, listen, I'm driving now, I've really got to go. Let's talk next week, all right? We'll do lunch."

"I'm not *doing lunch* with someone who screwed—"

The words cut off when Leslie's hand brushed the disconnect button on his steering wheel. He waved to the guards at the gate, then pulled out onto Colonial Farm Road, headed south toward Georgetown Pike. This late, traffic should be finished and he could be home in ten minutes.

Unfortunately, the phone rang almost immediately. *Unknown number?*

There were only a few people it could be. He answered.

"Collins here."

"Leslie. How pleasant to hear your voice."

Collins involuntarily stepped on the brakes, causing the car behind him to swerve dangerously. He got himself under control and driving again almost instantly. The cultured voice on the other end was familiar. Roshan al Saud—a member of the royal house of Saudi Arabia, and director general of *al Mukhabarat Al A'amah*—the Saudi Arabian Intelligence Agency. Educated at the best British boarding schools, Roshan gave off a polished, highly educated air which fooled everyone except those, like Collins, who had seen him torture captured Russian prisoners with a refined and frightening cruelty.

"Roshan! It is very good to hear your voice. You are well? I understand you're in the United States."

"I am, briefly. And I'd very much like to speak with you privately."

Leslie checked the time. "You're at your home?" he asked.

Roshan owned an exclusive thirty-room house less than a mile away from Leslie's.

"I am."

"I'm on my way. You caught me at the perfect time."

Collins disconnected the phone and drove. Traffic on Georgetown Pike wasn't heavy, but it wasn't especially light either. Sometimes, especially if there was rain or snow, you could get tied up here for hours. But it was warm now, a little humid, and after a long nasty winter, most Washingtonians were out relaxing instead of working.

It was fifteen minutes later when he pulled up to the gate of Prince Roshan's property. He slid down the window as the guard approached. The guard—a man in his early thirties with cold looking eyes and a thick five-o'clock shadow, stared at Collins for fifteen long seconds.

Then he said, "Mr. Collins, please pull up the driveway. You'll be met at the house."

Collins was familiar with the Saudi's routine. He'd been here as a guest many times before. As he parked the car and got out, he was startled to see that it wasn't a guard who opened the front door—it was Prince Roshan himself.

Roshan, like Collins, was no longer a young man. Roshan had once been the unofficial leader of the small group of western intel-

ligence agents working together in Afghanistan. Collins remembered riding together in a truck to Badakhshan province, at one
point hiding under the floorboards with Thompson while Prince
Roshan negotiated with the Russians.

That was a long time ago. Now, Roshan was portly, with prominent, almost puffy cheeks and a salt-and-pepper beard.

For official functions, Roshan wore robes and red and white
checked *keffiyeh*. But at home, he typically wore blue jeans and a
t-shirt. Roshan was a traditional Saudi man only when it came to
how he treated his wife and his public appearance. In private, he
indulged in all the luxuries Western culture could provide.

"Leslie!" Roshan said, a genuine appearing smile gracing his
face. "Come in, come in! It's been too long. How is Meredith?"

Leslie grimaced. "She's fine, Your Highness. Just fine."

"Come in. You know better than those niceties, Leslie. I won't
stand for titles." As he spoke the words, Roshan rested a hand on
Collins' arm, as if to emphasize the words and his affability.

"Roshan. You've always been a good friend. How is Myriam?"

Roshan led him into the house mumbling meaningless plati-
tudes about his wife. Myriam al-Saud effectively didn't matter.
Disenfranchised by the culture and law of her own country, she
had less role in her husband's life than the models who shamelessly
accompanied him to expensive dinners and shows at the Kennedy
Center whenever he was in Washington.

Roshan poured Collins a glass of Eagle Rare Single Barrel
Bourbon. Collins sniffed it, the smell of charred vanilla and old
oak and leather filling his nostrils.

He took the smallest of sips, then murmured, "This is very
good."

"Be my guest," Roshan said. He poured himself a drink and
tossed it back, then sat in the deep leather chair across from Leslie.

"My friend, we have a problem."

"We?" Leslie replied.

"Yes. *We.* The problem has several heads, and any one of them could harm both of us, and our countries."

"Thompson," Collins said.

"Indeed. He's sinking."

"We need to make sure we don't go down with him," Collins said. "There are a lot of loose ends. I'm particularly concerned because it looks like the oldest daughter may have information about Wakhan now. They broke into his office in San Francisco. God only knows what he had in there."

Roshan frowned. "Your people are responsible for the destruction of the home?"

Collins nodded. "Not agency. Independents."

Roshan frowned and his eyes narrowed. He looked away from Collins for a moment, then looked back. "Leslie, I'm concerned you've lost your nerve. Not just attacking Thompson's family, but by doing it so—ineptly. Letting a sixteen-year-old girl get away? What were you thinking?"

"You're aware of who the girl's father is?"

"Of course. He presents no risk to us."

Collins rolled his eyes. "He's the only person outside of our circle who knows what really happened at Wakhan."

"If he knew, none of us would be in our positions."

"He *knows.*"

"What makes you think that?"

Collins closed his eyes. "He confronted me about it."

Roshan sat up straight. "*When?* And why didn't you say anything?"

"I had it contained. That was in '84."

"Why is he still alive, then?"

"Are you serious? His cousin is the Queen of England. Besides, as I said, I had it contained. He was having his tawdry little affair with Thompson's wife. We didn't have to threaten him—we threatened her. That shut him up."

Roshan shook his head. "Not good enough. What are you doing now?"

"I had a team try to get him, but they missed. We'll try again. In the meantime, Thompson is thoroughly discredited, and Prince George-Phillip will be soon. Nothing they say will matter within the week. I'd expect the President to withdraw Thompson's nomination any moment."

"Good. And the rest of them? All this violence has done nothing but attract attention."

"We're backing off. Surveillance, but that's it. We planted drugs and money in the Thompson condo, and we've registered several accounts at friendly banks in the Caymans to Thompson. The IRS will likely find those within a couple more days."

Roshan nodded. "And Windsor? Do you really believe he is contained?"

Collins thought about it. The threat of killing Adelina Thompson was no longer going to be enough to keep George-Phillip quiet. That had probably passed years ago. Which meant they were going to have to find some new way of dealing with him. Or dispensing with him.

"I don't think so," Collins said.

"Leave him to me, then," Roshan said. "I have assets which make more sense for this. You focus your efforts on discrediting Thompson."

"Agreed," Collins said.

Then he took another sip of his bourbon. It really was quite good.

California. May 2.

The campsite was bathed in red and orange light, slanting through the redwoods, as Nick Larsden drove his 2008 Hummer into the camp. He scanned the area. It was an out of the way campsite, the facilities neglected and worn. The camp office, next to the entrance, was old and the white paint was peeling. Except for the beat up rusted truck next to the office, there wasn't a single vehicle.

Nick had been working his way up the coast all day, stopping at drive-thrus, campsites and any other likely place. An adult woman and her teenage daughter in a minivan shouldn't be that hard to find, but so far, he'd not had any luck. And he was pretty sure he wasn't the only person looking. The price dangled in front of him for finding the women was high.

Nick was a former soldier turned private investigator and later bounty hunter. Mostly he worked for ridiculously low fees, chasing men who were on the run after not paying alimony, so when the call came in, he didn't question it. Especially when the caller, a stuck prig with an Irish accent, indicated he was willing to pay a significant deposit.

"Where do you want me to bring them?" he had asked.

"When you find them, contact me for instructions."

That was more than a bit unusual. Nick suspected the caller wanted the women dead or missing. That was fine, Nick supposed, though he wasn't a big fan of making war on women. But sometimes you had to do what you had to do. When it happened, though, he was going to insist on the money up front. The original price had been enough for him to retire from this business for good. Nick wanted a nice place in the mountains, paid for, where he could hunt and have his dogs and not have to worry about the stress of day-to-day bullshit.

He slid out of the cab of the Hummer. An old man approached. He was short and scrawny, almost diseased, and his clothes didn't fit. Thick glasses revealed eyes that were oddly magnified.

"You looking for a campsite or a cabin? How long you staying?" the old man asked.

"I'm looking for two women," Nick said.

He held out a sheet of paper he'd printed that morning. Two separate photos: the one of the older woman looked like it came from a newspaper, and the one of the teenager was a selfie from her Facebook page.

The old man's eyes narrowed when his eyes hit the paper. *Bingo.* He'd seen them.

"I've never seen them," the old man said.

Oh, ho. He was going to make things difficult.

"You sure, old man? They're running from the law."

The man's eyes widened a little, and he sucked in a breath nervously. No wonder he looked so poor. Nick would have bet this guy played poker—and lost his shirt every time.

"I don't know what you're talking about," the old man said.

Nick sighed. He glanced around the campsite again, just to make sure. Not a soul around.

With violence so sudden the old man never saw it coming, Nick reached out and grabbed the old man's hand and twisted it. The first bone in his wrist snapped almost instantly and the old man screamed.

"Now tell me the truth, you old fuck. Did they come through here?"

"Yes! Yes! They slept in Cabin 3 last night. Left early this morning, before sunup. The girl was drugged or something. They paid me an extra twenty dollars! Now let go!"

Nick looked at the old guy for a second and frowned. "What else can you tell me? Were they still driving a minivan?"

The old man nodded urgently. "Plates was covered in mud. I don't know where they went. Headed north, I think, they turned right out of the camp."

Nick looked around the camp one more time, still absentmindedly twisting the old man's wrist, provoking moans from the man. He didn't suppose he'd find anything in the cabin, but he should check.

"Did she show you her license or anything? You got any record?"

The old man shook his head. "No. I'm supposed to. State inspectors. But ... Gawd, *please stop! That hurts!*"

Nick sighed. "You just failed your inspection," he said.

Then he reached out with both hands, grabbing the old man by the neck, and lifted him into the air, one forearm across the man's Adam's apple. He squeezed hard, and the old man twitched several times, then sagged, already passed out. Nick kept holding him, blocking his windpipe.

"Sorry about this, man," he said.

He held the man until he was sure. No pulse. Then he dropped him to the ground and walked to Cabin 3.

The door was unlocked. The old man hadn't cleaned the cabin, of course, but he didn't see anything of use. A woman's elastic hair band. And that was it. He shrugged. At least he knew they'd been here. Headed north.

Canada? He guessed so. But the odds of catching up with them were slim indeed with the information he had.

He shook his head, eyes falling on the old man again. What a waste.

CHAPTER TWENTY-TWO
Señora? Are you all right?

Adelina. May 3.

The pothole must have been large enough to swallow up a smaller car. As it was, the back end of the bus bounced in the air with a loud thump, and Adelina felt herself bounce right out of her seat for just a second. Jessica moaned and began to slide out of her seat. Adelina reached over and tugged her eighteen-year-old daughter back into her seat like she was a toddler.

The bus was crowded, and would have been reasonably well appointed, except that the air conditioning had failed sometime not long after Jessica's birth. The heat was a physical thing, alive with motion, like an unseen reptile under the surface of a Louisiana swamp, green and obscure, thick and dangerous. The upholstery in the seats was torn, and the baby two rows up from Adelina and Jessica had cried for the entire three and a half hour ride from Tacoma.

The passengers were a mix. At least two dozen men and women Adelina judged to be migrant workers. Hispanic, poor and tired. Two rows in front of her and across the aisle, a man slept with his head thrown back in the seat, mouth open, completely ignoring the squalling baby directly across the row.

The man fascinated Adelina. He wore blue jeans, threadbare but not torn at the knees and leather work shoes which had been resoled more than once, apparently by hand. He'd likely done it himself—

nowadays it was cheaper to buy a throwaway pair of shoes from Walmart, produced by near-slave labor in a third world country, than it was to have a pair of custom shoes resoled by a cobbler. The stitching along the edge of the leather sole was slightly uneven.

His sweatshirt was clean but old, the elastic near the wrists worn and loose, threads spreading apart, with deep stains in the elbows, which Adelina knew wouldn't come out no matter what he did. But it wasn't his clothes or his shoes that caught her attention. It was his craggy face, weathered, worn, his skin indistinguishable from the leather on his boots. Deep laugh lines radiated from his eyes and creases around his mouth. His mouth was open, asleep with the kind of abandon usually only seen in small children, despite the fact that the man was missing most of his teeth.

He looked not much different from her father, Juan Ramos, in the years before his death. Exhausted, yes. Tired from the weight of years of too much work and too much worry. But her father had also been content in the last years of his life. After he and her mother had separated, he'd been happy in a way she admired to this day. He laughed, he cried, and he loved life with an abandon she only wished she understood.

The man on the bus looked like that. He looked exhausted, and despite her poverty, her fear, her danger, she wanted to help him.

That was laughable. How could she help anyone now?

Closer to the front of the bus, four hikers rode together. They were in their early twenties—the two men with flannel shirts and brand new sandals, the women in color tank tops and too tight jeans. Two girls out with their boyfriends. Their backpacks took up too much space in the overhead racks, forcing everyone further back in the bus to jam their bags together, while the Birkenstock-clad college kids were largely unaware of the bus full of humanity behind them. Adelina thanked God that despite the problems her daughters had, despite the fact that they largely hated her, she'd sent them out into the world with a deep sense of caring and charity and love for the world around them.

The thought filled Adelina with a staggering sense of loss. She'd failed them in so many ways, and now she didn't even know where all of her daughters were. She'd seen the headlines. Andrea was missing along with Alexandra's husband. She'd never approved of Dylan, not until he'd made his cross-country trip to San Francisco to propose to Alexandra. But that had shown both courage and commitment, and he'd shown it even more in the way he'd supported Carrie after Ray died.

She bit back her tears and looked out the window. The bus was nearing Bellingham now, their last stop. She wasn't sure what to do from there. She had their passports, thankfully not the official diplomatic ones. In her experience, diplomatic passports did nothing to speed up travel, and often slowed them down. Because they were unusual, immigration officials everywhere tended to stop, look closer, and ask more questions.

Questions Adelina did not want to answer. When she crossed the border out of the United States, hopefully within the next twenty-four hours, she wanted it to be quick, routine, and no-nonsense. She wanted to attract no attention at all. She wanted no questions asked, until she got to the Canadian border officials.

The question was, could she make it? Despite the fact that she'd traveled to a dozen or more countries in the last thirty years, and lived across Europe, Asia and the United States, she'd never actually crossed the US borders into Canada or Mexico. Would they check her identification as she left the country? Would a routine check turn up the fact that she was missing and cause them to detain her?

She was afraid that's exactly what would happen. And if they did that, she didn't know what was likely to happen to her.

Well, she'd cross that bridge when she came to it. She craned her neck, looking off into the distance. Both sides of the highway were crowded with greenery, trees and lush bushes. Cars were passing them on both sides, the bus slowing down a little.

Her breath caught a little when the bus changed lanes to the far right, then slowed even further, the loud diesel engine decelerating with a whining sound. The bus slowed even further, then came to a stop. She craned her neck around, but couldn't see through the back—no windows, and the angle didn't allow for a decent view.

The heat inside the bus was oppressive, the smell of sweaty men filling the space.

Adelina forced herself not to panic when two men in dark green uniforms walked up along the side of the bus. They wore green Smokey the Bear hats and short sleeve uniforms with a bright yellow patch on one side. Customs and Border Control.

She swallowed. How could they have been found? She'd paid cash for their tickets and hadn't used her debit cards since leaving San Francisco. She hadn't shown identification to anyone since leaving San Francisco either.

The two men stepped aboard the bus, just as two more agents appeared, one of them female. The two who boarded the bus were a study in contrasts. The first, a tall man who obviously struggled with his own addictions. Balding, red faced, with a belly that cruised over the top of his belt much the way the bulbous prow of an oil tanker extended over the water, he looked uncomfortable and hot, with a sheen of sweat reflecting the outside sunlight.

His darker haired partner was shorter, more compact and far more muscular, with sculpted magazine quality biceps underneath a perfectly tailored uniform. Hispanic, he looked Puerto Rican or possibly Dominican, with dark skin and a thick carpet of hair. He reminded her of an older version of Eddie Vasquez, the college student and EMT who had been pursuing Sarah ever since the accident last year.

The shiny faced one called out in a voice intended to be authoritative but in fact just sounded hoarse. "All right, everyone please have your identification ready to examine. This is a routine stop, we're from Customs and Border Protection."

A series of curses ran through Adelina's mind even as Jessica stirred beside her. What would she do? What would they do? She was sure they were looking for her. Why else would the Border Patrol pull over the bus?

Why had she thrown away her phone? If she could have called someone—Carrie, or Julia, then at least they'd know her fate. Then she'd be far less likely to simply *disappear.* But it was gone, and there was nothing she could do about that.

The shorter Border Patrol officer repeated his partner's words in badly accented and translated Spanish. He might look at home in San Juan, but English was clearly his first language. Interesting he was the one doing the translating. It must be like being typecast as an actor.

The two agents had already stopped, dealing with the four Patagonia and Birkenstock-clad hikers with their manicured nails and three hundred dollar backpacks. One of the women, a petite blonde twenty-year-old in a Whitman College sweatshirt, was exclaiming out loud to everyone who could hear that *she was white.*

The shorter Border Patrol agent looked irritated and the woman's friends looked appalled. Adelina just shrank into her seat. She wanted this to be over as quickly as possible.

That didn't seem likely. The short agent had lost his patience. "Lady, either give me your ID right now, or you can do it at the station."

"I don't have to give you *anything*. I'm an American citizen, and I know my rights. I don't understand why you don't check out *him!*" As she said the words, she pointed directly at the old man two rows in front of Adelina, now awake and serenely watching the Border Patrol. Adelina could see a U.S. passport neatly resting in his hands.

"Crazy bitch," the taller agent muttered. He wiped a handkerchief across his forehead, then said, "I'm asking you a simple question. Are you an American citizen? Show me your ID. "

"My head," Jessica murmured. She squinted, looking up to the front of the car, and muttered, "Can't they be quieter?"

Chaos erupted. One of the two boys jerked to his feet for all of one half second. He immediately found the front of his shirt bunched up in the fist of the smaller Border Patrol agent.

"*Sit down!*" snarled the agent.

The bus driver leaned his head against the steering wheel, apparently giving up on going anywhere any time soon. The blonde girl shrank into her seat, suddenly realizing how serious this was. She was shaking and began to fumble in her purse.

"It's right here," she said in an unsteady voice.

"Yeah, lady, it's too late for that," one of the agents said. "Stand up, and step off the bus."

Slowly, the woman stood, her face serious. She stepped off the bus, and the two agents on the outside escorted her out of sight.

"Jesus," Jessica muttered. "What a stupid bitch."

"*Jessica,*" Adelina said, "I don't care how—misguided—that girl was. You don't need to use that kind of language."

Jessica started to tense and give her a scornful look—then looked down at her lap. "Sorry," she said. As if she'd suddenly remembered something.

The two agents were now systematically—and uneventfully—walking down the aisle. Examining passports and driver's licenses. Adelina watched as the agents made their way down the aisle. The legality of what they were doing was actually questionable. But that was beside the point. They were doing it, and she didn't have any choice but to comply.

The agents had reached the seats two rows in front of her and Jessica. On the left side, the old man. He smiled pleasantly and handed over his passport to the taller, sweaty agent. It looked worn, well used. The agent looked through it, eyes examining the photo, then looked back up at the old man.

"You're a U.S. citizen?"

"I am," the old man said.

"Where are you traveling to?"

Adelina knew well that the man didn't have to answer that. But he did. "My granddaughter lives in Bellingham. She's going to give birth to my first great-grandchild soon enough."

The sweaty agent wiped his forehead again, then said in a sour voice, "Congratulations." He thrust the passport back at the old man, and moved to the next row.

The shorter agent had moved past the couple with their crying baby, and was now only a foot and a half from Adelina.

In the row directly in front of her were two men, African-American, and both showed their driver's licenses.

"You're a U.S. citizen?" asked the agent.

"Yes, sir," both answered.

Adelina's tongue and cheeks were stiff, her neck aching. She had a hard time focusing as the agent asked more questions of the two men in front of her. Her heart was beating too fast, and a numb, tingly feeling began to expand from the tip of her tongue.

The sweaty agent was now at her row, talking to the two women directly across the aisle from Adelina.

"Mom," Jessica said.

Adelina was frozen, her mind turned inward to that cold February night a couple of months before her seventeenth birthday, when Richard Thompson had raped her. To the emotional torture he'd subjected her to. The psychological games. The one time he'd really beaten her, after he learned Carrie wasn't his.

She'd tried to love her daughters. But it was hard. Four of them, *his*. Four of them the product of rape and lust.

She looked at her wrists, and thought of Julia, who had once attempted suicide. Adelina would die before she went back. The pain in her chest was tighter and tighter. Cutting.

"*Mom*," Jessica hissed.

"Señora? Are you all right?"

Startled, she looked up. The shorter agent—the Hispanic one—stood in front of her. She didn't know how long the fear had paralyzed her. She didn't know how long the panic attack had gripped her.

"Sorry," she muttered. She reached in her purse and handed over her passport. Then immediately froze in terror. *She'd handed over the wrong passport.*

As the wife of a senior U.S. diplomat (and now Cabinet member) she carried two passports: one, her personal one, the other, her official diplomatic passport.

Her eyes, wide now, jerked to Jessica, who also sat frozen, arm extended, holding out her personal passport for the agent.

"You're a U.S. citizen?"

"Yes," Adelina croaked.

He looked at her passport. "Birthplace is Calella in Spain? Where exactly is that?"

"It's on the Mediterranean," she said. She coughed.

"You all right, ma'am?"

"The bus is hot, I just need a drink of water."

Jessica chimed in, "We're on a day trip and decided to take the bus instead of drive. Boy, was that a mistake."

The man gave Jessica an odd look, then his eyes went back to Adelina. He casually held up the passport. "Hey Perkins, you ever see one of these? Diplomatic passport."

The taller agent, an irritated expression on his face, shook his head. "We don't have time for that, Alvarez. If she's a citizen, move on. *Christ*, this bus is hot."

The shorter agent—Alvarez—chuckled, then handed the passport back to her. He looked at Jessica. "You two be careful. And get your Mom some water, she doesn't look good."

Both agents moved on to the next row, and Adelina sagged into her seat.

CHAPTER TWENTY-THREE
You Don't Understand

"**I don't** understand," Carrie said. "You're saying we're losing the safe house? The protective detail?"

Bear's jaw worked as he looked away from her. Teeth nearly clenched, he said, "It's out of my hands, Carrie. The entire investigation is being turned over to the special prosecutor and the IRS. I was ordered to stand down—in fact, I've been placed on administrative leave."

Carrie frowned. She didn't pretend to know the intricacies of government investigations and jurisdiction. But given that the IRS was investigating the family—and not the people who had attacked them—none of this seemed good.

"So when do we have to be out?" she asked.

"This morning," he said, his voice low.

Carrie sighed. Then she turned away from Bear and sank into her chair.

Julia, still sitting on the couch next to Crank, said, "We'll need to rent a suite, I think. The most secure hotel we can find, and we'll hire bodyguards."

Carrie shook her head. "Your accounts have been frozen, Julia."

"Only the business ones. My personal account's still accessible. It's enough to last a little while."

"Why are you placed on leave?" Sarah's voice, from the doorway, was aggressive, pitched a little loud and monotone.

Bear looked across the room at her. Then he said, "I was up late last night reviewing files related to your case, when the call came about the attack. Unfortunately I left the file out on my kitchen table—and someone broke into my apartment while I was out. The files are gone."

Carrie frowned and met Julia's eyes. Then she looked back at Bear.

"What was in the file?"

"Your father's State Department personnel file."

Sarah muttered something under her breath. Carrie couldn't hear it exactly, but it sounded suspiciously like *motherfucker*.

"So what do we do now?" Carrie asked.

"I want you to meet Anthony Walker," Julia said to Carrie. "I think he can help."

"The reporter?" Bear said. "That's a bad idea."

"I disagree," Julia said. "It's not like the government is helping us. Somebody is trying to destroy our family. We don't have time to screw around."

Carrie stared at Julia aghast. She'd spent more than a year avoiding reporters, ever since the calls started coming in when charges were filed against Ray. They'd been hounded by the media, caricatured, and it hadn't stopped after Ray's murder.

"I don't know," Carrie murmured.

Julia leaned forward and took her hands. "Listen—I know you don't want to, and I know why. I've been dealing with the press for years, I get it. But I'm telling you—this guy's straight up. And if anyone can get to the bottom of it, he can."

"This is a bad idea," Bear said.

"I don't know if I can trust a reporter," Carrie said.

"Look. Let's meet with him. If you decide you don't trust him, we don't have to talk with him anymore."

Carrie sighed. Her mind kept going back to Ronald Lafferty, the reporter from the *New York Post*. He'd harassed Ray for weeks, then shown up at the hospital during their three-day vigil after the accident.

Lafferty had penned a front page poison article attacking her and Ray less than a week after Ray's death. All so he could get his damn story. The story was filled with lies and innuendo with lots of descriptive detail, but little or no truth. Julia had offered to sue, and briefly tangled with the lawyers at the *Post*, but it didn't go to court.

Carrie sighed. "I'll talk with him. But I'm skeptical."

Bear frowned. Then he said, "It's your call, I can't stop you. But I think you're making a mistake. You can't trust some reporter."

"Can we trust you?" Carrie asked.

Bear flushed. "That's your call, too, now, isn't it? I'll tell you this much: I want to know who shot the mother of my children. You can cooperate or not, but I'm on this case until they shoot me."

Carrie turned to Julia, then to Alexandra, sitting quietly by herself. Alexandra gave a minute nod. Carrie nodded.

"All right. I'll meet with him. Bear—will you sit in on that too? We need all the help we can get."

George-Phillip. May 3.

Wouldn't it be wonderful, just once, to do something without fourteen layers of scrutiny?

The thought ran through George-Phillip's mind as he looked over the statement the flight attendant handed him, detailing the extensive charges either he, or the agency, or possibly the royal travel budget, would have to pick up for this flight. Ninety-two thousand pounds sterling for the roundtrip to Washington and back.

It seemed odd to him that Cabinet members—and, for that matter, members of the royal family, other than Her Majesty—often flew scheduled commercial flights. But increasingly the split personality of the British public meant restricted public resources. While the Queen always flew charter jets, or the shorter range jets of the 32nd Squadron of the Royal Air Force, all such flights came from the travel budget, which was limited.

The rest of the family typically flew commercial, except for special circumstances. Prince Charles had seen that such circumstances were increasingly rare, after his *six-hundred thousand pound* roundtrip to South America had caused significant public scandal. And that trip for an environmental jaunt—irony indeed. Now, as a result, George-Phillip had to figure out how in hell he was going to possibly *personally* pay for a charter flight across the Atlantic, which was required for official business.

Whatever. Let the newspapers bray. He wasn't flying his daughter commercial—not two days after an assassination attempt—and he wasn't leaving her alone in London.

Right now, Jane was asleep, stretched across the row of seats across from George-Phillip. Her nanny, Adriana, was in the row across from her, reading a paperback novel with two cupcakes on the cover. She'd been wide eyed, watching out the windows as the flight took off four hours before, and silent since then. Jane, on the other hand, had taken to her first flight as if it were her twentieth. She'd barely paid attention as the flight took to the air, instead keeping her nose buried in *Discovery Box*, her favorite periodical. That was actually fairly typical for Jane—she would appear to not pay any attention at all to new experiences, until the next day. To-morrow, she'd be able to talk about nothing else.

That tendency worried him. Because on the way to the airport this morning, she'd talked and talked and talked about waking up to the sound of gunshots two night earlier.

For the first time in the thirty years of his career, George-Phillip was considering retiring. Jane had already lost her mother.

For just a second, George-Phillip felt a lump of unhappiness. He'd lost the love of his life years ago. Then he'd married a good woman, a kind woman, a woman who he'd imagined spending the rest of his life with. But their marriage had lasted just three years.

He closed his eyes and gritted his teeth. He didn't have time for such nonsense.

Opening his eyes, George-Phillip flagged down the flight attendant. "Bring me a Pimm's iced tea, please, and a telephone."

"Yes, sir."

The phone came quicker than the drink, which was unfortunate. But he would have to settle for what he could. He leaned toward the window, looking out at the glare. Far below were the clouds, and below that, ocean in all directions. He looked back toward his daughter and his decision was made. When this crisis with the Thompson family was over, he was resigning from the government. He'd given thirty years of his life to the Queen. The remainder would belong to Jane.

Lifting the phone to his ear, he dialed.

"Aye," said the gruff voice of Oswald O'Leary.

"It's C," said George-Phillip. "Any updates?"

"Yes, sir, I do. One of our agents in California has a lead on Mrs. Thompson, sir. I'm told she's running south toward Mexico, and fast."

Damn it, George-Phillip thought. He'd have some influence if she were able to get to the Canadian border. Trying to cross into Mexico, however, would be hazardous. Security on the American border with Mexico was far more aggressive than the Canadian border—not to mention the dangers of drug wars and corruption, which had rocked the northern cities of Mexico in recent years. What was she thinking?

He sighed. He hadn't actually seen or spoken with her, other than a few short words, in sixteen years, and even then she'd changed a lot, twisted by anxiety and fear.

For the hundred-millionth time, George-Phillip found himself wishing Richard Thompson were dead.

"All right. Keep tracking her. I don't even know who all is after her at this point, but I want Adelina Thompson and her daughters protected."

"Aye, sir. I'll do the best I can."

They disconnected, and George-Phillip looked out the window at the clouds below. O'Leary would be on a flight to Washington the next day, but his role had become so important that George-Phillip insisted they take separate flights so one of them was on the ground at all times.

His affair with Adelina had been doomed from the beginning. He remembered those intense months in 1984 so clearly. She'd been terrified of Richard—terrified he would hurt her, even more terrified that she would lose Julia if they separated. They'd had the conversation too many times to count.

You should leave him.

I can't. You don't understand.

But he did. He understood she was terrified. But sometimes he wondered if her fear was warranted, or if it was all in her head.

He had stopped wondering after his investigation of Wakhan began to make real progress.

George-Phillip shook his head as he looked out at the clouds and the ocean far below. That had been the one and only time he'd ever broken the classification rules. In fact he'd violated the Official Secrets Act and every principle of his profession.

It had been an early-March day and the sun was dazzling over Washington, DC. Adelina had gotten away with an excuse of a nonexistent bridge game with equally nonexistent church friends. Instead, they met at an overlook high over the Potomac River on the George Washington Parkway. There, surrounded by forest overlooking Washington, DC, they could talk in private even as cars raced by on the parkway behind them.

"Before we go any further, there's something you must know," he had said.

"Are we going further?" she asked, raising one achingly beautiful eyebrow.

He said, "Regardless. You need to know that while my interest in you is purely personal, I do have a *professional* interest in your husband."

"Don't call him that. Not in private. Publicly he may be my husband, but privately, he is my jailor. My rapist. Don't you *ever* call him a husband."

George-Phillip had sighed. "Nevertheless, he is my target."

Her eyes widened. "Are you saying that you started seeing me in order to get to him?"

George-Phillip shook his head. "No. The two things happened independently of each other. But the bottom line is, something terrible happened in Afghanistan last year, and I believe Richard was involved in it."

"Nothing he did would surprise me."

"Did you expect him back from his tour so soon?"

She shook her head. "No, in fact, he originally said he would be in Pakistan for three years, and that I could expect to see him only occasionally for vacations." Her mouth curled into a bitter smile. "I'd looked forward to having him gone. But it turned out to be less than two years."

"When did you learn he would be coming back to the United States?"

"He called in mid-December to let me know he wouldn't be taking leave for Christmas. And that I needed to have the house packed and ready to move to Washington by the end of January."

George-Phillip had felt his heart sink then. The massacre in Badakhshan province had taken place on December 12. There was no question—someone at the U.S. State Department, or more likely the CIA, had ordered Thompson out of there following the massacre.

"Does that change anything?" Adelina asked him.

"Nothing could change what is between us," he had said. And he meant it. But it turned out to not be true. The next few weeks had been the most intense in his life. Was the affair sweetened by the fact that it was forbidden? He didn't know for sure. But he did know that in the nearly thirty years since then, he'd experienced nothing so emotionally intense as those weeks in the Spring of 1984 when he fell in love with Adelina.

Thirty years may have passed, but the intensity of the emotion never faded—it merely became a dull ache, one that was occasionally improved and even appeared to be in complete remission, but always returned. That was partly because he'd never known why it ended. The end came suddenly, without warning, and without explanation. On an afternoon in late May 1984, he'd called her and she didn't call back. Not that day, or the next.

Up until that point they hadn't gone more than a day without talking. George-Phillip worried, but didn't panic. Until the next day, when she didn't return his call for the third day in a row.

On the fourth day, George-Phillip was recalled to London for several days of meetings as a result of his report on the Wakhan massacre, and it was two weeks before he returned to Washington.

Two weeks during which she'd neither answered the phone nor returned his calls.

Frantic upon his return to the United States, George-Phillip rented a car and drove directly from National Airport to the Thompson condominium in Bethesda.

It was hellishly risky. But after three weeks without a response, he'd thought nothing but the worst. Was she dead? Had Richard finally done away with her? On his arrival at the building, he walked past the concierge as if he belonged there and stepped into the elevator and pressed the button for the penthouse.

Sixty seconds later he was knocking on the door of the condo in unison with the beating of his heart. He felt his pulse in his neck as he waited. The pulse in his neck pounded harder with each second.

An unfamiliar woman opened the door—not Jenny Sullivan, Julia's nanny. This woman was young—probably eighteen or nineteen, with long blonde hair.

"Can I help you?"

George-Phillip had coughed and said, "Is Mrs. Thompson in?"

The woman at the door said, "Wait right here." Then closed the door in his face.

He cooled his heels in the hallway. Ten seconds. Twenty. Thirty.

Finally Adelina opened the door. A ridge of tension ran down the center of her forehead like a furrow through the plowed field, the strain evident in her posture and in the flash of her eyes.

"What are you doing here?" she hissed.

"I just returned from London, and since you aren't returning my calls, I felt it necessary to come in person."

"I'm not returning your calls because I don't want to talk with you."

"Why?"

She rolled her eyes. She *rolled her eyes*. He'd spent weeks feeling shut out, frustrated. Concerned about her safety. Wondering if she was even alive. He'd felt ... angry. Afraid. Worried. And she rolled her eyes?

His face must have shown some of what he was thinking, because she stepped away from him, her face suddenly closed and wary.

"*Why?*" he asked. "Did I offend you somehow? Did I hurt you? Did *your husband* suddenly become the man of your dreams?"

Adelina's response was instantaneous; a loud ringing slap that stung his face. "How dare you?" she asked. "You know what he did to me."

George-Phillip staggered back. "And I know what you've done to me, Adelina. You've broken my heart."

"I never want to see you again," she said.

He closed his eyes, forcing himself to contain the overwhelming pain her statement brought on. "I don't understand you, Adelina."

She sobbed. "Please, George. Just go. Leave me."

She stepped back inside and closed the door. Twelve years would pass before he saw Adelina Thompson again.

CHAPTER TWENTY-FOUR
The Most Important Weapon

Alexandra. May 3.

"**E**xcuse me a moment," Alexandra said, stepping away from her sisters. They had just arrived at the Crowne Plaza in Arlington, where Julia had rented a suite.

"Hey," Carrie said, catching her eyes. "You okay?"

"Yeah," Alexandra replied. "I'm good."

She stepped into the bedroom at the end of the hall and dropped her bag on the bed, then took out her phone, urgently checking to see if he'd contacted her. Nothing from Dylan, but she had a friend request on Facebook from a Sherman Roberts. The name tore at her heart. Roberts and Sherman were Dylan's two best friends from the Army—both of them dead now.

She accepted the request then checked her messages.

His was obscure.

SHERMAN ROBERTS: Hey you. I was browsing profiles and saw yours and thought we should get to know each other. If you get my message, let me know.

She wondered if he was online right then. Maybe? She tapped in her response:

ALEXANDRA PARIS: Hi there. I don't usually talk to strangers.

His response was immediate. Her phone rang, but there was no caller ID.

She scrambled to answer it.

"Dylan?"

"Hey, babe. Where are you?"

"We've moved to the Crowne Plaza in Arlington, Virginia. The DSS isn't giving us protection anymore."

"Son of a bitch, are you serious? Why not?"

"They're not in charge of the investigation anymore. It sounds like that's the Justice Department and IRS. They're after my father. But Julia's working on hiring private security."

Silence at the other end of the line. Breathing. Finally, Dylan said, "I want you to make sure you've got a retreat. Fire escape. Anything. Make sure you've got a way out. And you need to buy a gun."

"Dylan, I've never fired a gun—"

"Alex. These people are serious."

She closed her eyes. Less than forty-eight hours before he'd killed two armed attackers while protecting her sister.

"Okay. Okay. I hear you, Dylan."

"Me and Sherman taught you how to protect yourself in a fight. What's the most important weapon you have?"

Jesus Christ, she thought. His voice was intense. "My brain," she whispered.

"That's right. You have to stay one step ahead. What's the plan from here?"

"We're meeting with Bear in a little while, and some guy from the Washington Post who Julia knows. She says she thinks he might be able to help us. Right now we need information."

"Right. We especially need to know who Carrie and Andrea's father is."

Alexandra sniffed. "Yes. You're right."

"I'm tossing this SIM card when we're finished talking. But I'll keep watching the Facebook account. Drop me a message and I'll call within a couple of hours. All right?"

"Dylan..." she said.

"Yeah?"

"Be careful."

"I will," he replied. His voice was sober. "I love you."

Julia. May 3.

The hotel telephone was loud and jarring, unsettling in a world where 99 percent of phone calls had a pleasing ring tone. Julia stood and walked to the phone and lifted it to her ear.

"Hello?"

"Mrs. Wilson?"

"Speaking," Julia said.

"There's a Mr. Anthony Walker here to see you."

"Send him up, please."

She hung up the phone and glanced over at Crank, who stood at the bar mixing a drink. "Fix me one, please?" she asked.

"Strong?"

"Yes. Better make it a double. What about you?" she asked Bear, who was standing in the corner sending an email on his phone.

"No, thanks," Bear said absently.

Carrie was lying on the couch nearby, her face exhausted, and Rachel stretched out across her chest asleep. The baby's eyes were closed, her tiny hands curled into fists.

Crank held out the glass to her, a vodka tonic. She sipped it, sighing in relief. Sarah was on the balcony, headset in her ears, her head moving as she listened to music. Alexandra had disappeared to her room the moment they'd arrived in the suite.

A knock on the door. Julia set her drink down as Crank opened it. He put a finger to his lips and whispered, "Quiet. Baby's sleeping."

Anthony practically tiptoed in, his eyes falling on Carrie and Rachel. Carrie didn't open her eyes, but said in an even voice, "It's fine as long as you don't shout. Forgive me for not getting up and introducing myself. I'm a mattress right now. An exhausted mattress. My name's Carrie Sherman."

"Anthony Walker," he replied in a bemused voice. His lips were curled up in a slight smile, and his eyes scanned Carrie longer than Julia was comfortable.

Intensely protective of her younger sister, Julia's eyes narrowed. "Anthony's a *journalist*," she said, in a none-too-friendly tone of voice.

Anthony raised his eyebrows. "I am. By the way, I've got a question for you. I know you guys ruled out Senator Rainsley. But—odd question, but the dates line up. And so do some other things. Do you remember George-Phillip Windsor?"

"Who?" Carrie said.

Anthony passed his phone to Julia, who stood to take it. A sudden squeeze in her chest hit when she looked at the photo.

Anthony said, "You recognize him."

In a higher pitched voice than she expected, Julia said, "That's George Lansing. He worked for the British embassy when we were in China. My mother—she had an affair with him."

"Let me see," Carrie said. "I never knew what he looked like."

Julia handed the phone to Carrie, realizing that the resemblance was too clear. "It's obvious now, but I never saw it before. That was a long time ago, and I had a lot going on."

Carrie's eyes widened when she saw the picture. Her hands started to shake, and she said, "I know him. He spoke at my graduation. And ... and ... he's the guy from the pictures. From Spain. I think."

"I don't know who George Lansing is," Anthony said. "Unless that was just the name your mother told you."

"Wait," Julia said. "You said—"

"I said George-Phillip Windsor. As in, Prince George-Phillip. He's like a second or third cousin or something to the Queen of England. *And* the head of the Special Intelligence Service."

Carrie let out a loud cough. "I'm sorry, but *what?*" The baby stirred, but Carrie shifted anyway, sitting up and trying to settle Rachel in her lap. "Are you saying *he's* my father? That my father is some ... somehow connected to the British royals? I *know* him—he gave the commencement address at Columbia when I graduated. I shook his hand."

Anthony said, "I don't think there's proof."

"Well," Julia said. "Tell us what you have."

Alexandra, standing in the door of the suite, said, "Yes. Tell us." Her face looked stunned, and she walked forward, facing Anthony.

Anthony looked back and forth between the sisters and Crank. "Okay. Here's what I know. The timing is right. I think they met sometime in the spring of 1984. George-Phillip was a junior diplomat at the British Embassy. I don't know where they met, but we can place them in a restaurant together in late February, 1984. In fact, you were there too, Julia."

Julia felt as if she'd been punched. "I was *there?* How do you know?"

"A gossip columnist spotted your mother and George-Phillip and wrote about it."

Julia felt her stomach churn. "A gossip columnist? Anyone I know?"

"Yeah," Anthony said, his voice apologetic. "It was Maria Clawson. From what I hear—and this is all hearsay—she dated George-Phillip briefly. Before he met your mother. And—well—she didn't take his rejection well at all."

"Jesus," Crank muttered. "That gossipy bitch smeared Julia all to hell twenty years later. What the hell?"

Julia took Crank's hand and squeezed it. "She's out of business now."

Maria Clawson was out of business only because Julia had personally funded a lawsuit against her. A nineteen-year-old college student had been raped by a popular football player on campus at the University of Alabama, and when she went public, the media came out swinging, Maria Clawson in the lead, smearing the girl. The girl won her lawsuit and a settlement big enough to permanently shut down Clawson.

"So I ate at a restaurant with this guy. Where did they meet?"

Anthony shrugged. "No idea."

"I can probably answer that," Bear said. He'd been quiet up until that moment, but Julia looked at him now. "In your father's State Department personnel file, we've got a photo of your parents along with George-Phillip. It was taken in the condo you live in now, in February 1984."

Carrie shook her head as she rocked Rachel back and forth. "The timing's right. I was born the next January."

"Right," Anthony said. "And then George-Phillip was in China for a year, from May '96 to May '97."

Julia closed her eyes. "That's the year I was—falling apart."

"The twins were born in April '96," Carrie said.

"And Andrea in June '97, which means she could easily be his daughter. Both of you could be."

Julia met Carrie's eyes. Carrie shrugged, her expression empty of emotion.

"I don't know what to think," she said.

"So Mom had an affair with some British prince who blew in and charmed her," Alexandra said sarcastically.

"I think it's crazy she stayed married, considering what happened," Carrie said.

"What exactly happened?" Alexandra asked. "He wasn't convicted of anything. He was *suspected*. They didn't arrest him. They dropped the charge."

"Yes, Alex," Carrie said. "Because he was a rich diplomat. You think he would have stayed out of jail if it hadn't been for that?"

"I am *not* the child of a rape," Alexandra shouted.

The baby started to stir, a rough cry slipping out. Alexandra covered her mouth.

"If I read her diary correctly," Julia said, "you are. And so am I."

"What about the twins?" Alexandra said. "You think they are too? Or is there some other affair waiting in the wings?"

Julia leaned forward, resting her head in her hands for just a second. Then she got up and walked over to Alexandra and faced her. Alexandra looked scared, her eyes an open window into confusion and shock.

"Alexandra, this is a shock to all of us. And we don't know the answers to a lot of this. But—just—right now, try to keep an open mind, okay? We're here for you. Whatever happened with our parents, we know who *we* are. We know what we've been through together. Okay?"

Alexandra took a deep breath. She nodded, silently. "All right," she whispered. "Sorry."

"It's okay," Julia soothed. "It's okay."

No one else spoke for a minute. Then Julia took Alexandra's hand and led her to the couch and sat down.

"Okay," Julia said. "So we have this Prince George-Phillip and my mother meeting in early '84. And we think he's likely to be Carrie and Andrea's father. We know they were together at least twice in '84, and I remember seeing him in Beijing."

"And he looks just like the mystery guy in my photo album. *And* he showed up at my graduation."

Anthony looked confused, and Julia said, "What mystery guy?"

Carrie sighed. "When I went to Spain with Andrea in 2002, there was a guy in two different photos—one on the beach and one in the town square. He's standing off to the side watching us, and neither picture was focused very well. But he looks a lot like your George-Phillip. I guess the deciding thing is height—is George-Phillip tall?"

"Really tall," Carrie said.

Anthony nodded. "Six-six maybe. Gangly. Hair and eyes like yours, but he's got these huge bushy eyebrows. Be grateful you didn't inherit those." The last words were said with a subdued grin.

Carrie laughed, a short, bark-like laugh. "I suppose. Now the question is, how do we get in to meet George-Phillip?"

"You don't," Anthony said. "He's the head of the British Intelligence Agency. It would be like asking for an appointment with the director of the CIA."

"Or the Secretary of Defense?" Carrie challenged.

"Hmm—good point. Except you don't have those kinds of connections in the British government. Do you?"

Oh, shit, Julia thought. For the first time in this discussion, she wanted to run. She wanted to just get up and walk out. Because *she* did have those kinds of connections in the British government. Or at least one.

Harry Easton.

Harry had been her first love, if you could call it that. Nineteen years old, a fourth year at the International School of Beijing when she started there at fourteen. He'd swept her off her feet. He'd treated her like dirt, pressured her into sex way too early, got her pregnant then dumped her. He'd ruined her life, at least for her high school and early college years.

He was currently the Deputy Head of Mission at the UK Embassy in Washington.

Julia only knew about that because of an article in the *Post* three weeks before, detailing the implementation of the latest trade agreement between Britain and the United States. Harry had been quoted in the article.

She sighed out loud, then said, "I know someone at the Embassy."

For the first time since he handed Julia her drink, Crank spoke up. "Fuck, no."

"Crank, it's necessary—"

"No. We'll find another way. He screwed you up way too much. I won't have you going to him asking for a favor."

Bear interceded. "What are we talking about here?"

Carrie sat up, clutching Rachel to her. "Julia, no. I can find another way."

Alexandra looked baffled, and Anthony's eyebrows drew together as he put together the story. "You aren't talking about—"

Julia spoke in a loud, sharp tone. Not a shout, but loud enough to cut through the sudden chaos. "Everybody be quiet! *I'll* be the one to decide who I talk with."

Silence from the others.

She took a steadying breath and said, "All of that happened almost twenty years ago. I'm going to go make the call." She stood, and Crank rose with her.

"Crank—I need to be alone, all right? *Please?*" She looked in Crank's eyes, trying to communicate through that gaze how much confusion and discomfort she felt. She needed to do this alone. She needed to process this call by herself, and not have to talk about it in front of other people.

He gave a minute nod. He understood.

She was ashamed of the sudden relief that flooded through her. So she leaned forward and kissed him on the corner of his mouth, then walked away from the group and into the bedroom, closing the door behind her.

She sat down on the bed and closed her eyes, puzzling through the feelings that flooded through her.

She was a grown woman in her early thirties. She ran a multimillion dollar corporation, moving hundreds of people all over the globe. She was competent, skilled, and in command of her own life.

But inside, part of her was still that desperately lonely fourteen-year-old girl who was abandoned emotionally by her parents, who'd gotten involved with a much older boy who took advantage of her loneliness and insecurity. Some days, even though she'd met the love of her life, she still woke up with a gaping pit of need that could never be filled. Even after twelve years with Crank, she still sometimes looked at him like he was a stranger. Not because of him, but because deep inside, she couldn't trust, couldn't open up, couldn't reveal the terrified little girl inside.

She didn't want to make this phone call.

So she unlocked her phone and dialed 411. An automated voice asked her for the listing she wanted. "Washington, DC. The Embassy of the United Kingdom."

A toneless voice, a computer, which had no understanding of the emotional weight of its words, said, "Stay on the line to be connected."

Two clicks, and then a ring. Another ring. She felt queasy and wrapped her left arm across her stomach. A third ring, then a pleasant female voice answered.

"Embassy of Great Britain. How may I help you?"

Julia cleared her throat. Then said in a voice far too tentative for her liking, "Harry Easton, please."

"May I ask who is calling?"

"Please tell him it's Julia Wil—Julia Thompson. He'll remember me from the International School of Beijing."

"Yes, ma'am, please hold."

Julia cleared her voice again. She would *not* let her voice shake when she was speaking with Harry.

Then his voice. The same melodious voice which had once whispered in her ear, *That wasn't so bad, was it?* Only now he sounded tentative and uncomfortable.

"Julia."

She cleared her throat, suddenly choked with anxiety. She couldn't force any words out.

"Hello? Julia?"

Get. A. Grip. She clenched a fist and said, "Harry. Hello."

"I was … surprised … to hear it was you." His voice sounded oddly tentative. "I've seen the news about your family—I'm sorry to hear you've had such tragedies."

Julia reminded herself that Harry Easton had no power over her now, unless it was power *she* gave him. And she wasn't going to do that anymore. Not after all these years.

"Honestly," she replied, "I didn't expect to be calling you. But I'm finding myself in need of a favor. And you're the person in a position to assist."

She heard him take a deep breath. He waited a moment, as if he couldn't find the right words to say. Then he responded in a low, sober tone, "If there is anything in my power, I will. I owe you that much, certainly."

Prepared for—arrogance, or anger, or contempt—Julia hadn't expected that tone of voice or those words. She flinched.

"I—" she started to speak, but cut herself off.

"Listen, Julia…"

"No," she responded. "You don't need—"

"I do," he said. "I … I've carried regret for many years for the way I treated you. I was so terribly wrong."

Julia wanted to scream with rage. She wanted to throw her phone across the room. She wanted to shout at him, or scream, or do anything she could to throw the words back at him, to not have to hear the remorse and sorrow in his voice. *He didn't get to be sad about what he'd done. He didn't get to ask for forgiveness.*

She shook. But she didn't say anything. Finally Harry spoke again.

"Julia, I'd never dare or presume to ask for your forgiveness. But all the same, I hope one day you'll offer it. I'm deeply sorry. I'd do anything to change it."

All of it flooded back. All of it. The shame and fear and sadness. The horror of walking through the halls of high school her senior year, with the words *slut, whore* whispered around her. The awful photo. The crushing shame, and the sharp pain in her wrist when she sliced it open.

She'd thought that she had left it behind. She'd thought that it didn't affect her anymore—that her career and her life with Crank had robbed those experiences of their power to make her hurt. But she hadn't. She hadn't healed, she hadn't walked away from it, and some of it still had the power to drag her right back.

But now she had a choice. Now she had a choice to move on and grow up and live her own life. It was the choice she'd made every day for the last twelve years, and the choice she was going to keep making.

There was no choice really. Not if she wanted to live the life she wanted. Because the only way to release the power Harry Easton had over her was to give up any power she might have over him. She heard the sadness in his tone. The shaking in his words. Somewhere along the way, he'd gained some—what? Wisdom?

She exhaled, letting out the tension. She hadn't even realized she'd been holding her breath. With that rush of air out of her lungs, she felt herself let it go.

"What happened?" she asked. "What changed?"

"Everything," he said. "But—the big thing was—I'm a father now. A little girl, she's three. And some day she's going to be in school and will be around boys and all I can do is pray she'll be treated better than you were. I'm truly sorry, Julia."

Julia closed her eyes. Something so simple, yet profound. A baby. Harry had no way of knowing that Julia couldn't have children. He had no way of knowing the utter rage she carried. A tear rolled down her cheek. Harry Easton walked away with some remorse, but he got to have a daughter. But thanks to him, thanks to the back-room abortion in that awful clinic in China, *she* would never bear a daughter of her own.

She didn't want to forgive him. She didn't want to let him off the hook. She wanted to reach through the phone and tear his guts out.

Julia closed her eyes. She thought of the affirmations her therapist had given her, and the prayers she'd learned to say. She sought the inner peace that was sometimes so elusive.

Finally, she whispered, "I forgive you."

Then she clenched her fist against her stomach, because she didn't know if she meant it. But even if she didn't, she had to act like it.

Harry gasped. Then, incredibly, she heard him sniff, as if he was tearing up. "I don't deserve that," he said, his voice broken.

She sighed. "Let it go, Harry. Move on. Raise your daughter, and protect her."

"I will," he replied.

"Now for the favor I need."

"Anything."

"My sister Carrie and I need to meet with Prince George-Phillip."

There was a stunned silence at the other end of the line. Finally he said, "Surely you're kidding."

"No, Harry. It's important."

"I don't—Julia, he's the head of the Special Intelligence Service. And a member of the royal family. I've got no power to arrange such a meeting."

"I need you to try," she replied.

"I would have to go well outside normal channels to arrange such a thing. Which means I'll need to give explanations."

She sighed, and said, "It's intensely personal."

"What personal business could you possibly have with him?"

She coughed. Then said, "This is related to the attack on my sisters. If you can get the message to him that Adelina Thompson's daughters want to meet with him, he'll know what it is about."

"Not *Richard* Thompson's daughters?"

Julia snorted a bitter laugh. "He'll understand either way."

"Then I'll do the best I can. Can I reach you back at this number?"

"This is my cell."

"I'll be in touch, Julia."

CHAPTER TWENTY-FIVE
Mister Oz

Dylan. May 3.

It was late afternoon, almost evening, as Dylan looked out the window of the kitchen. Mendoza sat at the table smoking a cigarette in front of an untouched deck of cards. Dylan imagined Mendoza's mother would give him hell later for smoking in the house. Andrea sat across from him, scanning through the Washington Post on the tablet they'd bought the night before. Along with the tablet and half a dozen disposable phones, they'd bought pre-paid SIM cards from several locations, dragging Mendoza along for a three-hour odyssey from store to store.

Dylan still worried that it would be dangerous to get online, but they had little choice. They needed information.

"Look at this," Andrea said. "It says your President is caught in an internal dispute about whether or not to rescind the nomination."

"Yeah?" Dylan said.

She slid the tablet across to him and he scanned the article. Dylan didn't follow politics at all, so most of the names mentioned in the article were unfamiliar. But one thing was clear—the President was caught in a bind, whether or not to support his nominee for Secretary of Defense. The confirmation hearings were set to begin in just a few days.

"I bet the President's hoping your father will withdraw."

"Richard Thompson is not my father," she said. Her tone was final.

"You know what I mean."

"I do. But I'd prefer you spoke with some precision. At this point we don't know who my father is, but we do know that man is not him."

"Okay," he replied. Slowly.

A large black SUV with flashy chrome rims was coming down the street. Dylan leaned a little closer to the window to see it. It came to a stop directly in front of the house and the door opened. A man got out—short black hair, black stubble darkening an angular face.

Dylan tensed, and Andrea followed his lead, rising half out of her seat. "Heads up, Mendoza. You know this guy?"

"Yeah. Relax. He's our delivery guy. Just stay here."

Mendoza stood and walked out of the kitchen. Andrea pointed to the other exit from the kitchen, a side door that led to a narrow space between homes. Dylan leaned back and unlocked the door, then carefully turned the knob to crack the door. He wanted to be able to move quickly if they needed to.

A minute went by, then another. Dylan could hear voices in the front entrance, Mendoza and the other guy, but he couldn't tell what they were saying.

A year ago, Dylan would never have doubted Mendoza. They'd served together. But things were different now. For one thing, Mendoza got hurt and left their unit early on. For another, the members of Dylan's platoon had turned on each other like frenzied sharks when it came time to save their own asses. Dylan trusted nobody but family now. Slowly and casually, he slid his hand under his shirt and rested his hand on the pistol grip of the weapon he'd taken from one of the dead killers. It was a .45 Glock patterned after the M1911 Colt automatic, and felt comfortable in his hand.

Andrea raised an eyebrow.

"Just being careful," he whispered.

The front door closed with a thump, and Dylan heard footsteps coming back toward the kitchen. His grip tightened on the pistol.

Outside, the guy with the SUV was walking back to it.

Mendoza froze in the doorway when he saw Dylan. "Paris—everything okay?"

"Yeah, man, it's all good."

The guy out front got in his SUV and drove away.

"I got your IDs. They're pretty good."

Mendoza dropped a card in front of Dylan and another in front of Andrea.

Dylan raised his eyebrows. It was a Tennessee driver's license in the name of Sherman Roberts. He flipped it back and forth. It looked real enough, including a bar code on the back.

"The bar code doesn't actually work. You don't want to get pulled over with that, all right? But it'll pass for hotels or whatever."

Dylan said, "This looks good. How's yours?"

Andrea passed hers over. It was indistinguishable from a real driver's license. Mendoza's *friend* had given her a couple of years, but the date on the license made her 18 rather than 21. That was good—she looked too young for that. They needed to stay as discreet as possible. He handed the card back to her without comment.

"We'll need to get going soon," Dylan said. "I don't want to put you in any more danger than I already have."

"Don't worry about me, man."

Andrea was already up.

Dylan said, "Let me check in with Alex real quick." He reached for the tablet and logged into Facebook and his new account.

He had a message from Alex.

Tell Andrea to Google Prince George-Phillip.

Weird. He showed the message to Andrea, whose eyebrows drew together.

"Do it," she said.

Dylan typed in the words on the screen. A moment later Google returned the Wikipedia results along with a photograph. Andrea, standing over his shoulder, cursed under her breath. Then she said, "That's the man who was in the photos from Spain."

Dylan looked through the Wikipedia entry. It was detailed.

"He was stationed with the Embassy in Washington, DC in the early 80s," he said.

"What about the 90s?"

Dylan looked up at her then pointed at the screen.

Her face stiffened. "He was in China."

"The resemblance is pretty strong," he said. "You and Carrie both look like him."

He scrolled down further.

She sucked in a breath and said, "Stop."

She hunched down next to the table, her face close to the tablet. The screen had stopped on a photo. George-Phillip, in a military uniform, complete with sash and medals. At his side was a little girl in a dress with red polka dots. The little girl had raven hair and green eyes. She could easily be mistaken as Carrie or Andrea's sister.

"I don't get it," Dylan said. "Your mom had an affair with this guy?"

"I guess so," Andrea said. "And not a short one. Carrie's twelve years older than I am." Her face settled into a thoughtful expression. She took the tablet and typed into it.

"I don't understand," Mendoza said.

Dylan nodded toward Andrea, then started to explain. But he stopped when Andrea let out a string of curses in Spanish.

"What is it?" he asked.

"He's coming to Washington," she said. "He has a meeting with the President tomorrow."

Dylan looked at her. "Okay, and...?" His voice trailed off.

She looked at him with calm eyes, and Dylan knew what she wanted to do.

"That's crazy talk, Andrea."

"I haven't said anything yet."

"It's still crazy."

"Crazy or not, if he's my father, don't you think it's time?"

Blaine, Washington. May 4.

Nick Larsden was frustrated.

Since early Friday morning he'd been on the road, working his way up the West Coast of California, then Oregon and Washington. A frustrating and probably futile search, he'd thought, until he stumbled on their campsite in California yesterday. Two hours after leaving the old man dead at his campsite, Nick had found the minivan. It was parked in the grocery store parking lot next to the Greyhound station in Medford, Oregon.

The license plates were a match, and more importantly, he'd found evidence in the van itself: the daughter had left piles of food wrappings, fast food bags and other garbage on the floor behind her seat. When Nick opened the glove box he found what he expected to find: the van was registered in the name of Richard Thompson. That must be the woman's husband. She'd abandoned her van and taken a bus, sometime that morning.

Nick followed the trail. From there it wasn't difficult to figure out. She'd probably arrived there at nine or ten am. The next buses north were to Seattle and Bellingham at ten and ten-thirty. And the Bellingham bus continued on to Blaine, on the Canadian border. He would bet anything the woman and her daughter were on that bus.

He had looked around the bus station. Medford had a tiny station and probably didn't have more than two dozen passengers a day. He'd flashed a fake badge at the woman behind the counter, identifying himself as a State investigator, then shown her the pictures of Adelina and Jessica Thompson.

Verification. He had been eight hours behind them, but the bus would be stopping along the way. Maybe he could catch up before they tried to cross the border.

Unfortunately, it wasn't to be. The bus started with an eight-hour lead, and got to Blaine ahead of him by three hours. There was no sign of the woman or her daughter.

So now he watched and waited, an unread newspaper in front of him at the cheap table in the corner of the McDonald's. The Sumas border crossing was only two hundred yards away, several lines of cars backed up waiting to cross the border. It seemed like a lot of traffic for a Sunday morning. The day was clear and bright, but a lot cooler than the San Fernando Valley where he lived.

His phone started to vibrate. UNKNOWN CALLER. Interesting. He picked it up and answered the call.

"Hello?"

The caller had a thick, gravelly Irish accent. "Mister Larsden, this is Oz."

"What can I do for you?" Larsden responded, his tone respectful but quick. It was a thin line—Mister Oz, who was obviously using an assumed name, had offered a million dollars for this job.

A million dollars. Larsden wanted that place in the mountains very badly.

"Your friends assured me you'd be able to accomplish this job. But it seems you are not making any progress."

Larsden gritted his teeth, then answered in as calm a voice as he could muster, "I'm in Blaine, Washington, I've traced them to the border. It looks like they're going to make an attempt to cross into Canada."

"Mister Larsden, they must not make it to Canada. Do you understand?"

"I may not be able to prevent that."

"You will if you want to continue in your line of work. Or any line of work. Do I make myself clear, Larsden? Adelina Thompson and her daughter must not make it to the border alive. I don't care what you have to do."

"Roger that." He dropped his voice to a whisper. "And what am I supposed to do after I start killing people in sight of the border guards?"

"I suggest that you make sure you are unseen."

Christ.

"Make it three million."

"Excuse me?"

"You heard me. When this job started you just wanted them caught. Now you've changed it to murder. If it's that important, then you pay."

Hesitation at the other end of the line. Then the response: "Fine."

"I'll be in touch," Larsden said, his voice back at a normal tone. Then he hung up the phone and stood up. No one in the dining room appeared to notice anything unusual. Now the only question was when would Adelina and Jessica Thompson show up? Or had they already crossed the border? He didn't have any way of knowing.

For now, he needed to find a good vantage point where he could take a concealed position with his rifle. It wasn't ideal, but he had few other options. He walked out into the parking lot, the breeze raising goose bumps on his skin. He checked his watch. It was 11 am.

The cars were backing up Cherry Street, away from the border crossing. Across the street was the pedestrian lane. A scattering of people walked toward the metal turnstiles, which marked the border. Once they crossed through, there was no immediate re-entry to the United States. Instead, the next stop was Canada's Customs station.

Nick paced the parking lot for a moment in frustration. They might have walked right out of the bus station and directly to the border. They might already be in Canada.

He didn't know why *Oz*, his unnamed benefactor, wanted to ensure they didn't make it across the border. But the job had come to him through Marky Lovecchio, an old Army buddy. When Nick got out of the army, Marky had gone on to a career in Special Forces. In 2006 he'd left the military for a private military contractor—the pay was a hell of a lot better, he said, and you got to pick your own weapons. Marky had a lot of contacts, and vouched for *Oz* and his ability to pay astronomical sums.

"I worked for him befoah," Marky had said. Even after fifteen years away from East Boston, Marky still couldn't pronounce his Rs. "He goes by *Oz*—I don't know his real name—but the cash is real enough. I did a couple jobs for him last year."

"Any idea who he is?" Nick had asked.

"Nah. I think he's some mucky muck in England. Or the IRA. I don't care who he is, his money's green."

That was all nice, but now Nick was stuck with a job that would pay well if he could complete it, and threats if he didn't. And there was no guarantee the two women had even come this way—

Wait.

His eyes followed Cherry Street back up the block. A turn next to the gas station led off to a couple of commercial buildings. Beyond that, some houses and woods. He took out his phone and pulled up the maps application. Harrison Avenue on this side of the border dead-ended into a farm, less than a hundred yards from Boundary Road on the Canadian side of the border.

There was nothing but a field there. *Was there even a fence?* No way to know from what he could see. But he imagined himself in the shoes of Adelina Thompson, running, fast. Trying to hide from the cops and from whoever was after her. To her, wouldn't it make a lot more sense to cross *anywhere* other than an official border crossing where she might be stopped and questioned?

As quickly as he could, Nick got into the vehicle and started it up. He drove to the exit of the McDonald's. Traffic—way too much traffic. Cars backed up from the border station right into the intersection. He nosed his Hummer into the intersection, provoking a series of wild honks from cars. He pushed forward, slightly bumping a rusted antique Oldsmobile.

In the distance, way down at the end of Harrison, he saw what he was afraid of.

Two women, one of them anorexic, walking in the shade of the trees as if they were just out for a stroll.

He laid on the horn.

CHAPTER TWENTY-SIX
One Shot

Dylan. May 4.

Dylan turned toward Andrea, easing his hands on the wheel a little. His knuckles were white.

"Once you get out, I want you to walk leisurely. Wait until you hear the horn honking before you do anything. Once you hear that, you'll have sixty seconds, tops, to make it over the fence. Then it's up to you."

She nodded, her face grim. She was wearing a tough pair of jeans and a heavy hooded sweatshirt labeled "George Mason University."

"Once you get in there, you look for the residence."

"Right. It's the two-story brick building. We looked at the satellite photos, Dylan. I'm not an idiot."

"You're anything but. But we're attempting something stupidly reckless, Andrea. You only get one shot."

She nodded. "All right."

"What do you do if the guards catch you?"

"Throw up my arms and yell that I'm seeking political asylum. Then tell everyone, loudly, that I'm Prince George-Phillip's daughter."

Dylan nodded. Traffic began to move and he hit the gas. Mendoza's old green Oldsmobile shuddered, spitting out a cloud of black smoke as it lurched forward. He glanced over at Andrea. She looked terrified.

"I'll be praying for you," he said. The words felt odd in his mouth.

She shook her head. "Bullshit you will. But I'll take it anyway."

"I can always try," he replied. "I don't *think* I'll get struck by lightning."

She chuckled. "I'm sure you won't." She craned her neck.

He followed the direction of her gaze.

On the other side of the street, headed Southeast on Massachusetts Avenue, traffic had slowed to a crawl, snaking slowly around a grouping of three police cars with lights flashing. Dylan kept his face impassive as he scanned the police cars. Two of them were District of Columbia police, and the third had a smaller logo on the door. As they got closer, he saw it clearly: Diplomatic Security Services. They were parked in front of the Embassy of Japan, and several uniformed police stood in front of the fence, blocking a group of twenty or so protesters from the front of the building. Ranging from their teens to an old lady in a wheelchair, they waved signs reading, "Stop the slaughter," and "Honk if you love dolphins."

A huge banner waved in the air, held up by two young men. The banner was full color, displaying a bloody beach strewn with the carcasses of dozens of dolphins.

Dylan flinched at the blood. He hated the sight of killing.

"You okay?" Andrea asked.

"Yeah. Fuckers." He honked the horn and waved at the protesters. "Almost there," he said. They were crossing a bridge now, heavy trees on both sides of the road. Dylan turned on his right hand turn signal then pulled to a stop just after 30th Street.

"Here's where you get out. You've got three minutes."

Andrea looked him in the eyes. "Dylan—be careful."

"Same to you."

She nodded, then reached over and squeezed his arm. She stepped out of the car, just as a cab behind Dylan started honking his horn. Dylan stayed there while she looked both ways, crossed to the yellow lines, then cut between cars and started walking down Whitehaven Street, a small street bordered by the Brazilian Embassy and several very large houses.

Once she was on her way, Dylan hit his left turn signal and pulled back into traffic. He drove intentionally slow, swerving the Oldsmobile slightly left and right, enraging the cabbie behind him. A moment later, he approached the British Embassy on the right side of the road.

Dylan had studied the satellite photos and images on Google as closely as possible. While those images told him nothing about the security setup at the Embassy, he knew that the first two driveways in front of the residence buildings were blocked with steel bollards before the fence and gates. He'd never get the Oldsmobile past those. The grass in between driveways was blocked with solid looking brick planters bordered by a well manicured lawn. It was attractive, but also functional.

The third entrance, however, didn't have the steel bollards. A solid looking gate stood between two stone pillars, with a small guard booth just inside the gate on the left. The stone pillars were capped by carved gryphons.

Just to add to the chaos when he arrived, Dylan turned on the radio at full volume. The sound of Jason Derulo singing *Talk Dirty to Me* blasted out of the car, the subwoofers in the trunk vibrating the windows of nearby buildings. Dylan came to a stop in the road, his left turn signal on. The guard stepped out of the booth, staring curiously at Dylan from the other side of the fence.

That lasted until Dylan turned and stepped on the gas, accelerating rapidly toward the fence.

George-Phillip. May 4.

The newspaper headline was troubling, but not nearly as troubling as some of the quotes inside the lead article. Heads would roll, and quite possibly some at the newspapers would be tried for violations of the Official Secrets Act, but that didn't erase the damage. In some ways it would make it worse. The Special Report had been online for less than ten minutes before the first phone call came in. George-Phillip had just finished breakfast. Now he sat staring at the screen on his tablet, wishing he'd waited to eat.

Special Report. MI6 Insiders Accuse
Government of Covering Up Afghanistan Massacre

This is a Guardian Special Report.

Related Special Reports:
    * Who Was Involved in the Massacre?
    * Interviews with Survivors
    * How the Tragedy Unfolded

On an ice-cold night in Afghanistan in December, 1983, the villagers of Bozai Gumbaz were huddled in their mud huts and yurts, large round portable structures used by the nomads of the steppes of Central Asia. For four years, war had raged in Afghanistan, following the 1979 Soviet invasion. But for the poor villagers of the

Wakhan Corridor, a finger-shaped protrusion from Afghanistan squeezed between Pakistan, China and the then-Soviet Union (now Uzbekistan), the war was remote. The villagers and herders of this region, once part of the Silk Road, had largely been bypassed by the war. With no roads, no structures, and few mineral resources, there was little here to interest outsiders.

Unbeknownst to the villagers that night, the war was about to reach out to them. Two unmarked helicopters left the mountains of Pakistan and crossed the Hindu Kush Mountains into the Wakhan Corridor. At approximately midnight on December 13, 1983, they came to a hover over the village. Survivors described a punishing whiteout as fresh snow was blown into the air by the rotors of the helicopters. No one on the outskirts of the village (those who survived) could have imagined what happened next. Villagers, standing in their doors and windows gawking at the helicopters, began dropping in their tracks. Men, women and children died within seconds, their village washed with a cloud of sarin, a deadly chemical warfare agent that can cause nearly instantaneous death to those exposed.

More than six weeks passed before word of the massacre reached the outside world, and three more months before the first outsiders reached the village. Two investigators from Helsinki Watch (now Human Rights Watch) trekked on snowmobiles from Pakistan into the country. What they found became an international crisis, with U.S. President Ronald Reagan denouncing the Soviets for using chemical weapons in Afghanistan.

Our investigation, however, has shown that the chemical weapons were provided not by the Soviets, as the entire world assumed in 1983, but by a group of American and Saudi intelligence officials led by the current Secretary of Defense nominee Richard H. Thompson (shown in a 1985 photograph, right). Further, according to confidential sources within the Special Intelligence Service, it was learned by The Guardian that current SIS Chief George-Phillip Windsor (second cousin to Her Majesty) was responsible for the investigation and later cover-up of the massacre.

George-Phillip closed his eyes as he read the last paragraph. His ability to influence events in Adelina's favor was about to come to a difficult end if he didn't get ahead of this.

Where did his responsibility lie? Was it to continue to protect a past Prime Minister, and by extension, the entire government? Was it to Adelina? Or to those poor villagers who had never had an advocate? Or, for that matter, was it to Jane, who had already lost her mother?

George-Phillip sighed. His daughter. She'd been the most cheerful of babies, always smiling and burbling and drooling. But after Anne died, she'd cried for months, inconsolably. He'd done everything he could, including taking a lengthy absence from SIS, but it wasn't until he'd hired Adriana Poole that Jane began to recover.

Adriana was flighty. Sometimes George-Phillip thought she was genuinely stupid. But she was also kind, and cared very much for Jane—no matter how indifferent she was to Jane's father. Like any man and woman in their position—a wealthy widower and a young woman of good stock, they'd both tossed around the idea, but quickly ruled it out. Two less compatible individuals had probably never existed.

He stood up and walked to the window, then looked at his watch. It was 2:00 pm. O'Leary should be in shortly. Not a day went by when George-Phillip didn't thank God he had the pugnacious little man working for him. He turned back to the article and read further.

According to the Guardian's sources inside the MI6, Prince George-Phillip led the investigation into the Wakhan massacre in the spring of 1984 while he was assigned as a medium-level attaché at the British Embassy in Washington, DC. His final report identified Secretary Thompson—then a low-level state department functionary—as the ringleader of a small group of intelligence officials responsible for delivering the chemical weapons to Ahmad Shah Massoud, the leader of an anti-Soviet militia operating in Badakhshan Province.

According to a senior MI6 official, Prince George-Phillip's report fingered those responsible, and then recommended burying the report.

George-Phillip muttered a curse. The last paragraph was patently untrue. He'd recommended confronting the United States publicly over the issue. But the Iron Lady had not only given the order to suppress the report, she'd also made a very persuasive argument. People today forgot that in the early 80s, the United States and Russia were poised to destroy the earth with their nuclear weapons. The Cold War was at its peak and George-Phillip's report would have created a tremendous propaganda victory for the Soviet Union and undermined everything the Queen's government had worked for.

The argument felt hollow with the retrospect of time, and the years of staring at the photos of the twisted and bloated bodies of children. He wondered how he would explain the decision to his child. Jane would know nothing of the Cold War and Ronald Reagan and Mutually Assured Destruction. She would understand only that children and their mothers had been murdered and a generation had passed and no one had done anything about it. No one had done anything for those children.

George-Phillip wondered how he would explain his actions to God, were he called to account today. He sighed. He had so many regrets. So many. He remembered one of his last conversations with Adelina, when he'd begged her to leave Richard and run away with him.

You don't mean it, she had said. *Your sense of duty is too strong to run away.*

He'd last seen Adelina in China a lifetime ago, in the fall of 1996. The American Embassy had hosted a dinner for the officers of the British and Australian Embassies along with their wives— even in the 90s, the diplomatic services of all three countries were still dominated by men. By that time George-Phillip was a senior intelligence officer, but publicly he was a junior attaché for the

Diplomatic Service. With his cover as a junior diplomat, he was required to attend such functions.

The meal had been tense, unusually quiet for a diplomatic function. All of George-Phillip's instincts had screamed that it was time to force the issue, insist that Adelina leave Richard. How was it even possible that the other Embassy personnel were not aware of the painfully obvious dysfunction of that family? Adelina mumbled through the meal, never taking her eyes off her plate, responding to queries about her health with only the barest of courtesies.

George-Phillip had frozen when he saw eleven-year-old Carrie for the first time. She stayed through the dinner then was escorted away by a governess. Unusually tall for an eleven-year-old, she had raven hair and blue-green eyes, and a slightly upturned nose that looked nothing like her mother or her father. She looked a great deal like his first cousin, Eloise Percy, right down to the glint of mischief in her eyes. Moments after the introduction, George-Phillip's eyes darted involuntarily to Adelina, whose face revealed nothing.

She'd never told him that Carrie was his daughter. But it was obvious, now that he'd met the girl. He didn't understand why. Nor could he erase the sudden surge of anger at the thought that he had a daughter who had been kept from him.

Adelina's eldest daughter Julia, fourteen years old, had a haunted, pale look about her face. George-Phillip had been alarmed to see that miscreant Harry Easton, the Ambassador's son, corner her after the meal, speaking urgently, his hands waving all over the place while she shrank back. Her curly brown hair was a disorganized mess, hanging in her eyes, and she kept her face pointed to the floor. Midway through the meal, she disappeared entirely, and so did Harry.

Neither Richard nor Adelina noticed. Adelina kept her head low, obviously terrified of Richard, who occasionally whispered urgent words in her ear. Every time he touched her she flinched.

George-Phillip had wanted to scream, because everyone else ignored all of it. He found himself questioning his own perceptions. Was everything normal and it just seemed wrong in his eyes? How could they just stand around and drink and laugh and enjoy themselves when everything was so obviously wrong?

He finally ran out of patience. Ronald Easton, the British Ambassador, was deep in a conversation with Richard Thompson, and Adelina had just broken away from a talk with the Australian Consul-General when George-Phillip approached her, his heart thumping.

"Hello, Adelina, how are you?"

She froze, her eyes darting to him, then away. She didn't say anything.

"You haven't called," he said.

"I'm pregnant," she whispered.

He swallowed. "You didn't tell me about Carrie."

"That's because I want to live," she whispered. "He put me in the hospital when he found out she wasn't his. I don't know what he'll do when he finds out I'm pregnant again."

"Is the baby—is the baby mine?" he asked, his voice low and urgent.

"Yes. Of course. I never *voluntarily* touch him."

Of course he knew that. He looked her in the eyes and said, "Adelina, you must leave him. He's destroying you *and* your children."

"You don't understand what you're asking. If you did, you wouldn't say that. I'd lose my children. I'd lose everything." Her face shifted to a smile and she said in a much louder voice, "Yes, I enjoyed the show very much! I'm hoping we can take Julia to see it, I think she'd love it. She's very musically inclined."

George-Phillip restrained himself from jumping back in disgust when Richard Thompson casually clapped him on the shoulder. "Prince George-Phillip, it's a delight to see you again."

"And you, Ambassador."

"Please excuse me," Adelina said. "I must find Julia, she seems to have snuck off."

George-Phillip grimaced. "I'm afraid she was speaking with Harry Easton a little while ago, and he's gone as well."

Adelina's lips pursed and she nodded. She stepped away, walking toward one of the side doors of the room.

George-Phillip found himself drawn into a policy discussion with Richard Thompson. It was bizarre and irritating, and as a diplomat he had to just bear it. Walking away from the American Ambassador just wasn't done. But where did she go? His eyes scanned the room over and over again, but she never reappeared.

She never reappeared. Not that day, not that month.

The diplomatic community was small, and word began to spread. Something had happened to Adelina. Or possibly one of her daughters. Harry Easton vanished from Beijing in June, sent back to London even though his father still had another year as Ambassador. Adelina Thompson wasn't seen at all, and when Richard Thompson attended functions without her, he would simply say that she felt ill.

Finally, in May of 1997, George-Phillip had reached the end of his assignment in China. He gave up any pretense of discretion and showed up at the Thompson's apartment the day before his departure. He knocked and knocked, and finally a young American woman answered.

"Miss Adelina ain't here," the woman said. "She can't see you."

"Tell her it's George Lansing."

"She can't see you," the woman said again. Then she leaned forward and whispered, "She told me to give you this, if you came. But she doesn't want to see you no more. Go back where you came from and leave her in peace. That woman deserve some peace."

She held out a thick, cream-colored envelope the size of a greeting card.

George-Phillip staggered away, walking down the block toward the entrance to the compound. It was late afternoon, and a black Ford pulled up to the gate—one of the many cars hired by members of the diplomatic community. Three girls stepped out of the car and quickly walked inside the gate.

The oldest, fourteen-year-old Julia, walked with her head down, her curly brown hair hanging almost in her face, books clasped to her chest. She kept her head down and rushed past George-Phillip without a word.

Behind her, twelve-year-old Carrie walked, holding the hand of her sister. The one Adelina had named for George-Phillip's aunt, Princess Alexandra. Carrie towered over the young and fair-haired Alexandra. For a moment she met George-Phillip's eyes.

"Good afternoon," he said to her.

"Hello," she said. She gave him a brief, impersonal smile, then tugged her sister along. "Come on, Alexandra. Let's get inside. I bet Grace made cookies again."

George-Phillip had walked away quickly, struggling to hide the tears that came to his eyes as he walked away from his daughter. His daughter that didn't know—would never know—that he even existed.

At the gate, the guard waved him out and he tore open the envelope.

It contained a note.

For my safety, you must never contact me again.

The envelope also contained an ultrasound. The baby was a girl.

Over the years since, George-Phillip had kept tabs on Adelina, of course, as well as all of her daughters. Through O'Leary, he'd kept a discreet eye on the girls, and when he learned that Carrie and Andrea were in Spain in 2002, he'd taken the very risky step of going there by himself to get an in person look at his daughters. He'd stayed in the background, but he'd longed to reveal himself to them. Four years later he'd made arrangements to give the commencement address at Columbia University the year Carrie graduated with her Bachelor's degree, and so was able to shake her hand and smile at her and say congratulations when she accepted her degree. She didn't know, of course. How would she? He doubted she even remembered his existence. He was just an old man who had spoken at her college.

He'd never had any indication Adelina wanted him to contact her. He'd never heard from her again. And finally he'd given up and moved on. He'd married Lady Anne, and they'd had a child, and then in due course his wife died. And now—more than anything—he wanted to know where his daughter Andrea was, where the love of his life Adelina was.

The knock on the door startled him. He turned away from the view of trees and large brick houses just on the other side of the fence.

"Come in," he said.

The door opened. It was Oswald O'Leary. He looked unusually flustered.

"What do you have?" George-Phillip asked without preamble.

"Nothing solid, sir, but one of our agents reports tracking her near the Mexican border. It seems she's trying to get across the border."

"And do we have anyone on the Mexican side of the border? In case she makes it across?"

"We've got a small team in Tijuana sir, watching the border crossing. If she goes across there, we'll get to her right away."

George-Phillip nodded. "All right. That's good news, I suppose. And how much is this all costing us?"

"We're up to four million, sir, I'm afraid. All the subcontractors. They charge a pretty penny in the States."

"Bastards," George-Phillip muttered. "All right. Keep going."

"Yes, sir." O'Leary started to turn away, then put a hand to the earpiece he always wore. His face tensed, a look of concern flashing across it.

"O'Leary?"

"A disturbance at the gate, sir. Nothing to worry about."

Jessica. May 4

"Here," Jessica's mother said.

Here was a muddy field, knee-high grass mostly trampled by cattle or illegal aliens or who knew what. What Jessica did see was obvious. A small concrete pillar about three feet high on the other side of the field marked the border. A road and some houses were just beyond.

A loud honk down the street caught Jessica's attention. She looked that way. Three blocks away, back at the intersection near the border station a gleaming black sports utility vehicle—a Hummer, she guessed—was nosing its way into traffic and snarling traffic. Her mom stopped and looked too.

"What the hell?" Jessica gasped as the Hummer bumped into another car, shoving it out of the way.

Her mother stood for just a moment, both of them tense.

The Hummer slowly pushed another car out of the way. The honking was coming from multiple vehicles now.

Jessica looked across the field, then back at the Hummer.

"Mom," she said, her voice quavering. "Run. Let's run. *Now.*"

Adelina, suddenly breathing rapidly, nodded.

Jessica grabbed her mother's hand and pulled, plunging off the street into the muddy field. Instantly her canvas shoes soaked through, the cold mud gripping at her feet like the undead trying to pull her under. Her heart sank. If the entire field was this muddy, it would take them all day to make it across.

More honks from the intersection.

Jessica felt panic descend. In the last few days someone had kidnapped her sister, attacked her other sisters, and bombed their house. Something had gone terribly wrong.

"Run!" she screamed as Adelina stumbled. She leaned down, putting her arms underneath her mom's and tugging her back to her feet. Hand in hand, they began to run across the field.

Thirty feet into the field, Jessica's left shoe was yanked off her foot by the mud. She didn't stop to do anything about it, because the Hummer was free of the traffic now, and speeding up the three blocks toward them, engine roaring. Instead, she kept moving as quickly as possible. Somewhere behind the Hummer and toward the border station, she heard a police siren.

They had at least seventy-five yards to go across the field. Jessica felt pain in her forehead as she ran, staggering, pulling her mother. Adelina was only fifty, but she wasn't athletic and had suffered a lifetime of stress. She struggled to make it across the field, her face turning red.

The sirens were getting louder behind them. Jessica hazarded a look behind her when they'd made it halfway across the field. The Hummer had bounced to a stop just off the road. The driver's side window rolled down.

Another police car appeared on the Canadian side of the border, screeching to a stop in the road. Two police officers got out of the vehicle.

Jessica screamed, "Help us!"

A loud crack sounded behind them, and a splat just to her right as a bullet struck the ground.

The two Canadian police jumped behind their car as the rifle shot rang out. The pain in her forehead sharpened, blooming down her neck and into her right arm. Jessica staggered.

CHAPTER TWENTY-SEVEN
The Darkest Valley

Adelina. May 4.

Adelina cried out when Jessica suddenly faltered beside her, sinking to her knees in the mud. Panic flooded her. Had her daughter been shot? Where? Behind her, she heard another shot, and a bullet grazed her arm. She pulled Jessica to the ground, then lay down on top of her, putting her body between the shooter and her daughter, praying the grass would be enough to stop the bullets.

"Help us!" she screamed.

More shots rang out, this time from the Canadian side of the border. These gunshots were higher pitched, not the deep bass of the rifle.

Jessica's face was grey, and her eyes were wide open. Her left eye was dilated, rolling around independently of her right eye, which was focused on Adelina. She was breathing heavily, her mouth moving, but no sound was coming out other than a high-pitched breathy wail. Her right eye was wide, terrified. Adelina couldn't see any injuries, no blood. *What was wrong with her?*

"It's going to be okay," Adelina whispered. "I'll protect you." She began to recite a prayer as she held her daughter's hand and looked in her eyes. "The Lord is my shepherd, I shall not want. He makes me lie down in green pastures … he leads me beside still waters; he restores my soul. He leads me in right paths for his name's sake."

Adelina flinched at the sound of another rifle shot. The bullet slammed into the mud six feet away from her. Another hit three feet away.

"Even though I walk through the darkest valley, I fear no evil ... for you are with me ... your rod and your staff—they comfort me..."

Sirens went off somewhere behind her, and she heard the rumble of the Hummer turn into a roar. Suddenly it was receding, and the sirens were following. She lifted her head and looked around, then directly at the Canadian police.

"Help me! My daughter's hurt!"

Across the field, two U.S. Border Patrol vehicles were parked, even as two police cars raced after the speeding Hummer.

Three Border Control officers were getting out of the vehicles and stepped into the field.

Adelina began to panic. She couldn't let the Border Patrol take her or Jessica. She leaned down, putting her arms underneath Jessica's armpits, and lifted her to her chest, backing toward the Canadian border.

She continued the prayer, silently, even as she pulled her daughter away from the Border Patrol, who began to run.

You prepare a table before me
In the presence of my enemies;
You anoint my head with oil;
My cup overflows,
Surely goodness and mercy will follow me
All the days of my life,
And I shall dwell in the house of the Lord
My whole life long.

Adelina staggered as she bumped into the concrete post marking the border. She fell to her back, dragging Jessica with her.

"I'm Adelina Thompson," she gasped. "My husband is the Secretary of Defense of the United States."

She saw the Canadian officers look stunned, even as the Border Patrol officers stopped just on the American side of the border.

"I claim political asylum. I need urgent medical care for my daughter. Please help me."

She looked the officer in the eyes.

He nodded then said to his partner, "Call for an ambulance," as he kneeled beside Jessica.

George-Phillip. May 4.

"What sort of disturbance?" George-Phillip asked. He glanced out the window. He could just barely hear the sound of a horn and the awful bass sound of a car stereo. The music sounded obnoxious, low and grating.

"Some drunk American crashed into the gate, sir. Nobody hurt. The security guards are dealing with it."

"Well, then. Keep me updated. It's Sunday, and I need to be with my daughter."

"Very well, sir."

George-Phillip left the small office. The official residence, which was reserved for visiting dignitaries, had four bedrooms on the first floor, plus several other assorted rooms—sitting rooms, offices and kitchens, along with a small locally hired permanent staff.

He walked down the hall by himself as O'Leary turned toward the exit. He reached his left hand out and opened the polished hardwood door to the playroom.

Jane was on the floor, humming to herself as she played with a doll set. Adriana was across the room from her, knitting a scarf or something.

As the door opened, Jane's face brightened.

"Daddy!" she cried, jumping to her feet.

She ran to him and he lifted her into the air. She threw her arms around him. He was always surprised by how solid she was, and tall for a girl her age. He held her in his left hand and tickled her, causing her to convulse with giggles.

"Miss Poole, I thought I would take Jane to the zoo this afternoon. You may come along if you'd like, or if you wish to have the day off to explore the city, that's fine as well."

Adriana stood and said, "If it's all the same to you, sir, I'll come along."

"The zoo? Take me to the zoo? Zoo!" Jane crooned.

"Yes. We'll go see the pandas, I think."

"And the lions!" Jane threw her head back and roared.

"She should have a bit of a snack first, sir, begging your pardon. She usually has a snack about 2:30."

"By all means," he said, sharply bothered by the fact that he didn't know that. He spent far too little time with Jane. It was time to rectify that.

He opened the door. At that moment one of the security guards appeared, running down the hall.

"Your Highness, please stay in the room for the moment."

"Excuse me?"

"There's an intruder on the grounds, sir."

At that moment he heard a shriek, then a loud thump just down the hall. A high-pitched voice, female, shouted, "Don't shoot! I'm looking for asylum!"

A male shout, then another thump, then he heard a scream. Then words he was stunned to hear, shouted down the hallway.

"I'm Prince George-Phillip's daughter!"

Silence. It sounded as if they had the female intruder subdued.

I'm Prince George-Phillip's daughter! It couldn't be. Could it?

"Step out of my way, please," George-Phillip said to the guard.

"Your Highness, wait until the area is cleared—"

"You heard me," George-Phillips said. He set Jane down, and said, "Stay back." Then he pushed his way past the guard.

At the end of the hall, two security guards had wrestled a young woman to the floor. One kneeled on her back, preparing to tie her hands with plastic zip-ties.

She looked up at him with big blue-green eyes.

"Let her go," George-Phillip said.

One of the security guards looked up at him, stunned.

"Let her go, right now," he commanded.

Both guards stepped back. Slowly, Andrea Thompson came to her feet, her wary eyes on George-Phillip and Jane. She was mussed, a little bit of dirt on her face, her black and turquoise hair tangled from wrestling with the security guard. He thought about what he'd read about her. How she fought her way free when she was kidnapped, and somehow climbed down from a twentieth floor balcony when killers were after her. This young woman, his daughter, had far more internal resources than he could have ever imagined.

Thirty years of painful regret welled up in George-Phillip at that moment. Thirty years of regret that he'd not been able to protect Adelina, that he'd never known Carrie or Andrea, and that he'd never been a part of their lives. Worse, he saw all the pain and fear in her face. Fear that he would reject her, that she'd be alone, fear that he wouldn't admit the truth. He felt his cheek suddenly twitching, his uncontrollable damned eyebrows working their own dance on his face, and then a tear ran down his cheek.

"Jane," he said, his voice low, shaking. He motioned for her to come out into the hallway. "I'd like you to meet your sister. Her name is Andrea."

Andrea's eyes widened and began to water.

Jane clapped her hands together. "Sister!" she shouted. She stepped fully into the hallway and ran to Andrea, wrapping her arms around the sister she'd never met.

Epilogue

Dylan. May 4.

I thought *the British didn't carry guns.* Dylan's brain was foggy. He hadn't been driving that fast when he hit the gate, maybe 15 mph, but the sudden impact had still jolted him hard. The music was still blaring out of the speakers, THUMP THUMP THUMP, obscene lyrics, booty calls, talk dirty.

He shook his head and looked back up into the barrel of the pistol.

"Step OUT of the CAR!" shouted the man with the gun.

"WHAT?" Dylan shouted. "I can't hear you!"

"Step out of the car *now!*"

Dylan heard sirens in the distance. Lots of them. The music changed. Pitbull and Ke$ha. Timber. Yelling. Going down. Twerking. *What is all that noise?* Dylan reached out and turned the stereo off.

"No need to be so freaked out," he said. "Sorry, I didn't mean to fuck up your gate—"

"*Get out!*" shouted the guard.

"Okay, okay, okay..." he said. He opened the car door and stepped out.

Immediately one of the guards slammed him up against the car. Dylan felt his ribs bruise. He didn't resist as they pulled his arms behind him.

He felt his mouth curl up in a slight smile, remembering Alex muttering, *What is it with you and cops?*

He needed to stall them and keep their attention for a few minutes, and give her some time to get into the residence. He didn't know if she'd made it yet—probably not, it was too quick.

Slurring his words, he said, "Where's Harry?"

"There's no one named Harry here, you wretch—"

"What do you mean?" he asked, still slurring his words. "Captain Harry. Er ... Captain Wales, I think they called him. I was in Afghanistan with him."

Take that, motherfuckers. Actually, he'd never been anywhere near Prince Harry, though he'd been in Afghanistan at the same time, at least from what he'd read in the papers at the time. But this was a good time to stretch the truth.

"I didn't mean to break your gate. He tol' me to stop by. He said any time."

The guards went into a huddle. Traffic on Massachusetts Avenue was at a complete stop now. Gawking drivers who were already slowed by the protest at the Japanese Embassy were now presented with even more of a spectacle with the fluorescent green Oldsmobile in the driveway of the British Embassy.

Good. Dylan was hoping this would all be sorted before the DC police arrived.

That's when he heard one of their radios. Shouts.

"Intruder spotted entering the residence. Full alert. Full alert."

The bad news was, that prompted the guards to knock Dylan straight to the ground. One of them kneeled on his back, his knee grinding into Dylan's spine.

"Take it easy, bud, I'm not resisting," he murmured.

Two extremely long minutes later, a radio call came. He heard an argument, but couldn't see anything with his face pressed to the grass. It was getting itchy down here. He hoped he wasn't going to jail again.

Then he heard a voice. "Let him up. We've got orders to let him in."

"What?" one of the other guards said. "Bullshit."

Mutters. More argument. Then he was hauled to his feet, and the guards were opening the gate.

"I'll drive your … your … car … inside," one of the guards said.

Their leader said, "Follow me, sir. You're to be taken to see the Prince, God knows why."

Dylan coughed, then composed himself. Unable to help himself, he winked at the security guard, and then followed him into the Embassy compound.

Adelina. May 4.

Adelina clutched the coat the police officer had lent her. It was cold, especially with the water and mud soaked through her clothes. The ambulance was so loud she couldn't hear what the emergency medical technicians were saying. But it didn't sound good. They'd run an IV and were checking Jessica's vitals as the ambulance raced down the highway.

One of the EMTs leaned close to her and said, "We're going to Abbotsford Regional Hospital."

"What's wrong with her? She wasn't shot."

"Ma'am, it looks like a stroke. How old is she?"

"Eighteen! She can't have had a stroke."

"There are good doctors at Abbotsford, they'll do their best to help her. But I need to ask some questions, all right?"

Adelina nodded, clutching the coat.

"Is she doing any drugs? Or alcohol?"

"None right now. She just got out of a drug detox."

The EMTs looked at each other, then back at her. "What was she using?"

"Alcohol. And ... crystal meth."

The EMT nodded. "That might explain the stroke. Is she taking any medication?"

"Ibuprofen. She's had terrible headaches. And she's eating enough for three people. I thought she was getting better!"

"She probably was. But your run across the border may have just been too much exertion. Meth can damage the blood vessels in the brain, unfortunately. How long have you two been on the run?"

Adelina sighed and thought back. Three days? Four? She couldn't even remember. "A few days."

The EMT nodded. "All right. An immigration officer will meet us at the hospital to discuss your asylum application. In the meantime, she'll be getting the best care possible. I promise we'll do our best."

Adelina nodded, looking at her daughter. Jessica's skin was grey, her eyes staring up at the ceiling. She was still awake and obviously frightened out of her wits.

Adelina didn't know what was going to happen from here. But she knew no matter what, she was never going back to Richard. She'd do everything she could to protect her daughters. She'd find Andrea. And for Jessica, right now, all she could do was comfort her. She reached out and took Jessica's hand.

To be continued in

GIRL OF VENGEANCE

www.ingramcontent.com/pod-product-compliance
Lightning Source LLC
Chambersburg PA
CBHW030642260626
47157CB00007B/2451